# THE LISTENERS

ANTHONY J. QUINN is an Irish author and journalist. He was born in County Tyrone and studied English at Queen's University, Belfast. His first novel, *Disappeared*, was a *Daily Mail* crime novel of the year.

# THE
# LISTENERS

## ANTHONY J. QUINN

HEAD
of ZEUS

First published in the UK in 2018 by Head of Zeus Ltd

9 7 5 3 1 2 4 6 8

A catalogue record for this book is available from
the British Library.

ISBN (HB): 9781786696069
ISBN (XTPB): 9781786696076
ISBN (E): 9781786696052

Typeset by Adrian McLaughlin

Printed and bound in Great Britain by
CPI Group (UK) Ltd, Croydon CR0 4YY

Head of Zeus Ltd
First Floor East
5–8 Hardwick Street
London EC1R 4RG

WWW.HEADOFZEUS.COM

*To two wonderful women, my mother Marie
and mother-in-law Anne.*

*Be patient with the childish storm
that blows through these pages.*

*Someday my dumb words will find the land
where your language of love is spoken.*

# THE LISTENERS

# CHAPTER ONE

Silence hung in the pine forest and in the sky framed by the black sides of the valley leading up to the mountain.

No matter how often she stood on her balcony overlooking the forest, she would never get used to its twilight stillness, the monotony of its noiseless needles and twigs, the uniformity of its shadows, the darkness that seemed to pour itself into the shape of a beast on soft pads drawing closer with the night. Beyond the railings of her home, there were no signs of civilisation, no other houses and no roads, not even a fence, just wave after wave of trees filling the valley to the sky. Somewhere over the mountain lay the border with England and its bright towns and cities, its pavements crammed with chattering strangers.

Long ago, she had convinced herself that all she needed was this valley of trees and its seamless silence.

It was just before eight o'clock, and she had one appointment remaining in her diary. She rose from one of the two large leather armchairs that had kept her company during her

1

years here. Sitting all afternoon and listening to her patients had made her feel stiff and tired. She pulled open the double doors and stepped out into the deep vista of trees and the peace she kept turning to whenever her clients absorbed all her strength. She listened to a silence as heavy as that of a stopped clock, time itself hanging on the brink as the last rays of daylight sank from the sky. So quiet the forest seemed to stretch out and press against her body.

She shivered, feeling the familiar tingle in her stomach, the mixture of fear and excitement that the forest always triggered inside her. She had moved to this valley in the Borders believing that it would help her reach the levels of concentration she required in her work. On nights like these, she wanted to turn the forest into a patient in its own right. The trees could not speak, yet somehow they whispered to her every evening. They did not move, yet somehow they drew closer, communicating to her in a language pitched too deep for the human ear.

She turned back into the room and went over to her desk. She glanced at her diary and considered her next appointment, the man who was due to arrive in five minutes, the weekly visitor who never smiled or laughed, who was fixated on pretending to be ordinary and maintaining an even temperament, but whose silences belonged to the deep end of mental imbalance. She felt unsure of herself. Where did this unfamiliar anxiety come from? She read her brief notes, reviewing in her mind her last meeting with him, and tried to put the unpleasant feelings behind her. He had been visiting her consulting room for more than thirty years now, one of the first people to sit in her leather chair when she had first qualified as a psychotherapist.

Strange to think that she had been listening to patients for all that time, tuning into their innermost secrets, taking her direction from the forest, reading its shapes and shadows on evenings like these. Nothing was as tempting as the territory of the human mind, and in psychoanalysis she had discovered a way of tracing mysterious paths through the uncharted terrain of human desires and fears.

Again, that twinge of fear, like a lone gust of wind passing through the forest, what was its source? She went over to the bookshelf and ran her hand along the row of academic papers and periodicals. She had trained with some of the finest traditional Freudian therapists and become a member of the Scottish Psychoanalytical Foundation before leaving to join a breakaway holistic society – a group of committed practitioners who had held onto controversial models of memory and childhood trauma. During her early years as a therapist, she had felt disorientated by the conflicting theories of psychotherapy, the changing directions and infighting between the various schools, until she found her own path. A patient's words and pauses provided the most legible route to their secret fears and desires. All she needed was this consulting room at the edge of a forest, a room to trap the silences. It was a field of study that no one had written about before, the intense silences that led you deep into the human heart, and was absent from all the psychiatric publications on her shelves. Unlike her colleagues, she had never been afraid of silence and its intimacy, of inviting it into her consultations and accepting the importance of it in her patients' lives.

Outside, the valley grew darker and her sense of foreboding intensified. She sighed and returned to the double doors and the balcony. She was under no illusions about the difficult session that lay ahead of her; a man who had grown more restless and irritated during their recent interviews. She had thought about ending their meetings in order to give her more time to write up her groundbreaking experiences as a therapist. Perhaps this will be our last session tonight, she thought. All I need is a little courage. She was approaching retirement and had only so many years left to record her original views on psychoanalysis, to do something permanent with her listening talent. All those years of patient note-keeping, laying down lines of insight and empathy like fine wine, would be lost for ever if she didn't write a book that would challenge the psychiatric orthodoxies.

She stared deep into the forest, but all she could see was a dark pit of stillness. Twilight was over. Her heart fluttered and, for a moment, she thought the fear would overcome her. She tried to rationalise her anxiety. Perhaps it was her way of appeasing the monstrous ego of her final visitor, offering him these moments of apprehension beforehand. She thought back through their previous conversations and felt the darkness draw closer.

When the knock sounded on the door, she hurried back into the room. She wasn't above quickly blessing herself before sinking into one of the leather chairs and suppressing the nervous tension in her chest by calling out in a loud clear voice, 'Come in.'

Immediately, she could tell from the way he walked into the room that he was out of sorts. He settled into the opposing chair, voluble from the start, wayward in his emotions, and the session raced ahead. She concentrated, hanging onto the ebb and flow of his words, nodding and replying, but he seemed to take little notice of her, and soon he was deep into a list of bitter grievances.

She leaned forward, trying to focus. She felt as though she were trying to contain a vortex that had to be fed constantly with her attention, a twisting funnel of imagined betrayals and slights. She attempted to soothe him with the correct words, but they came out garbled, her therapist's careful phrasing faltering.

The visitor's gaze was upon her. He had stopped speaking and was waiting for her to say something. The look in his eyes changed, turning cold and glittering. A creeping realisation came upon her. She tried to push it away but the look in his unblinking eyes remained. She could not tell what he was thinking, but she felt that her deduction was correct. Neither she nor any of the staff at the hospital had wanted to believe that this man had committed evil. He had hinted at it often enough, but no one had listened to the truth hidden behind his words and in his eyes. It was partially her fault, of course. She had not wanted to believe the worst. She did her utmost to remain calm as the realisation strengthened, trying to think clearly and say nothing that would give her insight away. The silence of the forest combined with the silence of her visitor. She reminded herself that she was in her leather chair, in this consulting room she had designed herself, a safe place.

He resumed his monologue, but this time his words were overloaded with contempt. The room filled with his hatred. She realised she was checking the clock on the wall behind him more often than usual, willing the consultation to end. *For the first time ever in his company, I am truly afraid.* With a rising sense of dread, she saw that he had noticed her fear. *Does he suspect that I have worked out his past? How much does he think I know? Enough to make me break my oath of confidentiality?*

She made a resolution that she would contact Dr Barker

as soon as he left. The director of the psychiatric hospital would know how to proceed, whether or not to inform the police about her suspicions. The thought gave her strength as the room reverberated to the sound of his voice complaining about how he had suffered all these years, misunderstood by everyone who knew him. The words floated through her mind. She glanced at the clock again. Only ten minutes to go. The closer she got to the end of the session, the more she relaxed. Perhaps she had nothing to fear from him, after all.

He had stopped speaking. The pauses in between his words were the worst part of the session, but the mood felt different. Had he noticed her anxiously checking the clock?

He resumed speaking. 'The truth is I haven't been able to say why I really came here tonight. The suspicions that are gnawing inside me.'

She asked him what his suspicions were about.

'Not about what. More about whom.'

'Suspicions about me?' she asked. His eyes glinted. She had committed her first indiscretion by rushing in too quickly.

'Yes. I don't know if I can explain them properly.'

She leaned forward slightly in her chair. 'Perhaps we should work through this in the next session. We can return to these feelings next week.'

'Does that mean you want to finish early?'

'I didn't say that... although it might be best if we leave it for now, especially if you feel such a block.' She felt a bitter taste in her mouth. Failure tinged with fear.

'This isn't how I wanted our conversation to end,' he complained.

'Nor I, but in the circumstances...'

'I've upset you,' he said, his voice turning raw and husky.

She sank back into her seat. She told him that nothing was

upsetting her. However, she wanted to know what was upsetting him. She wanted him to keep talking.

'Me? Why should anything be upsetting me? What are you suggesting?'

She did not reply and waited for him to keep speaking. Her eyes hung on his lips. She said she was interested in hearing why he was so suspicious of her.

'I think you know my secret.'

'What secret?' She spoke casually. She hoped he did not detect the catch in her voice.

'I don't know if I can trust you with it.'

'I'm a therapist; it's my job to be trusted. Who do you think I am?'

'I'm not sure.' He leaned towards her. 'Someone who might betray me.'

'I think you should come back tomorrow. We can talk some more then.'

'I hope so. But I don't know if I can trust you in the meantime. I don't know if I can leave you with these suspicions.'

She stood up with all the authority she could muster, all the authority that in her decades of practising as a psychotherapist had never deserted her before, and could be counted upon to neutralise even the most objectionable of patients. She walked to the door and opened it. She was about to turn towards him and repeat that their session was over when a sudden blow to her head knocked her to the ground, and she pitched forward, unable to break her fall.


When she regained consciousness, everything was black. Something had been tied over her eyes. She could barely hear. A ringing filled her ears, an internal disturbance that pressed

7

upon her eardrums. This bothered her much more than the fact that she could not see or move. She tried to ignore the rushing tide of panic that welled up inside. She strained her ears, and heard the sound of him very close, but poorly transmitted.

She was still in her consulting room; she knew that much. She could feel the cold of the night through the wooden floorboards. Slowly, the noises expanded and filled the darkness. The sounds of him, working on ropes as he tied her hands behind her back; and the sounds of her fear rushing up from inside. He paused and went quiet. She wondered why he had stopped. She searched for the silence in the room, the silence behind her thoughts and his, the silence she had been listening to all her life. She turned her head slightly and felt his breath on her neck as he went back to working on the ropes.

She was unable to move now. Her skills at listening were the only weapon left to her, her one means of working out an escape. She tuned in to his up-close movements, listening more intimately than she had ever done before with a patient. She detected sadness in his breathing, a shivery sense of gloom as he tightened the ropes. She heard his frustration, the damage at the core of his being. If only she had listened as intently in their previous sessions.

'I so wanted to be good,' he whispered tensely. 'I wanted to help you and your colleagues with your theories about memory and trauma. I wanted to help show the rest of the world that the therapies worked.'

His voice had lost its familiar complaining tone. It sounded possessed. She did not have the right word to describe the change in his voice, but she heard it clearly. It was the voice of evil, of barely repressed fury. As a psychotherapist, she had always discounted the existence of evil, believing every personality could be rehabilitated or redeemed, and that human nature was inherently good. She felt regret at her mistake, that she had failed to connect with this human being who now had the power of life and death over her.

He made her aware of his knee, pressing it gently against her neck. He brought his face closer to her ear, as though he were going to share another secret. 'Your patients will be silent no more,' he said. 'They will keep confessing to your murder long after your part in their stories is finished.'

Then there were no sounds at all. She kept listening, hoping for an end to the darkness, that somehow she would find a break in the silence. She kept on hoping, listening with courage and determination, and later, when she felt his hands tighten around her neck, the will to listen and understand still burned brightly within her, distinct and indestructible.

# CHAPTER TWO

Transfixed in the sunlight streaming through the tall windows, the male patients huddled together, looking blind and uncertain, their eyes puffed up by medication and lack of sleep. It was Monday morning in the library of Deepwell Psychiatric Hospital, and the trainee clinical psychologist Laura Dunnock was reading to her therapy group a passage from St Augustine's *The Confessions*, Book X.

> When I turn to memory, I ask it to bring forth what I want: and some things are produced immediately, some take longer as if they had to be brought out from some more secret place of storage; some pour out in a heap and while we are actually wanting and looking for something quite different, they hurl themselves upon us in masses as though to say, 'May it not be we that you want?'

No one in the room was a scholar of fifth-century divinity and the words seemed very delicate instruments with which to subdue her criminally insane patients. Yet the men must have recognised a greater power in the saint's prose for, as they listened to Dunnock's forthright voice, a transformation took hold.

The features of their faces, normally so blank and sagging in expression, grew deeper and stronger. She saw the light of awareness intensify in their concentrated gazes, the furrows criss-crossing their brows. Even the most resistant patients stopped fidgeting and listened. She read on and felt the charge of energy contained in the words communicate itself to the patients. These men might be branded as dangerous by psychiatric experts, but to Laura they were also the victims of traumatic childhoods, vulnerable individuals who had been too sensitive to survive the early cruelty of selfish and violent parents or other adults entrusted with their care.

She had been working with the group for six months now, and she was keen to publish an original piece of research on the effects of suppressed memories on criminal behaviour. It was this aspiration, glowing brightly within her, that had inspired her to choose that particular passage, believing that it would help her delve more deeply into the minds of her patients. The previous Monday, she had set the men a task. She wanted them to bear witness to the memories they had locked away, the memories they refused to fathom or confront. She was convinced St Augustine's words would give their thoughts the right push and set them off on their own inner journey to the truth.

The group met every week in the library because it was the most comfortable room in the hospital, the only library in that part of Scotland without a stolen or misplaced book, every one of them secure with its own catalogue number, colour code and place on the shelves, its reading history recorded in neat index cards. The walls had not been painted for years, but in the morning sunlight they looked sturdy and bright, a room that would never make Laura's patients scream in terror, nor did it reek of antiseptic or bleach. Its smells were warm and familiar, the scent of the printed page and dust jackets warming in the heat from ancient radiators. Laura inhaled, waiting until one of the men began talking, and then she leaned forward in her chair and listened carefully.

However, the patient had barely started when someone interrupted from the corner of the library.

'I need to say something,' said a ghostly tenor voice. Its oddness provoked a few smiles from the group as well as the barely disguised annoyance of the patient who had been interrupted.

The shelves were partially blocking Laura's view, and she craned her neck to see who had spoken. A head of unruly grey hair appeared from behind the hedge of books. A pair of large eyes with long, white eyelashes met her gaze. She was surprised to see that it was Alistair McCrea, a middle-aged, long-stay patient who had never spoken in the group before, and who was described in his notes as utterly friendless and alone in the world. Even in one-to-one therapy sessions, he tended to stutter badly, or weep uncontrollably. When he was not weeping, he wore a look of bewilderment, as though his life was already past and lost, destined to spend his days roaming the restricted corridors of institutions like Deepwell in shapeless T-shirts and jogging bottoms. He usually trudged to the library and sat in a corner, not listening to anything, clinging to his silences.

However, this morning his presence seemed more intense, his eyes bright and darting. She felt the keen interest of his gaze. She had read his history, the details of his abuse at the hands of an uncle, and the history of drug taking and housebreaking that had blighted his young adulthood. She imagined the scars he must carry. She thought of the frightened little boy inside him, and she wished she could reach out and reassure him. He took out several sheets of paper, and the sense that something had awoken in him grew stronger. He leaned forward in his seat and then tilted back, shuffling the set of handwritten pages that the courts were later to record as 'Exhibit B, The Confessions of Deepwell Patient Alistair McCrea'.

He rose and then sat down, almost spilling the sheets of paper. The medication round had taken place an hour previously, during which he had requested an extra Valium and Xanax to help him cope with his anxiety. However, she could see that the tablets had done little to stop the shaking in his hands.

'Where's Dr Pochard?' he asked. 'She was meant to see me this morning.'

In circumstances like these, Laura was trained to give as little detail as possible. 'Dr Pochard is otherwise engaged,' she said.

'Otherwise engaged?' He looked as though his worst fears had been confirmed by Laura's bland excuse. 'What does that mean?'

'It's really none of our business.'

'So you don't know where she is?'

Laura saw the look of fear increase in his eyes.

'The poor woman,' said Alistair, his voice dying away.

'Really, there's nothing to be concerned about. I'm sure Dr Pochard is perfectly fine.' She asked the patient who had been interrupted to resume talking but once again, Alistair spoke.

'I told you I've something to say.'

She asked if he wished to comment on what the other patient had said. When he replied no, his answer prompted an exchange of glances and threatening murmurs from the other patients. Laura sighed. Surely he understood the rules of the group. Only when the current speaker had stopped talking could another member talk, and then only if the comment was pertinent to the material being discussed.

He held up his pages and gave her a pleading look. It was the first time he had read in the group, and in the hope of encouraging future participation, she relented and invited him to continue, deciding to treat him to the most lavish display of therapeutic listening bestowed upon a patient since the days of Freud.

He clasped the pages to his chest and screwed his eyes shut. His lips moved as though he were rehearsing mutely the story he was about to relate, but then he stared at the pages for so long without speaking that she began to think they were empty and the words would never be spoken.

She smiled gently. 'If you like, I could read it for you.'

The agitation increased in his eyes. 'I'm afraid of how you will react.'

'You shouldn't worry about my reaction.'

'After you read it, you might not want me here.'

'But you're always welcome here, no matter what you've written.'

'You're very kind.'

'All I do is listen.'

'More than listen. More than that.' In a low, monotonous voice, Alistair told the group that he found it difficult to remember the events of his story, even though the latest act had occurred on Friday night. 'I have forgotten many things in my life, but some memories I can never escape. I want to confess the terrible things I have done.'

He said that he had tried to worm his way out of responsibility for his crimes, but now he wanted to be above board and tell the truth to the authorities. He hesitated, and then explained that for years his memories had felt more like fantasies or nightmares.

At first, Laura found herself a little thrown by the spookiness of his voice, the way it swooped up and down, and for a few brief moments she wondered what it would be like to be trapped alone in a room with that voice. She felt an unprofessional shiver of revulsion, her first during her time at Deepwell.

With a sudden, anguished sigh, McCrea announced to the group that he had murdered a red-haired woman on Friday night. He said he suspected the victim was Dr Pochard, and his suspicions had been confirmed by the fact that she had not turned up at the hospital this morning.

'I have tried to forget, but the images of what happened have remained clear in my mind. I can no longer shut my eyes to them. They are horrific and unbearable.'

He told them that the killing had been the moment when all his repressed memories had burst their banks. He said that Pochard was the latest in a long line of victims stretching back to his first sexual awakenings as a teenager. He had started writing down everything over the weekend, and the more he wrote, the more he remembered. He had written all night, but still he felt he had not explored all his repressed memories.

'I have tried to write down as many factual details as possible to help the police in their investigations,' he said, and then he began reading from his notes.

The attention of Laura and the other patients seemed to change McCrea. He stood tall and bright in the sunlight, his long, white eyelashes fluttering, his voice barely keeping pace with his crimes, the record of his trudging through dark forests, his days and nights as a murderer, his victims stumbling through the undergrowth, their sodden hair and clothes, the stone chambers he erected to contain their remains, the little memorials he made for the dead women he referred to as his beautiful-eyed birds. His descriptions were lucid and gripping, but his voice was beginning to tremble. He sounded on the verge of tears.

At the start, Laura's mind worked hard to keep up with his story, formulating appropriate responses, trying to sift between what was fantasy or hallucination, and what might be the truth. However, the more she listened to the details, the more uncertain she became, as though a void had opened up beneath his words. She shifted in her seat. Had her break-through moment arrived? The most shocking of hidden memories might be revealing themselves before her eyes. All those months of sitting beside patients, listening and making notes, observing and recording their progress, hoping to prove herself as an insightful psychologist, and now this revelation.

He had come to the end of the pages, but everyone in the room sensed the story had finished too abruptly, like a bridge hanging in mid-air. The group grew still and quiet, teetering on the story's brink.

She collected herself and returned Alistair's gaze with a pleasant smile. 'You've... I told you to write what was in your memory and nothing else. Do you remember? The memories that are difficult to talk about.'

'And I have told you them.'

'Are you telling me that you murdered Dr Pochard?'

'Yes. And I've been waiting all weekend to tell someone. I thought I could confess here.'

'Confess here? Why?' She could see that he was beginning to shiver.

'I thought the library was the most convenient place.'

The hairs stood on the back of her neck. What he was saying could not be true, she reassured herself. It couldn't. He had made it up. For a start, he was locked in his room every night, and he had not left Ward G all weekend. The entire story was a fabrication, a fantasy of his illness. However, she recalled a detail from McCrea's case history, something about him confessing to attacking several young women, but the police had never been able to trace the victims.

She asked stupidly, 'Are you sure you did these things?'

'Check with the police. They will be able to investigate everything.'

The patient next to him spoke. 'Come off it, Alistair, you've made it all up. I've heard these stories before. Your fantasies about chasing women.'

The rest of the group nodded and murmured. They seemed jealous and indignant at the way Alistair had stolen the spotlight. They tried to get a discussion going on their own memories and looked to Laura for encouragement.

However, she was unable to make a response or show any interest. The session was over. Her work would not proceed today. She had to collect her wits and work out how to deal with this unexpected development. She should report Alistair's claims to his caseworker and the senior psychiatrist on the ward.

She looked around the room, the bright sun on the solid rows of books, the curious faces of the patients, and the figure of Alistair McCrea staring at her like an angel of death, his eyes with their white eyelashes, challenging and provocative.

Afterwards, she saw two male nurses escort McCrea across an inner courtyard to the lock-up ward. Through a windowed corridor, she watched them open a door into one of the most secure rooms in the hospital. For a moment, Alistair turned back and looked out through the windows, as if savouring his last moments of freedom. She thought she glimpsed a look of peace fall across his face, before he stepped into the room without showing any sign of resistance whatsoever.

Then later, a strange car pulled up in the visitors' car park and two men got out. One of them was a senior psychiatrist at the hospital, but she did not recognise the other man. He was not a relative of any of the patients, nor did he look like a mental health professional. Laura guessed he must be a police detective.

That night, she did not sleep at all.

# CHAPTER THREE

Carla Herron had only managed to persuade her three-year-old daughter Alice to come along to the birthday party by promising her she could wear her red princess shoes. Now she tried, unsuccessfully, to get her to play with the other children, but the toddler clung obstinately to her hand, the delicate pressure of those sticky little fingers a constant reminder of the confinement of motherhood. Carla had never understood the point of birthday parties for children who barely got along with each other at nursery, and had yet to throw one for her own daughter.

In the kitchen, the other parents were drinking wine, even the oldest son of the hosts, a gloomy, sullen teenager. Another group had formed a huddle at the back door around a few smokers, who seemed glad of the company. The conclaves made the party more bearable, and Carla, who had started on strong coffee, was now drinking wine and trailing Alice behind her like a hostage.

'I want to go home,' her daughter pleaded softly, tugging at Carla's blouse.

'But they haven't taken out the birthday cake, pet. It's too early to leave. Why don't you give the present to Vicki and wish her a happy birthday?'

'I want my daddy,' said Alice. This time she dug her fingers into Carla's arm.

She tried to drag her daughter into the playroom, but the child wrapped herself around her legs, causing her to stumble into the father of the birthday girl, a dark, heavily bearded man called Derek Cavanagh. For a moment, she was pressed up against him, and had to take in a lungful of his overpowering deodorant.

'You're a police detective, aren't you?' he said, and before she could think twice about it, she had nodded and said yes.

When it came to work, she usually tried to be as reticent or as vague as possible, but Cavanagh was a neighbour and knew her from the morning runs to the nursery. She stepped back but he grabbed a glass of wine and sidled closer. Regretting her response and seeing the gleam in his eyes, she braced herself for an account of some morbid or bizarre crime, as men at parties tended to do when learning of her occupation. Already she could feel the innocent mood evaporating.

'Only someone with an enormous amount of common sense and maturity can be a police detective,' he said, nodding approvingly. He spoke like someone in the know, sharing a professional confidence with her.

The mention of her profession in those terms had an unsettling effect upon her. She felt a sense of gratitude mixed with despair. For a moment, the entire burden of motherhood lifted from her shoulders, to be replaced by another burden, that of her career.

With a quick glance, she appraised him, his probing stare, the deep lines on his forehead, the beard that almost hid his mouth, the head held high, a determined man who was used to asserting his dominance in social situations. She suspected that he had rehearsed his opening remarks like a chat-up line.

'If you knew some of my colleagues you might not think we were mature or sensible at all,' she replied. She thought of the bickering within her squad, the long faces on Monday mornings, the endlessly repeated taunts and jokes that tossed back and forth daily, the simmering rivalries that lay behind the banter, and the frustration when investigations stalled, like being stuck in a series of joyless marriages.

'I'm not talking about your colleagues; I'm talking about you.' He turned his face sideways to stare at the nearby room of laughing parents. Not an ugly man, she thought. As attractive as his type could be. She glanced down and saw the flash of his wedding ring, but for some reason he wore it on his right hand, the opposite to hers. She followed his gaze, into the room full of seemingly carefree people. Sometimes, it might be nice to forget common sense and maturity, she thought.

'There was a time when people had proper jobs you knew and understood,' he said. 'All these mothers and fathers moving down from Edinburgh, dressing like they're still in their twenties, running around with made-up-sounding jobs. Calling themselves analysts and consultants and managers of this and that, blowing their own trumpets all the time. You're different from all of them.'

'How?'

'You have an honest job, a real job. You're a grown-up in a way everyone else here can never be.'

Carla relaxed a little at being called a grown-up. Yes, she could handle that. She liked thinking of herself as just a grown-up. That was the challenge facing her. For too long, she had judged herself in terms of being a good or bad mother, or a competent or incompetent detective, alternating between the high-pressured roles like some sort of depersonalised two-headed being.

'And what do you do for a living?'

'I teach at the university, but I used to listen to people all day. I was a psychologist with my own private practice for fifteen years.'

'Did you find it hard to leave behind your old job?'

He shrugged and moved closer. 'I never stop listening, even at parties. You know, I've been listening to you since I first saw you. Before you uttered a word.'

The father of another of Alice's classmates passed them by with an ironic smile. Carla worried that the other parents had noticed their closeness, the intimacy of his voice.

'What do you mean?' she asked sharply.

'A good psychologist listens with more than just his ears.' His eyes brightened. 'The other senses have a vital role. For instance, you have a way of gathering your hair that is very expressive.'

She felt the intensity of his gaze again, as though he were reading her face, her body, listening to her inner thoughts through the channels of visual communication.

'There's more wine in the kitchen,' he said, breaking the tension. 'Would you like another glass?'

She hesitated, and then couldn't make up her mind.

'Just one? You're off duty, aren't you?'

'I've already had a glass. Don't let me stop you though.'

'Shame. You know, I watched you come in through the door with your little girl and I thought you looked very unhappy.'

'I'm not unhappy.' She spoke in the coldest voice she could

muster. She had nothing else to say to him and wanted to move away with her daughter in tow, but the corridor was packed at that moment.

'I'm sorry if I made you uncomfortable.'

'No, you haven't made me uncomfortable.' She could feel Alice gripping her wrist, digging her nails into her skin. 'If I'm uncomfortable, it's not your fault.'

He tried to change the subject. 'I've often wondered what makes me keep listening to people, trying to analyse them. Do you ever think about detective work in that way?'

'I'm too busy to think like that,' she said. However, the truth was she thought about it often, not every day, but frequently enough to question the motivation that had led her straight to the police training college six months after the birth of her first child.

'I suspect you have some trauma, a memory that keeps haunting you.' He probed with a natural lightness that must have been perfected during countless hours with his patients. She heard his breathing change. She was being read, again, systematically through his senses. His nose twitched as he took in her scent, waiting for her silent messages to reach him. She felt a crawling sensation around her neck. The fingers of her right hand stretched out and gripped her daughter's hand. Her back shifted against the wall, but there was no place of retreat in the crowded corridor.

'You don't need to say anything more,' he said with a little smile as though they were sharing an intimate joke. He turned his attention to Alice, saying, 'What a lovely little girl.'

She stood back, allowing a couple of harassed mothers to pass through the corridor, and then her phone rang. Seeing that it was her chief inspector, Simon Bates, she excused herself from Cavanagh's company.

'I hope I'm not disturbing you, Carla?' said Bates.

'No, not at all.'

The sound of his voice made the air in the corridor seem suffocatingly domestic. She hesitated, adjusting her voice to the correct professional tone, feeling the gears of her life shift painfully. 'What is it?'

'Something has just come up and I thought of you.' He began describing the case, an apparent confession to murder made by a patient at a local psychiatric hospital. Carla passed the phone to her other ear, and led Alice into the main room.

'You still haven't given the present to Vicki,' she whispered, giving her a little nudge. She sidestepped a helpless mother who was hovering over a boy throwing a tantrum on the floor, his limbs flailing and kicking against her.

'So you're putting me in charge of the investigation?' Carla asked. Alice followed her with her gaze, pleading mutely that she stay with her, but Carla made a discreet exit and slipped out the front door.

'I wouldn't call it an investigation at this stage,' said the DCI. 'Patients at that particular hospital are always claiming to have committed crimes. Most of them are living in complete fantasy land. However, the hospital authorities have a duty to bring the claims to our attention.'

'What should I do then?'

'Keep an open mind. Go over the details of the patient's story from the beginning to the end and make sure you don't miss anything. Then write the report and have it on my desk by Thursday morning. I'll evaluate what action to take from there.'

The DCI said he was also assigning Harry Morton to the case, to help oversee her interview with the patient. The psychiatrist at the hospital who reported the confession was a

Dr Robert Llewyn. Bates had worked with him in the past, and trusted his judgement. He went over the information that had been passed to the police, and then ended the call. She put away her phone and went in search of Vicki's mother, Deborah.

Mercifully, there was no sign of Cavanagh, and the corridor had emptied of people. Through the half-opened door of the kitchen, she glimpsed a group of children's faces, and then the door slammed shut as if a sudden gust of wind had caught it. She stood in the corridor, without anyone, child or adult, paying her the slightest bit of attention. To occupy herself she located Alice's coat from the hangers and waded deeper into the house. She murmured hello to a group of women but none of them replied. She began to see the party from Alice's point of view, dragged to a strange house and trapped in a series of rooms with barely known schoolmates. More than unsettling, it felt oppressive.

Framed by the door into the garden, she saw Deborah with Vicki and Alice, their backs to her. As she drew closer, they turned back into the house. Vicki was frowning as usual. However, it was not Alice holding Deborah's other hand; it was a different child altogether with freckles and a sulky face. Carla looked at Deborah as though she were a thief who had substituted her child for another.

'Where's Alice?' she asked, realising that ten minutes must have passed since she'd last seen her.

'Oh, I think she went into the garden with Derek to look at the bees.'

Cavanagh kept bees as a hobby and had promised the children a tour of the hives. She walked down through the garden and, before she knew it, was amid the buzzing flashes of the bees. From inside the white hives there rose a hectic roaring sound, drowning out the laughter and shouts from the party. She hunted through the clumps of wild flowers, brambles and nettles, her efforts sending bees into the air and whirring down the hedge, but there was no sign of Alice or Derek. The moments ticked by.

She went back into the house. Amid the pink balloons, the festoons of birthday bunting and the mingling mothers and fathers, she thought she glimpsed a child's soft hand gripped by a hand that looked more like a wrinkled claw. She heard a cry like Alice's and pushed through the crowd. She turned her head, searching the sea of faces, hunting for another sign. She saw a flickering movement, what appeared to be a child's bare legs running for dear life down the garden, but the image remained indistinct and she was not sure if it was her daughter or not. More sounds trickled through the murmuring conversation. A girl shouting and crying. Was Alice trapped somewhere? She listened carefully, but the plaintive sounds grew faint. Then a rush of children's voices engulfed her as the birthday cake appeared and everyone began singing 'Happy Birthday'. Still there was no sign of her daughter.

She looked in all the rooms of the ground floor and then checked the bedrooms upstairs, the bathrooms, the wardrobes, the closets, and all the drawers of the cupboards, even the ones that were too small for Alice to crawl into, as though her daughter might have been pulled through the thinnest of apertures, and every chink of darkness had to be exposed and investigated.

She returned to the party and asked Deborah for help. The conversations between the parents seemed to fade. Following behind her, Deborah's face grew uneasy, frowning with the effort of her reassuring words, which were beginning to sound false to Carla's ears.

She stood still, trying to collect her thoughts. She should have kept her daughter at her side. She was the only adult Alice knew at the party. She had forgotten her role as a mother, trusting that her child would stay close by and not move from the one spot. The faces of the other parents began to blur into bright points, their glasses and the bald heads of some of the fathers, and the queasy realisation came to her that the men were all strangers to her. She thought of ringing her police colleagues and organising a search party. However, the relaxed behaviour and advice of the other mothers counselled her to delay raising the alarm. They all seemed to have coped with disappearing children before. Everyone was looking for Alice now, and Deborah kept reassuring her that she could not have gone very far. They searched through the house again. In her distraction, she even glanced into the mirrors in the bathrooms and bedrooms, searching for a trace of her daughter, seeing only her own face, blazing now with maternal fear.

She made her way to the bottom of the garden and looked back at the house. From here, she could see the building in its entirety. She checked all the windows on each of the floors, scanning the glass panes. Her eyes fixed upon a dormer window in the roof, its drab curtains making it seem cold and remote from the rest of the house. Somehow, she had not been able to access it from the inside. All her attention grew focused on that blind-looking attic window, the frames of the glass panes like the bars of a tiny cage, the roof closing in from above, with just enough space for a little prisoner in red shoes to be hidden away from the rest of the birthday party. She felt the house's weight tilt above her, bees whizzing past her face, and then she was running back up the garden and through the kitchen doors. She hauled herself up the stairs. At the top of them, she found a small door, hidden behind a plant stand, which led to a narrow flight of steps. As she climbed them, Deborah grabbed her by the arm.

'Wait. That leads to Derek's old counselling room. He always keeps it locked. No one's been up there for years.'

'I need to check inside,' she said. She pulled free and wrenched at the handle, but the door did not budge. She rattled it harder. This was a secret room, hidden away at the top of the house. No other way to describe it.

'All right,' said Deborah. 'I'll get the key.'

She returned with an ancient-looking key. She carefully inserted it into the lock. As soon as the handle gave, Carla pushed forward and the door flew open. She stumbled into a small dark room dominated by two large leather chairs set at an angle to each other and covered in dust, but no sign of Alice. She went over to the window and pulled back the shabby curtains. The grey light diluted the shadows. The room was like a museum to an abandoned career with Cavanagh's achievements as a therapist proudly on display, certificates framed and hung on the walls in positions of prominence. A younger Cavanagh stared out from photographs with other serious-faced people. Shelves of dusty journals lined one of the walls.

'Satisfied?' asked Deborah, standing at the door.

From below, the front door slammed shut and a voice shouted up, 'I've found her. I've found her. She was hiding between the cars on the street.'

Carla rushed down the stairs and into the hall, where she met the relaxed, dark eyes of Derek. He was holding Alice in his arms. Her daughter looked just as she had done when Carla had last seen her. There were no marks on her skin or signs of disarray in her clothing that might have suggested an abduction. Her expression was wide-eyed but composed, no message in her features to suggest an ordeal or that anything untoward had happened to her.

Alice said nothing as Carla lifted her from Derek's arms and held her tight. The blankness of her response did not completely dissolve the dread in Carla's stomach. She thanked Derek and Deborah, and the other parents. Everyone smiled at her and Alice, even the children. Slowly the party mood returned and the children went back to laughing and shouting, glad the celebrations were not yet over.

However, Carla was in no mood to stay. She said her goodbyes and carried Alice into the street. It was a bright afternoon in the town of Peebles, and the pedestrians she met were happy and smiling. Having Alice in her arms should have been a cause for happiness, and she ought to have returned their smiles, but she felt frightened and also strangely elated. A pressure built up behind her breastbone, intensifying into a form of euphoria. Some deep instinct had been stirred up in her soul, and she gathered Alice tighter to her chest, running the rest of the way home.

She met her husband in the hallway and decided not to mention what had happened. He was rocking their six-month-old son, Ben, in his pram, and the house had not been tidied from breakfast time. David's face was rigid with frustration as he tried to settle the baby to sleep. However, as soon as he saw Alice, he bent down to her with a look of concern and asked, 'What happened to your other princess shoe, pet?'

To her surprise, Carla saw that one of Alice's feet was bare.

'The man took it,' said Alice.

'What man?'

'The man with the beard. He said it was dirty.'

'Then we'll have to go back and get it.'

He stared at Carla. 'Are you OK?'

'Yes,' she said, tight-throated, even though she felt as though she was going to start shaking again. She told him what had happened at the party, how Alice had been missing for about twenty minutes. As she spoke, she felt the pressure return under her breastbone.

When she had finished, David knelt down beside Alice. 'What happened at the party?' he asked.

'I was hiding in the street, and then the man found me.'

'Anything else?'

'I had cake with chocolate sauce. Vicki says her mummy cooked it for her. She said home-made cakes are the best.'

David half-patted, half-caressed her head. 'I think Vicki is right. Home-made is always the best.'

Later, over a coffee, David told her to relax, reminding her that nothing bad could have happened to Alice. He watched her with a look of concern.

'I didn't look after her,' she said, shaking her head. 'I let her out of my sight for too long. I was negligent in front of all those other parents. There was a moment when I felt so out of control and dangerous I could have torn the house down.'

David gave her his full attention over his coffee. It had been a while since she'd felt the force of his cool blue eyes.

'I've never seen this side of you before,' he said.

'What side of me?'

'Your crazy maternal side. You've come back from a three-year-old's birthday party like a wounded animal.'

'Our daughter was *missing*. I thought someone had taken her. And it was my fault. I left her alone in a house full of strangers.'

'I don't know how child kidnappers operate, but I'd have

thought it unlikely that a stray one was invited to a children's party.'

'Children disappear all the time, even in towns like this,' she said. However, even as she spoke her voice weakened, knowing what she had said wasn't entirely true.

David rolled his eyes. It was clear he did not believe predators roamed the streets of snug little Peebles, waiting for the chance to snatch an unsuspecting child. She recalled those terrible moments in the garden and then climbing the stairs to the attic, and tried to analyse her feelings. The intensity triggered inside her had been strong enough to turn her understanding of motherhood on its head, and make everything else seem meaningless. Where before she had lived and moved easily in the world of maternal instincts, now she saw that it was the world of maternal instincts that lived and moved within her with a frightening force. Not knowing the whereabouts of Alice was all that had been necessary for the meaning of her old life to be lost, and everything she had striven for to cease to matter.

She rose in the middle of the night to check on Alice and Ben. When she returned to bed, David murmured, in between a bout of snoring, 'Sleep now, go back to sleep, now,' as though he could sense her inner fears. She snuggled up against him, but all she could see in her mind's eye was the cold attic window and its shabby curtains, and somewhere hidden within, a tiny red shoe covered in dirt.

# CHAPTER FOUR

Carla usually found conversation with her colleague Harry Morton tough, and his reticence when they drove on the A72 out of Peebles to Deepwell Hospital diluted any enthusiasm she might have felt at being handed a fresh assignment.

'Ever been to Deepwell before?' she asked.

He nodded with his usual aura of weary resignation. His furrowed face leaned towards the windscreen as he changed gears, his long hair falling down his bearded cheeks, as though he were deliberately trying to prevent Herron from reading his expression or glimpsing his eyes.

'What was it like?'

He paused, thinking, and then he turned to her briefly, his stiff, mask-like expression impossible to read or get close to in any way. She had only exchanged a few words with Morton in the six months she had been working in Peebles and knew practically nothing about him personally. Other officers at the station found him distant and off-hand, even arrogant, but she regarded him with more than a trace of pity. He lacked the swagger of confidence that emboldened the other male officers in the team. Instead, she sensed something miserable and fragile about him as he clung to his aloof manner.

'You'll see when we get there,' he said.

Well, don't take too bloody long, she thought to herself. Her thoughts changed direction, rehearsing various lines she might say. She remembered a joke by a mentally ill shoplifter she had helped arrest during her first post in Edinburgh. The man had been caught at an off-licence, shortly after absconding from a psychiatric hospital. When Herron had read the charges to him, he had replied, 'It's not a frontal lobotomy I need, it's a bottle in front of me.' It was a good line, but she couldn't summon up the nerve to tell it to Morton. She was afraid he would not react at all, and that he would just stare at her with that morose expression of his.

That doesn't sound like you talking, her father used to say when she tried to fill the silences between them with a ready-made story. However, the greater the quiet in the car, the more she felt compelled to say something. She even contemplated sticking her tongue out at Morton's profile to provoke a reaction. She kept wondering what he really thought of her as a detective and colleague. Perhaps he was annoyed at having to partner a newly recruited officer on one of her first assignments.

The road began to rise and descend through a landscape of hills and sheep farms. After several miles, the only signs of habitation were stone structures of unknown purpose, tumbling cairns, low-slung ruins taken over by sheep, and ancient hill-forts stranded in a sea of heather. At the bottom of a valley, she saw what might have been the remnants of an entire village swallowed up by the poverty of a previous century. She closed her eyes. When she opened them again, the landscape had grown more forested, and it was raining. The smell of pine trees drifted into the car. They were heading southwards over the hills, but the encroaching forests made the road appear directionless. Morton did not seem to have noticed that she had fallen asleep. She began to suspect that perhaps the older detective had no particular opinion about her capabilities. Perhaps he had passed no judgement upon her as a detective or a human being, and had a complete lack of interest in her feelings. She relaxed at the thought that nothing she could say or do would get a reaction from this world-weary policeman.

A loch appeared on one side of the road, the water bright in spite of the rain, and then they were back in the murk of the overshadowing forest, which stretched from hill to hill, con-necting with other plantations of pine and sprawling across the border uplands. Perhaps Morton's company was the escape she had unconsciously needed, she thought to herself, a mother of two young children, who four years ago had been happily teaching in a primary school in Glasgow, ensconced in newly married life. While she had not envisaged staying there for the rest of the life, she had not planned on changing schools any time soon, let alone leaving her profession entirely and moving to the countryside. But something had happened after the birth of Alice, and from one day to the next, she had resigned her teaching post and enrolled on the fast-track detective training course at the police college in Edinburgh. She had been so busy with her new career and the children that she had not had time to reflect on this before. How did I end up with a sullen inspector in his forties for company instead of a class of hyperactive nine-year-olds? Why have things turned out for me like this?

Her unanswered questions hung between them as they arrived at Deepwell Hospital, an imposing building of rain-darkened granite that looked as though it had settled for the same moody stillness as Morton and the surrounding forest. They drove into a courtyard where a sign directed visitors to a small car park.

When they reached the entrance, Morton held the door open for her. At the front desk, they asked for Dr Robert Llewyn but the receptionist said he no longer worked there. The two detectives looked at each other blankly. Morton was about to ring back to headquarters and check the contact details, when a short, thickset man wearing a white coat came walking up behind them and introduced himself as Dr Liam Barker.

'I'm the director of the hospital,' he told them. 'Dr Llewyn was here as a locum, covering while I was on leave.'

He led them through two sets of security doors and into a courtyard garden.

'I'm not quite sure what happened during my absence,' explained Barker. 'But let me assure you, this so-called confession is a sign of Alistair's illness returning. A flare-up of old symptoms and nothing more. We've given him sedatives and antipsychotics. He needs to rest and avoid any excitement.'

A team of gardeners stiffened in mid-movement and watched the detectives, their weeding tools suspended above the black earth. Only their eyes moved. The sight of Herron and Morton walking past seemed to halt their normal reality amid the hybrid roses and herb containers. Herron concluded they must be patients rather than professional gardeners, men and women only partially in touch with the real world. One of them, a woman, caught Herron's attention. She had bulging eyes and hair so sparse she was bald in places. She lowered her head slightly, and grinning, pointed two fingers at her protruding eyes, as if urging Herron to take a look in there. Her arms showed thin scars, glowing pink and sullen in the sun.

Herron dragged her attention back to Barker. 'What prompted the confession?'

'He was undergoing a new treatment plan. Unfortunately, it seems to have awoken his dormant fantasies.'

An alarm sounded somewhere as they stepped into another part of the building and down a long corridor.

'What kind of treatment plan?'

'We were reducing his medication and encouraging him to take part in group therapies. The hope was to return Alistair to the community. I've explained to him the unfortunate legal consequences of his claims, and understandably he is very agitated.'

A door buzzed open for them and Morton commented on the amount of security.

'We take every precaution when it comes to the patients. Ours is the only facility in this part of Scotland prepared to handle the most dangerous patients.'

'You have murderers and sex attackers here?' asked Morton.

Barker nodded. 'While they're here, they get treatment to help them understand what might have made them disengage from the normal rules of society. We believe that with the right psychological tools we can eradicate violent crime from society.'

Morton surreptitiously rolled his eyes at Herron, and then he asked if there was anything to suggest that McCrea might in fact be telling the truth.

'I've already interrogated him. He gave evasive answers to my direct questions. He told me that he is now unsure of having attacked anyone. He said he had come to the conclusion that Dr Pochard was his victim only because she wasn't in hospital yesterday.'

'What about Dr Pochard?' said Herron. 'Has anyone checked on her?'

'She's on annual leave this week, and not answering her mobile phone.'

'So you don't know for sure if she's OK?' asked Herron.

Barker sighed. 'Jane rarely answers her phone when she's off duty.'

'Where does she live?'

He frowned and hesitated but then he told her Pochard's address.

'I'll go and check it out this afternoon,' said Herron.

'You're being very thorough,' said Barker. 'But I doubt you'll find much sign of her. She's somewhere deep in the Trossachs right now, if I'm not mistaken.' He explained that Pochard had arranged a walking holiday up north with Professor Eric Reichmann, who was flying over from Switzerland to join her. Reichmann was the founder of the European holistic society to which Pochard and most of her colleagues at Deepwell belonged.

They had reached an oak door at the end of a long corridor. A brass plate in the middle of the door read, 'Director of Staff, Dr Liam Barker'.

Herron asked, 'Aren't you worried that something might have happened to Dr Pochard if she's not answering her phone?'

Barker turned to look at her, his hand stiffening on the door handle. 'If something has, then it has nothing to do with any of my patients. None of them left the hospital over the weekend.'

His hand rested on the handle, waiting for Herron to speak again. She had sensed an inner resistance to answering her question completely honestly. When she said nothing further, Barker pushed open the door and led them into his office.

He cleared his throat and straightened his back as he took his seat behind the desk.

'McCrea has made claims in the past that he attacked young women,' said Morton. 'Rope and handcuffs were found in his car before he was admitted here.'

'Which he never used. Instead he drove himself straight to the police station and confessed to the dangerous fantasies that were haunting him. He was guilt-ridden and frightened by the thought of what he might do. That doesn't fit with the profile of a serial killer who has repressed his memories. Alistair does have a criminal record, but there is little evidence of violence against women in it.'

Barker handed them a typed sheet summarising what McCrea had said during the group therapy. The detectives read it in turn.

Herron spoke first. 'So it is your professional opinion that Alistair McCrea's claims are purely the result of his illness?'

'You've read them yourself. What do you think?'

She had to agree with him. McCrea's descriptions were florid and disturbing, more like visions or nightmares than anything that might have any basis in reality. 'I have to ask you to confirm your statement,' she said. 'It's necessary for the paperwork.'

Barker nodded impatiently.

'Anything else that makes you doubt their authenticity?' asked Morton.

'No, but I'm certain I'm correct.'

'About what?'

He stared at the two detectives with deadpan eyes. 'That Alistair is a deeply disturbed and lonely individual who will confess to anything to get attention.'

'Has he confessed to anything similar in the past?'

'He's confessed to countless crimes during his time here, crimes he could not possibly have committed.'

'What sort of crimes?'

A shade of tension fell over Barker's face. 'Those are confidential matters and I really can't say.'

'We're police officers, investigating a confession to murder,' said Morton. 'Nothing is confidential in the circumstances.'

Barker began talking about patient privacy and the code of conduct governing psychiatrists. He sounded clever and professional, but Morton cut him off.

'I understand you are trying to uphold your policies on patient privacy, but your actions could be construed as obstruction,' he warned. 'I suggest you drop words like "confidentiality" and "privacy" when talking about what your patients may or may not have confessed to.'

Barker sighed. 'Alistair has written many confessions over the years. Confessions involving murdered women and hidden bodies that do not make sense and cannot be backed up by any concrete evidence. I will not try to summarise them for you. I would not know where to start. They're all recorded in his case notes, of course.'

'May we have a look at them?' asked Herron. 'We sent you through a written request first thing this morning.'

Barker sighed again. It struck her that his sighs were like a clock, counting down the reserves of his patience. A while went by without any of them saying a word. Realising that the officers were determined to see the notes, Barker eventually sent his secretary to get the file.

'In the past,' said Barker, 'the therapeutic side of our treatment programme was too focused on getting the patients to delve into their memories. Revealing stories of abuse or even confessing to abuse and violence could lead to a reward of sorts, greater attention from sympathetic psychologists and stronger medication. Unfortunately, Alistair fell into that trap.'

'Why weren't these previous confessions reported to the police?' asked Herron.

'There was no need to do that. His psychologists were quite sure he had fabricated them.'

'If the claims weren't properly investigated, how could his psychologists be sure?'

'You're police officers. With all respect, you don't understand the nature of mental illness. Right now, Alistair is heavily sedated with benzodiazepines and incapable of distinguishing truth from fantasy. Your involvement here will only interfere with his therapy.'

'We haven't come to interfere with his therapy.'

'But you're the police; your very presence here is interference.'

Herron heard the trace of venom in his response, the first hint of a rift between the world of law and order and that of psychiatry.

The secretary returned with a file on McCrea's background and history, and Barker passed it over to the two detectives. Herron quickly read the notes. Amid McCrea's descriptions of his life as a petty thief and drug-taker, the serial break-ins and the shoplifting, there were hints of a darker, more violent world, murder plots concealed within conspiracies, women who had disappeared, their body parts hidden in forests, and mysterious visitors to the hospital who used torture on the patients. However, the accounts were entangled in garbled visions that kept returning to a forest trail, a body of calm water through the fir trees, and a pile of stones with a woman's head buried within. There were other disturbing images in his notes, including one of a pit of water with two snakes threshing together that turned into the bodies of two police officers, one female and the other male, bound together by ropes. Herron flinched a little.

Against Barker's advice, the officers insisted on interviewing McCrea. Barker looked aggrieved by their determination. 'You really think these fabrications merit a police investigation?'

Herron smiled in an effort to ease his annoyance. 'We can only decide that after we interview him.'

'Alistair is at home in this hospital,' said Barker. 'To him it is a secure place. He is safely medicated, surrounded by routine and order, much more than he could expect in the outside world. You are free to interview him. However, it must be on his terms. He has insisted that he will speak only to a female detective.'

Herron wondered if the chief inspector had known about this demand from the very start. She looked at Morton and he nodded at her, so she agreed to McCrea's request.

'Let me give you a piece of advice, Sergeant Herron,' said Barker, leading her onto Ward G. 'You will never be able to keep up with Alistair. Even when you're interviewing him, his mind will be busy fabricating another fantasy besides the one he is telling you about, another crime that he never committed, because he has finally got the attention of a police detective.'

# CHAPTER FIVE

The first police interview with Alistair McCrea was conducted by Sergeant Herron in the music room on Ward G. A pale light, diluted through the blinds, shone on the soundproofed walls, and on the pale face of the patient, who was seated at an empty table in the centre with two male nurses sitting cross-armed behind him.

Herron's first impression was of a tall, fragile man, who would not survive long in a police interrogation room. At first, he did not seem to see her. His eyes scanned the room, as though it were already filled with people. She sat down at the table and leaned towards him, smiling warmly. His eyes met hers and then rolled down to her neckline before widening as though he had received a jolt of electricity. She felt it then, a tingle of fear, as his eyes took her in.

She began by introducing herself and explaining that this was not a formal police interrogation.

'But you are going to investigate?' he asked. His voice was deep, but querulous, with a whine of self-pity in it.

'Oh no, we can't investigate unless you tell us a good deal more than what is in this confession of yours.'

McCrea contorted in his chair. Was it surprise or disappointment she saw in his pale eyes? 'Then you don't believe me. No one will believe me, no matter how many times I say it.'

'Persuade me that your story is true, Alistair. Tell me what happened to Dr Pochard. And the others? What were their names? What did you do with their bodies?'

McCrea groaned, leaned forward, and then flung himself back into his chair. The male nurse who had been staring out the window turned his head sharply towards the patient.

'The doctors say that your confession is a symptom of your illness.'

'It's not,' he replied. 'I'm telling you that it happened. I have proof. That's why you should take me seriously.'

'What proof?'

'Dr Pochard is missing.'

The nurses remained calm and untroubled, indifferent to McCrea's protestations.

'You see, I keep having hallucinations that it's happening again. I see her head tipping backwards and falling out of my hands.'

'What if the entire incident is an hallucination? Is that possible?'

'I wish it were.' He gave a cry of despair as though he were seeing the murder again, not as the perpetrator, but as a helpless witness, forced to endure a recurring glimpse of murder. She saw in his bloodshot gaze the certainty of his vision, that a woman had been killed and he was responsible for her death.

'I'm telling you the truth,' he said. The eyelids retracted; his eyes were full on her, opaque and haunted, seeking an audience for his visions.

'Then tell me how you got by hospital security?'

'I don't know. I can't remember.' He seemed about to weep. 'Will there be an investigation?'

'That's not for me to say. Others will decide if one is warranted.'

'If you don't investigate, I'll have to do something about it.'

'What do you mean?'

'I might go to the newspapers.' His eyes gloated. 'Yes, I think I will go to the press.'

'You said in your confession that you can't remember kiling your victims, but that you've dreamed about it.'

'Yes, many, many times.'

'Did you base your confession on your dreams?'

'My dreams are all I have to base my memories upon.'

'And you're convinced that these events actually happened.'

'Yes, but I'm not sure if I was the murderer.'

'You don't know?'

'That is the difficulty I have. As soon as I start trying to remember what happened everything is twisted and distorted by my illness.'

Herron thought she understood what he was trying to say. 'But how am I to unlock the truth and make you remember?'

'By not asking questions like that. Because as soon as I try to put my memories into words they become unreal and I push them away. They get mixed up with my fantasies and hallucinations and then I can no longer believe in them as facts.'

'But that's impossible. I'm a detective. It's my job to ask questions, not entertain suspicions about dreamed-up murders.'

'Then my memories are guaranteed to drive you to distraction.'

'Memories or dreams about memories.'

McCrea hesitated. 'My dreams are always rooted in memories.'

'Then tell me what you remember. No more word games.'

McCrea placed his hands over his ears and closed his eyes. 'I remember burying their heads in a pile of stones.'

'Where?'

'There are trees all around, and a lot of water nearby. Or at least the sense of water.'

'A forest by a loch?'

He frowned. 'I can't think if you keep asking questions.'

'I need the name of the place.'

'What if I can't tell you? Will you still investigate?'

'Not to chase figments of your imagination. Not when there are real criminals running along the streets.'

'I keep having the same dream. I'm chasing someone through a forest.'

'Describe the forest to me. What kind of trees are there? Is there a road or a landmark nearby?'

He closed his eyes. 'I'm trying.'

'That's good.'

'When I look through the trees, the view keeps changing. Sometimes I see a caravan park my parents took me to near Callander, then I see a summer camp with lots of children. I think it's in Cardrona Forest, outside Peebles.'

'What about the loch? Is there a jetty or boats? An island perhaps?'

'Yes, an island. Definitely an island with rocks and more trees.' He brought his hands up to cover his eyes.

'Who are you chasing?'

'I'm not sure.' His breathing hoarsened. 'A woman like you.'

'What do you mean?'

He lowered his head. 'There are lots of memories of women being chased that I don't dare to believe in yet.'

She sensed the eyes of the two nurses upon her, checking her professional performance against their assumptions of how a detective should behave in the circumstances. She felt stiff as a dummy in her work clothes, exposed between the experienced nurses and this disturbed patient.

'What happens next?'

'In my dream?'

'Yes.'

'The track goes past a waterfall covered in the roots of dead trees, and then the forest changes as I go deeper. The wind picks up and the trees start thrashing through the air. Some sort of storm is raging through the branches. Then the commotion changes and I see the disturbance is her, the woman struggling in my arms. A bird cries out from the treetops and I realise it's her screaming.' Alistair rubbed his eyes. 'I hold her head in my hands and then she bites my middle finger.'

'And then what?'

'Her head rolls away onto a pile of stones and I wake up. I find myself here in this safe place. I remember that I am a patient on Ward G of Deepwell Psychiatric Hospital. That the staff are trying to protect the world from my violent fantasies.'

McCrea's story was more outlandish than she had expected. Yet his sense of remorse seemed genuine. She was careful not to appear too interested, remembering Barker's advice that McCrea was an attention-seeker. She was well out of her comfort zone and Barker was the expert, after all. Still, McCrea's emotions felt credible, even if the physical details did not, and she was intrigued. The crux of the puzzle was finding concrete evidence. She explained to him that if he could tell her the precise location of one of the bodies, then that would prove once and for all if he was telling the truth.

'So unless you find a body you won't believe my confession?'

'It's not up to me. I'm not in charge of the investigation.'

'So there is an investigation?' A gleam appeared in his eyes.

'Not a formal investigation.'

An alarm bell sounded, a siren that rose and fell, and she could hear people running down the corridor. There was no way of telling what was happening, only that it was an emergency.

'Has there ever been a police report that matches my nightmare? One where an eyewitness might have seen something strange in a forest but not known what it was?'

'If they didn't know what they'd seen then the report was probably never recorded.'

When she saw the look of disappointment in his face, she promised to ask her colleagues and check through all the archived logs, even though she was convinced any search would be fruitless.

'I've made my confession,' he said. 'I'm guilty until the courts prove I'm innocent, isn't that how it works?'

'No court in the country will put on trial someone's nightmares.'

'Then there is no one who can take away my guilt.'

The longer the session went on, the more she pitied McCrea. A large part of him was lost to the real world. A man who could only make himself conspicuous by confessing to a terrible secret he had concocted from his nightmares and repressed fantasies. Her time was almost up, but before she could leave, McCrea tried to delay her with a final puzzle. 'My middle finger still hurts where she bit me. If I made all this all up then why does it still hurt so much?' He held up his right hand to her, but none of his fingers looked injured or painful.

Exasperated, she told him that the staff on the ward would help if he were in any discomfort.

She rose from her seat and signalled to the male nurses, one of whom led her back through a set of corridors. The lino floor gave way to carpet and a hush descended. They marched back to Barker's office at a brisk pace, the doors banging shut behind them like traps, and then they met the woman with the scars on her arms. She was making small plodding steps down the middle of the corridor, forcing the female care assistant who was accompanying her to stop and wait. She halted right in front of Herron. The care assistant, who was sweating and wheezing slightly, made a half-hearted attempt to move her on, but the woman stuck out her elbows and stiffened her body. She stood there, as if suspended, and then she leaned closer to Herron.

'Do you know Inspector Monteath?' she asked in a dry whisper.

Herron said she had never heard of him.

'But I saw him talking to you earlier. He comes here when he's off duty and Dr Barker has gone for the day. Tell him I've got a clue for him.'

'What clue?'

Her eyes grew vague. They seemed to search for an answer and then lose it. The care assistant made another attempt to move her on but she resisted with her thin arms. 'They were re-enacting a murder on Ward G,' she said.

'Whose murder?' Herron had an absurd image of the doctors and patients performing a grisly charade.

She said she did not know. The care assistant grabbed her by the elbow. 'Come on, Mary, it's time you had your tablets.' She winked at Herron. 'She's been watching too many crime dramas on TV.'

But Mary dug in her heels. 'You think I'm crazy,' she said to Herron, her face turning pale and distraught.

'No,' said Herron softly.

Suddenly Mary smiled provocatively at her. 'Then you must be crazy, too.' Her face grew so tight with grinning it looked ready to burst.

'Come on, Mary,' said the care assistant again, dragging her along the corridor. 'You're wasting people's time.'

Before she was wrenched out of sight, Mary shouted, 'At least Inspector Monteath is not a fraud. Unlike the others.'

'Unlike who?'

'Dr Barker and the rest. They're all frauds, passing themselves off as something they're not, persecuting me every day.'

The male nurse raised his eyebrows and gave Herron a look that warned her not to say anything else. They walked through another set of double doors.

'Mary's a lonely woman desperately trying to get attention,' he explained. 'A stranger's face is like fresh meat to her.' Then, dropping his voice to a whisper, he added, 'To survive in this place you have to be at least a little bit crazy.'

'She said I was crazy, too,' said Herron.

'Don't worry, you're not crazy. Not even a little bit.' He gave her a wink. 'You'd never survive on a ward like this.'

His comment prompted a smile from Herron, and then, as if taking her into his confidence, he said, 'You know, Alistair was waiting all morning for you, asking had the police arrived, were they really on their way.'

'Why is he so keen to have the police involved?'

'He wants to make sure he stays on Ward G rather than go back to the community. The doctors were planning to release him at the end of the month.'

'But what if he's arrested and taken into custody?' she said. 'At the very least, he runs the risk of wasting police time.'

'Alistair's plan B is to keep spinning you a story so absurd and vague that no court would ever believe it.' The nurse opened the final set of security doors and pointed her in the direction of the reception. 'He wants you officers of the law to give up eventually and leave him to his own devices without ruining his comfortable relationship with Ward G and its pharmaceutical cabinet.'

# CHAPTER SIX

It was raining when the detectives left the hospital. They hurried down to the car park without looking back. Herron seated herself in the passenger seat and Morton drove off. Behind them, the hospital disappeared in the downpour. Morton was aloof, colder than before, and the trees seemed to hem in the road more tightly on the way back to Peebles. The rain drummed on the roof and against the windscreen.

She expected him to ask her how the interview had gone, but he did not show the slightest degree of curiosity. They were meant to be working together with him overseeing the interview, and she thought some form of communication or candour was needed between them. Besides, Morton had twenty years' more experience than she had, and had visited the hospital before. He was bound to have something useful to say. Her thoughts groped for a way to initiate conversation, troubled by Morton's reticence. She sensed no outlet in the vista of ramifying trees and constant rain, but she was unwilling to say nothing.

'Do you think McCrea is making it all up?' she asked.

'You're the one who interviewed him, not me. And it's you who has to write up the report for Bates.'

'You don't want to contribute to it in any way? After all, you were meant to help me with the interview.'

'No.'

'At least you could tell me your impressions.'

There was no answer from Morton. He seemed to be concentrating all his energy on driving. Several minutes passed. The downpour darkened.

'What awful weather,' said Herron, giving up any attempt to extract Morton's opinion. It seemed too much to ask. She peered sideways at his lank hair, his beard and his glowering eyes. Much too much.

After a few miles, he shuddered slightly. 'To tell you the truth, all I could think of was how lonely McCrea must feel in a place like that, surrounded by mad people and cold-faced bastards like Barker.'

He didn't say anything else after that. Herron wanted to tell him about the odd impression she'd had that McCrea was telling the truth, or at least a version of the truth, but she was afraid the wrong words might slip out, stupidities she might regret uttering to a senior colleague not known for his patience with new recruits. She had excelled on the training course, but still she felt unsure of herself, and of the larger world of policing and crime. Her weaknesses and strengths felt inseparable. She was the fast-tracked female detective, whose bright talent might easily be shattered by a careless word or action, and who had to be treated with extreme caution by her older male colleagues. Was that the reason for Morton's reticence?

It was only when they were pulling into the police station's car park that Morton spoke again. 'Words can sometimes be the devil,' he said. 'They get people into all sorts of trouble. If I don't have anything useful to say, I'd rather say nothing.'

She nodded, grateful at getting such a succinct reply, wondering to herself how on earth she was going to work with a partner so reluctant to use the powers of speech. There was an unnerving solidity about Morton and his few announcements, which she noticed to an extent in the other officers at the station, a sense that their judgement was always accurate and beyond doubt. Morton's behaviour demonstrated his great confidence in his place in the world as a middle-aged detective in a small Scottish town, but it also showed his flaw, his inability to test his opinions with others and invite opposing points of view or ideas. What if one day a detective like her were to prove him wrong? What would happen then? Some sort of violent inner explosion, she suspected.

In front of Herron, framed against the forest stretching up to a bleak hillside at Dawyck, stood Dr Pochard's wooden lodge. It looked pretty with its large windows and overhanging balcony, floating amid the surrounding pine trees like a little island, a final refuge of civilisation before the harsh Borders landscape set in. There was even something enchanting about the darkness in the forest, she thought. It was the kind of place she would like to retire to or go on weekend retreats. She wondered what was so comforting about a secluded timber house enclosed by trees. Was it the return to the wild and the simpler charms of nature that it seemed to offer her troubled mind?

After leaving Morton at the station, she had travelled the winding A72 road to Lyne Station on her own. She had crossed the river Tweed, and taken a small side road away from the valley floor, feeling calm settle upon her thoughts, the professional and domestic worries slipping behind her as the track rose into the leaf-purified air.

The lower floor of the house was completely dark, the sun-light only reaching the windows on the first floor. She tried the doors and lower windows. They were all locked. She rang the doorbell and called Dr Pochard's name through the letter box. From inside, she could hear the sound of an extractor fan, which struck her as odd, if Pochard had indeed left on holiday. She walked round the building and saw a car in a little side garage, which also struck her as unusual.

She was drawn to the burnt-out remains of a fire at the bottom of the garden. A thin sour stink emanated from the ashes, which she surmised were a few days old. She poked through them and studied the blackened scraps of paper. The pine trees swayed slightly in the wind as she read what appeared to be the remnants of Dr Pochard's notes on her patients. She picked over a notebook that had escaped the worst of the blaze, but was now sodden and disintegrating. She could see that Pochard had been a careful listener, recording all the little details of her patients' lives, the nuances of their emotions, precise descriptions of their dreams, more like little biographies than patient notes. However, the fire and rain had made it impossible to draw the fragments into a coherent story. She flicked through the pages, recognising the names of some of her patients from the media, actors and writers and even the odd politician. In one of the last pages, Pochard had written in shaky, strained handwriting, 'This is a total setback for Deep-well. I can't let everyone down. The therapy with the patients should continue. No doubt about it.'

At the edge of the fire, she found the imprint of a boot, size nine or ten, she guessed, smudging a collection of half-burnt notes and photographs, the imprint like an angry verdict on Pochard's life's work. She saw the photos were of forest clearings, some of them with figures huddled together for the camera. Immediately, she recognised the figure of Alistair McCrea in one of them, framed against a row of trees. He was half looking back at the camera, his long white eyelashes clearly visible in the low sunlight, seemingly exhausted, grimacing in the light, while the other figures stood around him as if waiting for something. One of them was the male nurse from Ward G.

She poured all her attention into the photographs. They seemed to document some sort of excursion from Deepwell Hospital, but what was the exact purpose of the trip? The only thing she could construe was that staff had taken a deeply troubled McCrea on a walk through a forest. What did the path through the pine trees represent? Not a venture into freedom, but something much darker.

Most of the photos were empty of people. Snapshots of different waterfalls and piles of stones, upended roots, contorted branches, all trying to tell her something as though the photographer were attempting to bleed secrets from wood and rocks, and always the presence of water in the background, silent and solitary.

A psychotherapist who had burned her notes before going off on holiday. A set of photographs taken by a photographer who seemed as obsessed with forest clearings, piles of stones and waterfalls as McCrea. She wondered what Morton would do in the circumstances. She listened to the stillness of the house again and decided she needed to speak to him. She could not tell if there were sufficient grounds to be suspicious about Pochard's safety, but she was sure that she needed to speak to someone. She rang headquarters, but Morton had already left. She called him on his mobile. In the background, she could hear the muffled sound of his car radio. She told him what she had discovered.

'There's no sign of Dr Pochard, as we expected,' she said. 'But I found some half-burnt photographs and notes in her garden. I think you need to take a look at them.' She described the scenes, their similarities with the landscapes of McCrea's confession. 'I find it disturbing that the photos match descriptions from his delusions.'

'Why?' There was a hint of harshness in his tone.

She wanted to voice the troubling thought that was running through her mind, that somehow Pochard had fallen into the trap of McCrea's nightmares, a trap that had snapped shut upon her.

'It seems like some sort of warning,' she said. 'Whoever took the photographs was searching for something.' She struggled to put her fears into words. 'It's as though they were trying to summon up McCrea's nightmare from the forest.'

'You make it sound so sinister and mysterious. It doesn't have to be that way. There might be a perfectly ordinary explanation for the pictures.'

The pine trees began to whisper in a strengthening gust of wind. All around, she felt the shadowy weight of their branches.

'No,' she replied. 'In this case, it is that way. I'm sure something bad has happened to Pochard.' She stared at the doctor's house, the empty gaze of its windows and the glass reflections of the pine trees swaying like restless curtains. She knew there was something to be grasped in the convulsions of the trees, something fleeting in the quietness of the house and the mystery of the discarded photographs, but she wasn't skilled enough to listen and understand.

'There's something you learn with experience,' said Morton.

'The most reasonable explanation is usually the one that turns out to be true, even when there are sinister possibilities lurking in the background. In this case, you are worrying too much about a patient who was locked up in a secure ward and had no possible means to do any harm to this doctor, who, I suspect, will turn up perfectly well in a day or two. You must learn to distinguish between the possible and the impossible in our line of work.'

'I still think we should put a call-out for Dr Pochard. Ask her to make contact with the police and clear up any concerns about her safety.'

After a pause, Morton asked, 'Do you remember what the boss told you about this case?'

'It's not a formal investigation.'

'Correct, and what else?'

'He wanted a report on his desk by Thursday morning.'

'The order still stands. I'm sure Bates will look forward to reading your findings. In the meantime, take my advice; stick with the most reasonable conclusions.'

Morton said something else, but the call grew inaudible and then she lost the connection.

# CHAPTER SEVEN

Although Carla could not work out exactly what was troubling her, she could feel it sharply and distinctly in her skin and nerves. The interview with McCrea had disturbed her in a way she had never experienced before. She could not be satisfied by Morton's advice, and she refused to draw the most reasonable explanations for Dr Pochard's disappearance. Her instinct told her that something ruthless and violent had befallen the psychotherapist. It made her greedy to know more, to track down McCrea's nightmarish clearing in the forest. This is good, she told herself. This craving to keep investigating, to keep digging. It thrust her out of her tame routine as a mother of two children into something much darker and deeper, something she could really explore, a world of unknown limits and dangers where everything had been set in mysterious motion.

That night, she pored over Pochard's photographs while nursing the baby to sleep. She spread out several maps of the Borders area on the floor and began dividing the terrain into sections. She listed the sites in each section that roughly matched the photographs and McCrea's description. After an hour she had collected dozens of locations worth investigating further, but had only covered a small portion of the Borders. Doubts began to assail her when the breakthrough moment did not arrive. How was she meant to find the clearing McCrea had described and which seemed to closely resemble the one in the photographs? She was an inexperienced investigator who had been handed the case, she now suspected, because Bates had believed it would go nowhere. She was unsure of what she was doing, and still trying to learn the basics from Morton, who seemed resolute in his determination to ignore her.

Several times, she read the notes she had made from her interview with McCrea and his case history. She felt as though she was working at the very edge of her consciousness, and that McCrea, for all his irrationality, had deliberately placed the location just beyond her reach. Not only did memories change over time, but so did the landscape. Both were in constant flux. Did the path through the trees and the clearing still exist, and what about the pile of stones itself? She pushed aside the depressing thoughts and continued with her painstaking work, poring over the maps. She thought she might go mad herself, sifting through McCrea's delusions and memories, searching for a clear signpost amidst the confusion.

She switched on her laptop and clicked on Google Earth's icon. She zoomed in on the topography around Peebles, searching for more context, another anchor in the landscape. Holding down the shift key, clicking and dragging upwards, she was able to rotate her view so that she could see towards the horizon instead of straight down. Her shoulders were hunched and her neck ached, yet inside her head she was as alert as a bird of prey. What was she looking for? A crime scene, or the innocent path taken by a group of psychiatrists and their patients on a day trip? She enlarged and changed the view, hoping to find a location that would match the features of the photographs. However, one forest path was much like another, and the views of lochs blurred into each other. She kept clicking the mouse, rotating the view, switching back to her printed maps whenever she wanted to find a new forest to explore.

Several times, Ben woke and she had to lift him in her arms. Patiently, she settled him back to sleep. She heard David downstairs trying to meet Alice's unending list of bedtime demands, and with a sense of blessed relief, pulled the screen closer and immersed herself in the landscape of the Borders. A wall fell away from her domestic existence, and a feeling of escape flooded through her. This was work but it was also turning into something else, a drug that made her feel invincibly tall and omniscient. The aerial images must have been taken late in the year. Along the ridges and valleys surrounding Peebles lay the browns, oranges and yellows of dying vegetation. She followed the course of the Tweed river, black and meandering, and its tributaries, and then she crossed the crest of high hills that ran south of the town. The roads dwindled into rough tracks until the only signs of civilisation were a few isolated farms lost amid the pines and deserted lochs, a lonely landscape of contrasting shades, heathery hills and dense forests, darkness and light, a completely clear canvas for her enquiring mind. She followed the patterns on the screen, down and down into hidden valleys and wells of silence, and then she came upon a shadowy wall of mountain and bare rock. Still the landscape withheld the secret she was so determined to find.

A flicker of movement at the door made her spin round, and she saw David standing at the doorway, staring at her with a look of mystification on his face. Ben had started crying again and was wriggling in her left arm. With her free hand, she was scrabbling at the computer mouse. All about her feet were strewn pieces of paper and discarded maps.

'Sorry, I didn't hear you,' she said. 'What did you say?'

'I didn't say anything.'

'Oh, right.'

'When are you coming to bed?'

'I don't know.'

They stared at each other for a moment or two, and then he stepped back into the landing like an actor reluctant to enter the stage. Their exchanges at this time of the night were often like this, full of hesitations and exhausted silences.

'I'm getting close to a breakthrough,' she said.

He paused and sighed. 'You know you never properly explained to me why you suddenly decided to be a police detective. How did having a baby make you want to completely change your direction in life?'

'I'll try to explain some other time. Not now.'

'I think you did it because you felt cheated and exhausted by motherhood. All the breastfeeding and those sleepless nights didn't live up to the glossy magazine articles.'

She raised her eyebrows. Wasn't it clear she put motherhood before everything else, that her children were at the forefront of her existence? But rather than get annoyed, she simply shook her head. 'When you have a baby,' she told him, 'your dreams either slip away, or they become the driving force that spurs you on.'

'Are parents of two small children allowed to have dreams?'

'Everyone has dreams,' she said. 'What about you? Why did you become a stay-at-home dad? Was it because you decided you no longer wanted to be a classroom teacher and would rather mark exam papers at home? And now you've got what you wanted, you're jealous because I have a life outside the house.'

She tried to place Ben into the cot, but he raised his arms and began crying vehemently. She lifted him back into her arms and looked at David. So far, he had not shown the slightest bit of interest in their crying child. He stood frozen at the doorstep as if her accusation had rendered him completely impotent, turning the room into a place of shame, a threshold he could not cross without forsaking every shred of his male dignity.

Eventually, he shrugged his shoulders. 'I'm not jealous at all, Carla. I'm just worried about you running after your other life and exhausting yourself.' He scanned the floor of discarded paper. 'But if this is what you want, then so be it.'

'Yes, this is what I want.'

There was nothing more to be said. They waited until the baby had stopped crying.

'You're off work tomorrow,' he said. 'Let's make the most of it and go somewhere nice.'

She pulled a face. 'I need to stay here and finish this.'

'OK then, have it your way,' he said and closed the door behind him.

She let the baby fall asleep on her chest. Then she went back to Google Earth and her notes, feeling the inner rush return as she searched for the location of McCrea's stone pile. She tracked north and then east, following even the unclassified roads into the forested hillsides. Several times she got lost and had to return to her printed maps, stretching her tired fingers and giving them a chance to recover from scrolling through the endless screens. Eventually, she narrowed her search to half a dozen sites that seemed worthy of investigation. Among the most promising was the forest at Cademuir in the Tweed valley. It had a secluded glen named the Pilot's Trail after two downed German pilots who had taken refuge there during

World War II and were only discovered when smoke from their fire gave them away.

Soon the house was completely silent, the children and David fast asleep. All the lights were out, but the glow of the computer screen shone on her hands, making her skin seem transparent. She kept working after midnight, feeling proud of her diligence and determination. This was her refuge from everything else, she realised, her hiding place, and yet it linked her to the darkest place imaginable, the mind of a man who fantasised about murder.

She caught David studying her face while they lay in bed the following morning. His features were slightly bloated, his hair unkempt, and his eyes were staring at hers, not in the usual intimate way, but as if he was searching for something, as if the person he was looking at had become a stranger. Since when had he started looking at her in that way?

It was Wednesday, her day off, and she spent the first part of the morning going over her notes again. David did the weekly shop, and then, after lunch, took Alice for a check-up at the doctor's. Meanwhile, Carla decided to take Ben with her and investigate a loch near Cademuir, one of the locations she had pinpointed on Google Earth. She hoped the baby would be distracted by the sights and sounds of the water, and allow her enough time to search for a setting that might match McCrea's descriptions.

By the time she reached the loch the temperature had dropped. She could sense the darkness of a winter twilight mustering in the dank reflections of the trees. Gripping the buggy tightly, she pushed it along a track that ran beside the water's edge. In spite of the cold, Ben was enjoying his escape from his father's company, laughing at the wild ducks waddling over the stones, and pointing vigorously at the paths ahead.

Since moving to Peebles, she and David had taken their children everywhere, visiting all the parks within a wide radius of the town, getting to know even the most obscure nature trails and out-of-the-way beauty spots in Cardrona Forest. On a run of easy Sunday afternoons that had felt like the most charmed of her life, they had visited the ruins of Cardrona Tower and the iron-age hill fort at Caberston Forest, setting out their picnics on patches of heather, the baby flopping on his belly, Alice rolling through the purple sprigs, and the river Tweed snaking below, disappearing into forests that filled her with curiosity and the hope of longer excursions into the countryside. Come to think of it, there was hardly a bench with a view of the Tweed valley that she had not sat on, with the buggy in one hand, pushing it gently back and forth, willing one or other of the children to sleep.

She pushed the pram harder, veering away from the loch and its reflections, which seemed to have been dredged from a dark corner of McCrea's imagination. It struck her that his confession had changed her relationship to the country-side. Picturing his footprints under the trees altered every-thing. The sunlight playing in the overhead trees went, as did the gentle sounds of the birds calling to each other, and any sense of peace or refuge amid the trails. The forest became the domain of his deranged mind, the paths wretched and shadowy, contaminated with deliriums of repressed violence. She took this darkness as a sign that she was on the correct track. However, she spent an hour pushing Ben's buggy along the trails, and could see nothing comparable to McCrea's clearing and pile of stones. The baby's face grew paler and more watchful.

She rested at a large stone overlooking the loch and Ben stared at her with a serious look.

'Hello,' said Carla, smiling.

Ben made some babbling sounds. He seemed hungry. She felt a sudden sorrow at not spending more afternoons with him. It was her day off, and she owed it to her children to push aside everything else and give them her undivided attention.

It was getting late, and she had to decide whether to go back to the car, or continue with the search. The wind picked up and the trees leaned and creaked against each other. She took the path that led into deeper undergrowth, setting off at a faster pace, trundling the buggy over the rough ground. The sound of a waterfall became increasingly audible. She followed a track leading deeper into the forest. Through the branches, she saw a cascade of water flinging itself from a rocky outcrop in the hillside. It was the sort of landscape she wanted her children to grow up in, but today it felt overshadowed. The lie of the path, the forest crammed with wind, the waterfall in full flow, and the gnarled roots of the ancient trees crawling over the rocks, all seemed to mimic the photographs and the sketch map she had made in her mind of McCrea's confession.

She pushed on, panting and puffing, the path rising steeply. She could not stop; she was completely entranced. Rain began to fall, cold and drenching, and she had to take shelter under the threshing trees. She pulled the waterproof cover over the buggy, and Ben stared at her, eyeing her warily, as if to ask, what dangerous underworld have you dragged me into?

She surveyed the twisted roots at the waterfall and was convinced they belonged to the same scene McCrea had described in his nightmare. The rain fell heavier and the sky darkened almost to blackness. For a moment, the movement of the trees ceased, and a line of sight opened up. The view through the trees seemed eerily calm and stable. What was that collection of stones to the right of the waterfall? A cairn or stone chamber of sorts dimly visible in the almost supernatural light.

A tremble passed through Ben's pale face, his features resembling those of a little animal of the forest, big-eyed, staring up at her from his hiding place. Another tremble passed through his face, and this time it shook his entire body before convulsing into a protracted wail. She should turn back now and make sure he got fed; the search for the cairn would have to wait until later. She could feel the buggy shaking with his wriggling limbs and frenzied protest. It was time to act like an attentive mother to her baby, for Christ's sake, and concentrate on meeting his needs. Wasn't that the most important thing right now? Why let a wild hunch and her detective's ambition put that beyond her? However, she ignored the crying, and kept staring at the waterfall scene, full of fascination for what lay further along the track. She felt she was so close to finding the location McCrea had described. Her heart beat faster as Ben's wailing increased; her hands gripping the pram, but still she did not turn back. How long could she keep ignoring her baby's desperate wail? What was she thinking of?

A lone figure appeared out of nowhere on the path and began walking towards her, a small, dishevelled man with a black, suspicious gaze. Her spine ran cold, and suddenly she felt fearful for her baby's safety. She turned the pram back down the track and glanced behind her but the figure had disappeared. What sort of person had he been? A tramp or some kind of troll, a guardian of the waterfall or a figment of her tired imagination? Distracted now, shaken deep in her maternal soul, she looked at the trees overshadowing the waterfall and the writhing roots. Slowly the scene began to lose its sinister glow, but still she felt afraid. The low sun returned and the paths steamed with the secret smells of the forest. Ben dozed off, exhausted by his crying fit, his little forest self hidden away behind his sleeping face.

She pushed on, hurrying back along the steep path, the buggy rocking from side to side, down through the trees and into a normal dripping wet evening in the Borders. When they were both in the safety of her car, she took out her phone and rang David. She was hoping that he might come and take Ben back home, allowing her to return to the waterfall for one final look, but she couldn't get a signal.

She drove home at speed, the heather on the wet hills resembling a churning sea.

That evening, it took her ages to get Ben and Alice fed and into bed. Both children were restless and completely oblivious to her presence as she sat beside their beds, willing them to settle down for the night. She paced around the room, tidying away clothes and toys, and then sat on her chair again. In her distracted state, she read them the same story several times. As soon as their eyes closed, she pulled the blinds and shut the bedroom door softly behind her.

She knew David was downstairs waiting for her in the living room, the door closed and the TV quietly on. This time of the day was the only private time in their routine when they could chat or complain to each other without the children hearing. However, this evening, she changed back into her work clothes and hunted out the car keys.

In the bathroom, she caught a glimpse of her reflection, a thirty-two-year-old spent-looking woman who had just got her children to sleep and should be heading to bed herself, rather than embarking on a wild-goose search based on the confession of a mad man. The exhaustion in her face was nothing new, but tonight her eyes stared back at her, terribly animated and dark. McCrea had handed her this dangerous new edge, she thought, the feeling that she had been liberated from the evening conveyor belt of feeding, toileting, sleeping and the anxious hours turning in bed, ears pricked for the slightest whimper from the children. Her overriding instinct was to protect her babies, but another part of her must be hardwired for danger and violence, she realised, otherwise why did she find McCrea's confessions and their descriptions of the forest so electrifying?

Before stepping out, she shouted in to David that she was heading out again. His exact words she could not make out, but the tone of his voice was as flat as a recorded message.

'I don't expect you to stay up,' she shouted and slipped out the front door.

However, before she could take off in the car, David appeared, knocking the glass of the driver door. 'Wait, we're meant to be going out tonight,' he said.

She rolled down the window, blinking at him.

'The babysitter's due in half an hour,' he said.

'You're kidding me.'

'No, we're going to the new Indian. The table's booked for nine.'

'Impossible.' She tried to smile sympathetically at him, but the expression felt painful and uncertain. 'Something important has come up.'

When he saw she was not going to get out of the car, he grimaced. 'What's the point trying to organise a night out any more when it's clear you'd rather be at work?'

'We can do it some other time. When this investigation is over.' She listened to him sigh. Why was she treating him like this? Why didn't she relent, apologise and postpone the investigation for another day? What was wrong with her?

He stood there, staring at her in his socks.

'There's no point standing in the cold,' she said.

'I know,' he replied and slinked back into the house like a dog that had just watched the cat steal its dinner.

# CHAPTER EIGHT

She followed the trail with her torch, hoping the battery would not run out. It was barely a path now, only a couple of feet wide, and uneven with tree roots and half-buried stones. She had been exploring the darkened loch and its adjoining forest for more than an hour, trying to find the track that would lead her back to the waterfall and the mysterious cairn of stones. However, where her map told her she would find the waterfall, she could only make out the dim outline of pine trees and overgrown rocks. She double-checked the notes she had made. This was definitely the place. She pulled her coat tighter around her, and set off deeper into the forest. She worried that this was not a proper search for a crime scene, and that she needed a team of officers and sniffer dogs to guide her to the right location. She was just wasting her time, and should head back home, but she was reluctant to leave after having come this far. Tired, she sat down on a fallen tree trunk and tried to get her bearings. She had already lost her sense of judgement and was now in danger of losing her sense of direction.

The moon came out and filled the forest with a silvery web of light and shade. She noticed that the path had been enlarged slightly, the weeds brushed back on both sides. Someone had been walking back and forth here. She pushed on, her pace quickening, and then she heard the waterfall ahead, hidden behind the trees. She stood for several moments with the sensation that she was no longer alone. She felt as though a stranger had entered the scene and was watching her. She turned sharply but there was no one there. The wind rose and the dappled undergrowth filled with nocturnal contours, shadows multiplying and receding under the swaying branches. She felt a pang of homesickness and a gnawing sense of separation from her children and husband. Thinking that ringing home and speaking to David might soothe her nerves, she took out her phone and tried to place a call, but there was no signal.

She pushed on, following the track towards the waterfall. She froze when she saw the figure of a man standing in the middle of the clearing. For an instant, she thought she had turned McCrea's cryptic vision back onto himself, and that in following the path to the waterfall she had summoned up his ghost and was about to witness the traumatic scene that haunted him. However, when the figure turned towards her, she saw it was the man she had spotted earlier that day. Disturbed by the detective, he staggered away. A tramp groping about in the undergrowth for a hiding place, she thought. However, when she saw that his right hand was bandaged and there was a stump where his middle finger should be, she shone her flashlight into his face and ordered him to stop.

'What are you doing here?' she asked.

'Just watching.' He sounded annoyed at her question. 'Who are you?'

'Carla Herron. I'm a police detective. I want to know what you're doing here.'

'Taking a trip down memory lane.' He blinked in the light of the torch. 'Is it forbidden to walk through a forest and think of the past?'

'Not at all.' She lowered the light from his face.

She could hear the ragged sound of his breathing. He seemed anxious now. 'Don't think your coming here is going to help things,' he warned.

'What do you mean?'

'You're too late.'

'Too late for what?'

'To stop what happened here.' He looked as though he was scanning the trees, but his eyes were shut tight. 'I'm so over-whelmed by memories I can hardly think straight.'

'What are you talking about?'

'The pile of stones you're searching for is over there to the left. Follow the ridge through the trees.'

She walked in the direction he pointed, the ground rough and steep in places, the path barely distinguishable from the undergrowth. She waited, looked back and saw he had disappeared. She waded deeper into the forest. The sound of the waterfall grew in volume, thrusting through the darkness, fed by invisible streams in the hillside. She kept walking and the forest rose above her in the night sky like the shelf of a cliff. After a while, she saw the waterfall tumbling in the moonlight, the jumble of rocks and the gnarled tree roots. A hundred yards further, and she came upon a cairn of stones emerging from the vegetation. She stood, feeling the tension rising in her body. What was this place? A stone cairn hiding a secret? It was certainly the same pattern of landscape features in McCrea's confession, no doubt about it. She walked towards the cairn.

Half-covered by the stones, she found a cardboard box. She read the words on the lid, Number One Delivery. She put on a pair of gloves from her coat pocket, and with unbelieving hands, she lifted the box from its hiding place. The sides were sticky and sodden. Its bottom collapsed and out dropped the contents. She shone her torch amid the cobwebs and forest litter. At first, she could not make out what she was looking at. Something unreal and grisly. She peered closer, forcing herself not to look away. She shivered and recoiled, taking several steps backwards. Later she would tell her colleagues that it was the most sickening sight she had ever witnessed. What lay before her was a chunk of jagged flesh and long red hair flowing into the darkness. The disembodied head of a woman, her eyes closed. It was her blood that had soaked the cardboard box and the detective's hands. Something else rolled out of the box. A bloodstained finger, swollen and grey, dropped onto the ground. There was something distasteful about the way it lay next to the head, the discoloured nail pointing blindly into the darkness. Herron almost collapsed. She reached for her phone but still there was no signal. She had to wade back through the darkness and on to the road, before she was able to put the call through, feeling beads of sweat roll down her spine, the hairs on the back of her neck pricking, and her ears ringing as though the bloody head was screaming at her.

# CHAPTER NINE

Afterwards – in the hours before dawn – Detective Chief Inspector Bates and Inspector Morton joined Herron to squint through the shadows at the scene. Herron could see from the way the two men clambered around the clearing, and the heaviness of their breathing, that they were troubled, yet excited, by the grisly finding. She watched them from the periphery. The DCI kept glancing at her as though her discovery of the decapitated head had made her an object of pity rather than admiration.

'If McCrea hadn't told his story it might have been a long time before we found this place,' said Morton.

'What does that tell us about his link to the body part?' asked Bates.

Morton went to the edge of the clearing and stood there for a while, his long hair and beard getting wet, his hands clasped behind his back, staring into the early morning darkness and the hanging mist.

He turned back and joined them with an air of calm

authority. 'Perhaps it's not really that strange,' he said. 'The key is that lots of people knew about McCrea's story. Staff at the hospital, patients, perhaps even relatives. Who's to say that whoever did this hasn't cleverly organised it to resemble the confession?'

'As a way to throw us off his scent,' said Bates, nodding.

Dawn crept through the trees, revealing a forest floor of dark, jutting things, rotting tree trunks and upended roots. After a pause, Morton said, as if speaking to himself, 'Yes, that's what must have happened.'

The DCI cleared his throat. 'That's what I think too.' He turned to look at Herron. 'What do you make of it?'

The two men watched her as the mist rose slowly through the trees.

She chose her words carefully. 'The brutality of it, the way the head was arranged here with the finger, suggests someone who is organised and very clear about what he is doing.' She paused. 'However, if the tramp with the missing finger is our main suspect, why did he hang around? He should have stayed away, rather than linger in the forest like another signpost.'

'Another signpost?'

A morbid thought had struck her, that her journey to find the woman's head had been mapped out for her in advance, with McCrea and the tramp stepping out from the shadows like ghosts of a murder-to-be, guiding her along the way. She felt the tingle of a mysterious intelligence operating in the darkness, a killer reaching out to her and whispering of his dark deeds.

'Yes, pointing the way to the scene. Like McCrea's confession and the photographs at Dr Pochard's house.'

'Listen,' said Bates, 'when you're writing up your preliminary report of what happened, keep the finger confidential. And don't let it slip to the media. We should use it to help eliminate fantasists like McCrea. That sort of detail is unusual.'

'McCrea knows about the finger already.' She recounted his dream of the woman biting his finger before her head rolled out of his hands.

'But he doesn't know that a finger was left behind,' said Bates.

'He knows it's important in the context of the scene. The bitten finger keeps recurring in his dreams and his notes.'

'Dear God, is there anything new about this crime scene? Anything McCrea hasn't already mentioned?'

She thought about it for a while. 'We need to speak to McCrea again and go over his dreams. We need to find what links he might have with the tramp.'

The DCI gave Herron a strange smile and said, 'Look, Carla, this has changed everything.' His words sounded more polished than anything else he had said that night. 'Your diligence is to be highly commended, but the entire investigation will have to begin again from scratch. The tramp is our main suspect, but we will have to re-examine McCrea's confession and any assumptions we made about it. We can't allow ourselves to be influenced by psychiatric professionals and their opinions on McCrea's illness. The truth might turn out to be very difficult for them to swallow.'

Herron exhaled a long breath into the cold morning air.

Bates adopted a more confidential tone. 'Which is why I am taking you off the investigation. Morton is in charge of it now.'

She could feel the heat rising in her face. Her curiosity had been strongly aroused by the crime scene. Surely, the DCI could sense it, her eagerness to hunt down the killer.

'But I'm already deeply involved in the case,' she told him.

'You should judge me on my performance and decision-making to date, rather than my lack of experience.'

'There's no discussion on the matter. This looks to be a murder scene. Only the investigating officers should be here.'

Her face, which had glowed with excitement, and then annoyance, now drained of all colour. She fought to control her feelings. 'You can't just kick me off the investigation.'

'Yes, I bloody well can.' Bates glared at her, anger gathering in his eyes.

She tried to protest further, but could not find the words, cut off by Bates's blunt dismissal in a way that felt so stark and absolute. She felt betrayed. Her doubts about her capabilities enveloped her like the mist, shutting her away from the crime scene through which she had so confidently strode minutes previously.

Bates had turned his back to her, and was speaking to Morton in a more familiar manner. 'They've released too many of the psychiatric patients in this bloody country,' he said. 'You see them mumbling and shouting on every street corner.'

Morton, however, was gazing at her in a sympathetic way. 'I don't agree with your decision to take Sergeant Herron off the case,' he said, the stubbornness gleaming in his dark eyes. 'I think she is the best candidate we have to lead the investigation.'

Bates blinked at the senior detective in surprise. 'Listen, Morton, I had no idea this case would turn out to be so serious when I assigned it to Herron. The thought of having a completely untested officer running the investigation is enough to keep me awake all night.'

'The fact that she is untested should not be a problem. What's key is her intelligence and her emotional rapport with McCrea. I think she's the perfect choice; after all, it was her that brought us here.'

'But she has no experience tracking murder suspects. I never imagined that McCrea would actually lead us to a body.'

'When it comes to interrogating disturbed patients in a hospital, no one on the team has that much experience.'

'Quite. Up till now, our suspects have tended to be sane and at-large.'

'So this is the first time for the entire team. We're all on new ground.'

Morton swept his eyes over the clearing, the police tape clinging to the bushes, the trees tossing against the sky and the trampled paths leading up to the stone chamber. Forensic officers in protective gear were crouching and crawling through the undergrowth. Deep in the forest, an animal, a fox or a badger, gave an incomprehensible yelp.

'All murder investigations have their points of similarity,' said Morton, 'and I've investigated many, but this one is completely different. The crime scene has been constructed for us. The person responsible has spent time making it mysterious; he's working us. Sergeant Herron led us here. She understood the path of the killer. Having her lead the investigation makes sense.'

With the air of someone going against his better judgement, but who could also not stand beating around the bush, the DCI replied, 'OK. Let's compromise, and say that both you and Herron will lead the investigation. You can also have Ian Shaw and Brian Rodgers to help with your inquiries, along with the usual teams. Is that all right with the two of you?'

Morton looked at Herron and waited until she nodded in agreement, before nodding, too. He gave her a little smile as if to acknowledge their victory.

Bates wagged his finger. 'McCrea sounds like a tricky bastard. I want you to keep both feet on the ground and in step with Morton. Don't believe anything McCrea tells you and don't go off running on your own following hunches. Stick to the facts and don't underestimate McCrea.'

The three of them stared at the clearing. They could hear the roar of the waterfall, a damp breeze against their faces. Only one thing was certain in Herron's mind: no matter how the woman had died, it had begun with McCrea and his confession. If she were to unravel the mystery, she would have to return to Ward G and dig out the tunnel the killer had carefully filled in behind him.

David hardly spoke to Carla over breakfast that morning, not looking at her and limiting himself to responding in the most taciturn way possible to her descriptions of the forest scene. She apologised for letting him down the previous evening, but still he did not look at her. Not a good sign, she thought. Better leave him be. He crouched over his bowl, a handsome man with slightly greying hair in a wrinkled black T-shirt stained with baby food, shoulders hunched as he sipped methodically at his porridge. He seemed too old to be sitting at the table in such an untidy state. He lifted the spoon towards his mouth, hesitated, and for the first time that morning, turned to look at Carla. His eyes glinted, reminding her of Alice's just as she was about to throw a tantrum. Not wanting a confrontation, she rose quickly and checked that Alice was ready for nursery and then she put on her coat. On the way back downstairs, she glanced into David's study. Coursework assessments were scattered all over his desk, some lay open and were half-marked, and others were stacked in untidy bundles. There were more bundles of papers in the living room and in the kitchen, where David was cleaning away the plates. In the hall, she picked up and then accidentally dropped her keys. The noises in the kitchen stopped.

His voice floated into the hall. 'Where are you off to?'

'Work.'

'But you've been working all night.'

To David the investigation was just another assignment but to her it felt like the most important battleground of her career so far. 'I'm sorry,' she said, 'but I have to go.'

'I'm surprised you even know what time of day it is.'

She craned her neck to catch sight of the clock in the kitchen. 'Twenty past nine.'

'Honestly though, you're going to be exhausted.'

'Probably. Don't forget, the nursery needs to be paid for last month.'

'I haven't forgotten.'

She also reminded him that Ben had his first vaccination appointment at ten thirty.

'For Christ's sake, I'll get nothing done today.' He scowled at her. 'Early morning is the best time for me to mark papers, but you've ruined it. I've been too distracted worrying about where you were.'

She got the impression he was finding home life more and more frustrating and was storing up his annoyance so that it could be directed at her. Still wearing her coat, she helped him load the dishwasher, but he'd done most of the work already.

'Am I supposed to do everything at home?' he complained.

She turned towards him. His face was pale and his eyes glittered. Was it frustration she saw there? Not frustration but anger. He seemed to be staring right through her.

'I'm trying to help you before I head back to work.'

'But your work is spreading into our family life, right into the centre of our home and marriage. Can't you see? It's ruining everything.'

She fixed the chairs in their places, her lips shut tight. After all she had been through that night, she had imagined that David could hold the fort at home, step into any breach, but she had been wrong. She should have known better. He was quiet again, head down. Was he sulking? Sometimes it was impossible to know what his feelings were. She gave the table a quick wipe-down.

'What is it you want?' he asked.

'I want what you want. A happy family life.'

'No, that's not what I want. All I want is for you to do your fair share of the housework.'

Whatever it was she was working for day and night, it was not for arguments like these that were becoming alarmingly common. He probably had every right to be grumpy, but didn't she deserve better than these petty outbursts of his temper? She said goodbye and made to leave.

'That's fine,' he called after her. 'Run off back to your detective friends.'

# CHAPTER TEN

Now that Herron was one of the lead detectives in a murder investigation, she knew instinctively that she would have to prioritise the search for the murderer over her home life and family responsibilities.

One cold meaningless forensic report about the forest clearing followed another, interspersed with short discussions with Morton that failed to draw any conclusions. None of the reports gave up what she most wanted to know. Was the decapitated head Dr Pochard's? She forced herself to keep going. There was nothing else she could do. She felt as though they were hovering at the distant edge of the investigation, with everything far away and murky, and only the grisliness of the head speaking to them powerfully.

In the meantime, Morton agreed to open a file on the disappearance of Dr Pochard. A preliminary investigation of her house, however, had thrown up no clues, no signs of life, nothing, apart from Pochard's appointment diary and the car left in the garage. Herron's attention had been snagged by the

comment the psychotherapist wrote under her last appointment on the previous Friday. She had been due to see a patient
referred to only as 'S'. Underneath, Dr Pochard had written
the cryptic line: *I'm at my best when the forest turns its silence
towards me.*

They managed to put together a brief profile of Pochard,
based on interviews with her colleagues at Deepwell. She was
unmarried and her only relative was a sister living in Edinburgh,
whom her colleagues were trying to contact. After qualifying
from medical school, she had specialised in psychiatry, and
had held a position at Deepwell for most of her working life.
She worked long hours and lived with regular habits. She had
never been known to do anything out of the blue before.

Bates interrupted the meeting in the vulgar, impatient way of
a boss with not enough to do but worry about the weaknesses
of his staff and how they might reflect badly on his reputation.
He sat down in a chair opposite them, put his hands behind
his head, and said, 'Update. Please.'

Morton stared at the wall, while Herron rifled through her
notes.

'Well, what progress have you made?' demanded Bates.

The hours since the discovery in the forest had passed too
intensely for Herron for much besides puzzlement and frustration. Nor had she been expecting Bates to put her and
Morton under the spotlight so soon. His usual level of involvement in important investigations was to roar and shout, and
then run off to some mysterious meeting he could not get out
of. An invisible uneasiness seemed to have seized Morton.
The silence grew and Bates glared at them. Come on, get a
grip, Herron told herself. She cleared her throat and leaned
forward, holding her notebook firmly.

'I'm sure it's her,' she said. 'I mean, Dr Pochard.'

'How have you come to that conclusion?' said Bates.

Now it was Morton's turn to clear his throat. 'All we know for certain at this stage is that it's the head of a woman.' His tone was reflective rather than dismissive of Herron's certainty. 'Forensics are working to establish how and when she died.'

'Are you even sure this was a murder?' asked Bates.

'It's possible she may have died due to natural causes, and someone may have removed her head after death.'

'Go on,' said Bates, pointedly ignoring Herron.

'We're checking to make sure a corpse hasn't gone missing from anywhere,' said Morton. He summarised the unclear picture of what was emerging from the forest. 'It's plain that whoever left the box in the clearing made sure not to leave any clues lying round. We're now fairly certain that the decapitation must have occurred somewhere else.'

'What about Deepwell?' asked Bates.

Morton counselled against them drawing any hasty links to Deepwell. The only connection between the two was the words of a mentally ill patient locked away from society. However, he had to agree with Herron that even if the head did not belong to Pochard, the strange confession of McCrea and the secret atmosphere at Deepwell pointed to something murky going on.

Herron was about to speak, but Morton gave her a warning look. She felt herself blush with annoyance.

'Just remember this is a police station,' said Bates. 'Not some sort of madhouse like Deepwell. Stick to what we know for sure. First establish identification of the head and then progress from there.' He rose from the seat. 'I expect the two of you to have this sorted very soon. It shouldn't be too bloody difficult to work out where the head came from and who it belongs to. After all, isn't that how we recognise our fellow human beings, for Christ's sake?'

That was as far as they got on the first day of the investigation. Herron hoped that the mood of tension and frustration would lift the instant she arrived home.

David was standing in the hallway late that evening, glaring with disapproval at the clock on the wall. He seemed pent up with impatience.

'Is this what it's going to be like from now on?' he asked. 'Me looking after the children all day and now the evenings as well?' He looked as though he were staring into a terrible future, one he would rather not contemplate. 'I thought you'd be home ages ago.'

At first, she did not react, hunkering down to greet Alice who had come running down the stairs in her pyjamas.

'There's a lot of pressure on the investigation team at the minute,' she explained, walking into the kitchen. 'Until we get a breakthrough we have to do a lot of work in a short space of time.'

She told him about the absence of any firm clues and the mood of confusion that had descended upon the investigation.

'What do you mean? Don't you think you're going to solve it?'

'I hope so. I don't know.'

'You don't know? Don't you realise I can't keep this up? Working from home, managing all the routines with the children, day in, day out, hanging on every evening, waiting for you to come walking through the door.'

He was angry, but she did not know if his anger was meant for her or the children, or her career, or even life in general. His feelings tended to build up in a secret male place and often he got angry with everything at the same time, even the bland newsreader speaking on TV, or whatever programme they happened to be watching.

'You were the one who encouraged me to join the police force,' she said. 'You believed in me. You said I'd make a great detective.'

'I still believe in you.'

'No you don't. You'd rather I'd fail. You'd rather have me home on the dot of five thirty and let someone else on the team make the breakthrough.'

'What if another big case comes up, or you get a promotion? You'll just step into your new role without any qualms and bury your old life. While I'm still tied to the house and the children.' He turned his back on her. 'It's like you've forgotten everything about our lives before the children came.'

'Is that it? Do you miss the time we had together?'

'Yes, I do.' He began stacking plates into the dishwasher. His anger seemed to change into an equally strong feeling of sadness. 'I have to hand it to you, Carla. The way things have worked out. You got what you wanted, the children and a career. While I've had three years of insomnia and near insanity being stuck at home every day.'

'Our family life is about more than that.'

'Yes, but you've won the battle of the sexes. You've got your womanhood sorted. You got the career while I got the nappies and the projectile vomiting.'

She saw the disappointment and envy in his face. 'Don't generalise this. This is about me and you, and the children. You're a father now. Surely, that means something precious. It must give you a sense of achievement and pleasure?'

'Just tell me when the two of us can go to the pub and have a nice lie-in the next morning.'

Most evenings all she wanted to do was collapse in front

of the TV with a large glass of wine, rather than go out. She could see that David was indoors too much, hovering around the children all day, witnessing all their moods and difficulties, seeing to all their needs. 'What if you got a break from the children? Would that make things better?'

'I'd prefer more of your company, but it would help.'

'Then we'll have to find a nursery that will take the two of them.'

'Ben is only six months old. He's too young for a nursery.' David had strong feelings about institutionalised childcare of any sort.

'Yes, he is too young. But if it gives you a few hours break during the day…'

'You're happy to send him to a nursery at his age?'

'Not really. But I can't drop the overtime right now. We've no choice.'

'Well, I'm not happy. Ben is far too small. There must be another solution.'

He fetched a bottle of wine from the rack. He uncorked the bottle and appeared keen to mollify her, as if he had recognised it was his fault for getting angry. He poured her a glass and then one for himself.

'Don't worry about failing to catch the killer,' he said. 'I know you'll get him soon. Now drink up and relax. I'm going to come up with a better solution to the childminding. Just leave it with me.'

# CHAPTER ELEVEN

Next morning, Carla dashed up the stairs and turned off the tap she had left running. She stepped into the bedroom and grabbed her purse, trying not to look at David, who had come down with a virus overnight. However, he was already awake, sitting up in bed and staring at her with bloodshot eyes.

'Morning,' she said.

'I forgot to tell you. Alice has been asking about her missing red shoe. She won't go outside without it.'

Oh shit, she thought. It was still at the birthday party house. 'You'll have to pop over and get it yourself. I've no time to stop.'

She had already prepared Alice and Ben's breakfasts, and left out their clothes for the day. Then she had got dressed in the dark, trying to enjoy the early morning idyll of peace while everyone was still asleep.

She slipped into Alice's bedroom to say goodbye and to her alarm found that she had a temperature. Ben cried robustly when she checked on him, but thankfully he had not come down with anything. She nursed him back to sleep with a fresh bottle, thinking that it was becoming clearer by the day how much Ben took after his father, the same angry tone lurking in his voice, the same petulance hiding behind the surface. She had just settled him into the cot and closed her eyes briefly, preparing for the important day ahead, when her mobile rang.

'Morton, here. Did I wake you?'

'You'd have to ring much earlier to stand a chance of that.'

'Forensics have finally identified the head in the box. The victim was Dr Jane Pochard.'

She held her breath.

'And the finger?'

'They're still working on that. I wanted to call you first thing. Dr Barker has been informed. He has agreed to help with the investigation in any way possible. He's ready to speak to you this morning.'

'Anything else I need to know?'

'Nothing yet. Her sister is helping us. The connections to Deepwell are troubling.'

She asked about the man with the missing finger. Was there any more information about him?

'Not yet. I'm organising the search for him right now, but I can go with you to Deepwell, if you like.'

'No, I can take care of it myself.'

'I suspected you'd say that. There's a lot we still don't know about what is going on at Deepwell, so be careful. McCrea's confession might lead us in the wrong direction entirely. Don't draw any conclusions too soon. There's something about McCrea that doesn't add up.'

She wanted to say that nothing about that place added up, but he had ended the call.

David was standing behind her, still dressed in his pyjamas.

'Hi,' he said, waving feebly. Alice was clutching his hand, her shoulders hunched. Carla could feel a family crisis looming.

'I want you to stay at home,' said Alice, grabbing her leg.

Carla had no weapons to keep at bay the domestic responsibilities gathering in her wake other than sweeping promises and words of distraction. 'Daddy's here to take care of you,' she said. 'He's going to get your party shoe back today.'

'Will I have a big birthday party like Vicki?'

Carla felt the hot flesh of her daughter's fever-ridden face press against her body. Her determination faltered. She held her daughter's slender arms, and said, 'Of course, pet. You can have as big a birthday party as you like.'

'Will you come to it?'

'I promise you I'll be there.'

'Will there be lots of presents?'

'A birthday party is meant to be a surprise. That way you enjoy it more.'

'A surprise?' Alice's eyes widened.

She squeezed Alice to her tightly and said, 'Yes, a big surprise.' Deftly, she passed her back to David, who looked at her coldly, as if to say that words and promises were no replacement for parenting.

From the bedroom upstairs, Ben began wailing at a pitch that seared her ears. It was half past eight, and she had to leave.

# CHAPTER TWELVE

Deepwell's rain-stained granite building had grown secluded and sinister-looking, its windows squinting in the wet light, as Detective Herron drove up the approach avenue.

She found that getting inside was more difficult this time round. Staff were no longer allowed to come and go as they pleased, the security man explained to her as he examined her ID, and only visitors with special permission were allowed to enter.

The sound of footsteps receded before them as he led her down a long corridor to the medical director's office. Was it the claustrophobic echo of their feet, or those of invisible staff reverberating in hidden corridors, noises trapped as though in a deepening tunnel? When she entered the room, Barker was conversing with two other men dressed in white hospital coats. The director offered her a seat without introducing his colleagues, one of whom gazed uneasily at Herron. Immediately, she felt at a disadvantage, that forces within the hospital had already discussed how to manage the disturbing news of Pochard's death.

The two men stepped out of the room without a further word. Gesturing towards his colleagues, Barker explained that staff at Deepwell were finding it difficult coping with the tragic news. 'Jane was a very hard-working psychotherapist,' he said. 'This is the most terrible act imaginable. I can't believe it.' He added that the hospital would do its utmost to assist the police with their inquiries.

Herron nodded. 'Good,' she said, 'because first, I need to establish if there is any way Alistair McCrea could have escaped from Ward G and returned without staff knowing last Friday night.'

Barker cleared his throat. 'Ward G is our high security unit. If there had been any breach we would have already informed you.'

'What if you weren't aware of the breach?'

'There is no question of that. My staff have reviewed the CCTV footage. We have checked everything, all the door locks and security systems.' Barker stared at her and bit his beard. 'I gather it was you who found her. How was she killed?'

'Brutally.'

Barker kept looking at her, expecting more information.

'You found her entire body, I take it?' His gaze was probing.

She understood his motive. He had fired off the question because he wanted his worst fears either confirmed or denied.

'She was found more or less how McCrea described. Only her head was there.'

'How terrible—' His voice broke off, and a part of him disappeared from the conversation, retreating into a corner, clinging to the hope that his hospital's reputation might still emerge unscathed. His eyes grew hooded, and his voice fainter, as though it were trying to hide among the piles of patients' notes and academic publications on his desk. 'I've allotted you an hour with Alistair. In the meantime, I'll instruct the secretary to get you any files you might want to see.'

When and where does a suspect lie? These were the two most crucial questions for a detective conducting an investigation. In the ordinary course of events, an officer could grope towards the truth. The hidden facts of the investigation existed as a clearly defined zone of knowledge, like a chessboard, a space of moves and counter-moves that was straightforward and strictly regulated. In the police training college, she had been taught the codes of practice for interviewing suspects and witnesses, special techniques to elicit the truth and assess whether or not the interviewee was lying, but all these methods were based on the assumption that the truth did exist, that there was a set of answers underlying the game of words between the interrogator and the interrogated, the struggle between verbal and non-verbal communication, the little blinks and shifting of the eyes, the tactics of secrecy and evasive answers. But what if there was no subjective truth to be discovered? In all her training, there had been no preparation for what lay waiting for Herron when the nurse unlocked the door and she entered the music room on Ward G.

McCrea was perched at the edge of the seat, slanting away from her, his shoulders hunched, staring at the blank wall, as though trying to make himself invisible.

'The police are here, Alistair,' said the nurse.

McCrea looked up at her with his pale face and white eyelashes, but he showed little sign of recognition. She felt as though, in his world, she was nothing more than a shadow, indistinguishable from the other shadows that came and went. He began to shuffle his feet uncomfortably when she greeted him and explained the purpose of her visit.

'You remember who I am?' she asked.

He paused before saying yes, and then added, 'I'm afraid.'

'Afraid of what?'

'My memories.'

'What memories?'

'I don't know. I can't remember. That's what frightens me.'

'But you must remember.'

Wordlessly, his face told her that a part of him had been locked away in darkness. At first, she was unable to fathom his sense of confusion. Then she realised. He was drugged, heavily drugged. His mind had been eased into a chemical straitjacket.

'Dr Pochard's remains were found in a forest clearing last night. The pathologist has estimated that she died sometime on Friday night. Are you surprised?'

'Yes.'

'Why?'

He looked up at her briefly, his eyes half-closed, and his long white eyelashes like a blindfold. 'I only ever saw her head in the pile of stones.'

'What about the rest of Dr Pochard's body?'

'They won't let me have it. They've taken it away.'

'Who?'

'The other people in the forest. They won't let me see their faces and I don't know who they are.'

'What are they doing?'

'Walking around the cairn, spying on me, checking behind the trees and under the stones.'

It filled her with a strangeness she could not absorb. His thoughts were confused and uncertain, but she knew that

McCrea had a crucial link to Dr Pochard's murder. An investigation that had not really been an investigation and a confession where the truth had been mixed up with the volatile dreams of a psychiatric patient were now linked to a real murder inquiry. Of all the possible outcomes, this was the least expected. McCrea confessing to a murder he could not have committed. What other secret clues might lie in his confession? Herron was not willing to assume the worst conclusion, that somehow McCrea had committed the murder from his secure room on Ward G, either directly or indirectly. She had the impression that McCrea was too ill to convince anyone else to murder Dr Pochard. But the sheer implausibility of him recounting the murder scene in such detail worried her. She knew that he had repeated the same gruesome images in his earlier confessions.

'Have you any idea what happened to the rest of her body?'

'Haven't I told you enough?'

'Is it hidden somewhere? Can you think of the terrain?'

McCrea began to rock back and forth.

'The police need your help. You must help us find her body.'

When McCrea didn't reply it occurred to Herron that the patient sitting opposite her belonged to a puzzle he couldn't solve himself, perhaps because he was only a tiny part of it.

'I need your help, Alistair,' she said. 'It was clever and very good of you to warn us that Dr Pochard had been killed. Right now, you're the only person who can give us the help we need.' She felt the urge to kneel at his side, to penetrate the veil of his long lashes.

'I don't want to remember.'

McCrea lowered his head further. Herron knew it was important to keep his attention and not let him slip further into a drug-induced haze.

'Remember what?'

'The rest of the story. For months, it didn't make sense to me, but now it feels horribly true. I don't think I can bear the strain. What about the other patients? Can't they help you with the details?'

'What other patients?'

'I'm not the only one who remembers killing women in forests. Stories like mine have been going round Ward G for months. Why don't you read the other ones?' He raised his head and she saw his face full on, the long eyelashes hiding the strange look in his eyes. 'Billy Chisholm was the first of us to talk. He made a full confession to the staff. If you read through his notes you might find a clue.'

'Is Billy here on Ward G?'

'Not any more.' He watched her carefully. 'He managed to bluff the staff, even Dr Barker, and got himself released. No one madder than Billy ever got out of here before.'

'Isn't it odd that Billy confessed to the same type of crime?'

'No.'

'But the two of you must have talked about it.'

'We were ordered not to.'

'By who?'

'Dr Barker. After Billy and me, other patients started giving the same confession. But they were only trying to get staff attention. At least, that's what Dr Barker accused them of. He went to great trouble to keep everything under control. First, he stopped the therapies that Dr Sinden had set up. And then he got rid of Sinden.'

'Who's Dr Sinden?'

'A memory expert. He used all sorts of ways to help us bring up our repressed memories. He thought that with enough therapy all the missing bits would come back.'

'What sort of therapies?'

'Drug therapies, hypnosis, regression, role plays, even re-enactments. For weeks, we had sessions with him every day.'

'What do you mean re-enactments?'

'He used smells, sounds, photographs to trigger our memories. He even took Billy and me on trips into the forests.'

'Did Billy ever talk about his plans when he left hospital?'

'One of your colleagues asked me that already,' said McCrea.

'A colleague?'

'Yes, a detective. He was here for most of the morning. Didn't introduce himself or say goodbye. He left just before you came.'

'What was he like?'

McCrea shrugged. 'A middle-aged man in a black coat with its collars turned up and a hat. I couldn't see his face. To be honest, I was afraid to look in case there was no face there.'

Again, she wanted to get up and kneel by his side so that she could see his eyes more clearly.

'He had pictures of the crime scene. He wanted to charge me with aiding a murderer. He said I was a monster hiding behind my mental illness.'

'Did he ask any other questions?'

'Only did I know where Chisholm was. I told him Billy had left the hospital but he wanted to know where he'd gone and did I know his address. I said I had no idea. He said not to worry and it wasn't important. He told me he'd be in touch and then he left just before you arrived.'

Herron made a mental note to check the story with staff. She suspected the detective had been an hallucination. By now, the strands of hair on McCrea's brow were tangled in sweat. She had an unpleasant flashback of Pochard's red hair, sticky and darkened with threads of blood.

'If you read Billy's confession you might find clues about the other bodies.'

'You mean there are others?'

'Yes. Did I not tell you? Billy had lots of plans when he left.'

'What sort of plans?'

'I don't know exactly, but ask Dr Barker who else has gone missing from Deepwell.' McCrea's face suddenly turned ghoulish. 'Maybe now you'll listen to my story. If someone had believed me earlier, Dr Pochard wouldn't be dead.'

McCrea's descriptions of the forest clearing had matched the murder scene, but there had been something veiled in his recollections, his words evasive. Herron now suspected that the entire fantasy was second-hand, borrowed from a darker, more dangerous mind entirely.

'You've got it wrong, Alistair. Dr Pochard's death is not part of your story. This is someone else's story, not yours, someone who is no longer locked up here, someone like Chisholm.'

'Then how has my memory slipped into his story? My mind keeps circling around the scene in the forest. I can see it as if from a distance, as if I'm looking into the past.'

Herron was too tired to provide any explanations for McCrea's confusion, and her time with him was ending. He had given her the openings she needed to quiz Barker about. Two new names – Billy Chisholm and Dr Sinden – which she felt would bring her closer to the truth.


A nurse opened the door and led her back through the security doors. Herron asked him about the detective who had visited McCrea earlier.

'He must be talking about Monteath,' replied the nurse. 'What did Alistair say about him?'

'Only that he sat in the corner for most of the morning and asked some questions.'

'That fits. Monteath usually sits in the corner and listens in on his thoughts. It's not a good sign that Alistair is talking about him again.'

It was the same name that the female patient had mentioned to Herron during her first visit to the hospital. 'What do you mean, not a good sign?' A detective who did not say much, it reminded her of a close colleague.

'Monteath exists only in the borderland between Alistair's fantasies and the real world. He's a delusion. All this stress caused by Dr Pochard's death, there's a real danger he'll have another breakdown.'

Herron wanted to ask him more about Monteath, but the nurse would not be detained any further.

'I'm sorry,' he said, 'I've the medication round to do now. You have no idea how agitated the patients get if there's a delay with their tablets.'

She could imagine well enough. She turned and walked back down the corridor, wondering if there was anything McCrea had said that would stand up in a court of law. It was clear that he was shut inside a world that was emptied of all rational meaning. Not for the first time, she thought of Ward G as a separate mental state, one where the sterile surroundings and boring daily routine had been replaced by sinister plots and fictions fabricated by the patients who roamed freely in their imaginations, while the hushed, orderly team of doctors and nurses were the true inmates, locked up inside their beliefs about mental illness and their therapeutic practices.

# CHAPTER THIRTEEN

Barker came marching down the corridor to meet Herron and escort her back to his office. She would have liked more time to digest what McCrea had told her and unravel what had been going on in Ward G, but Barker gave her the impression he wanted her off the hospital grounds as soon as possible.

'I take it you'll want to see McCrea's notes again,' he said.

'His notes aren't the only ones I want. I have more questions for you.'

'Yes?'

'McCrea says there were other patients on Ward G who made similar confessions.'

Barker frowned. 'Is this really relevant? These are confidential matters.'

Once again, Herron felt a flicker of annoyance at the way Barker kept erecting professional barriers, in spite of his promise to help in any way he could. 'I shall decide if it's confidential or not,' she said. 'You're in charge of this hospital and you have a legal right to protect the privacy of your patients, to lock away their case histories and treatment plans, and prevent whoever you like from probing too deeply. With one exception. The police. Especially in the middle of a murder investigation.'

'I haven't locked away any treatment plans,' he said, without batting an eyelid.

'What about helping the inquiry by explaining what exactly has been happening on Ward G?'

They were back in his office now. Barker sat down heavily in his seat and hesitated. He looked as though he were pulling together thoughts from corners of his mind he wanted to keep hidden. 'The delusion obsessing McCrea that he is a secret murderer is a not a creation of his own illness,' he said eventually. 'It is much more perplexing than that. The delusion operated on a group level on Ward G. It could only be described as a form of collective madness, one that I did my best to cure.'

'So several of your patients made bogus claims that they were murderers. How did you interpret this behaviour?'

'In order to survive on Ward G, patients like McCrea and Chisholm needed to keep a fantasy playing in their minds. These delusions are always in the background, like an orchestra repeating the same comforting melodies, drowning out the harsher sounds of reality.'

'But why concoct a fantasy about murder in the first place?'

'Why not? The patients are cut off from everything else. The only links they have with the outside world are through the internet and television, and both are awash with images and stories of murder and attacks on women. They are among the most shocking tales we tell ourselves. My therapeutic approach was to interrupt their fantasies rather than treat them as a clue to suppressed memories.' Herron could detect a note of hostility enter his voice. 'Their shared delusion was completely out of control, in my opinion. My approach was to close off the affected areas and stamp it out, like a forest fire.'

Herron was interested in his interpretation. It was perplexing, and, more than that, fascinating. However, Barker's interpretation still did not explain the most confusing fact of all: how had this delusion turned into reality?

'McCrea told me about a patient called Billy Chisholm. Where is he?'

'No longer under our care. About a month ago we released him to a halfway house under the supervision of one of our doctors and the mental health team. We don't leave patients to their own devices. The problem is Chisholm absconded last week, and no one has seen him since.'

Barker chewed on his beard. What was he not telling her? she wondered.

'The doctor who was looking after him, I take it it was...'

Barker finished the sentence for her. 'Dr Pochard.'

'Did it not concern you that Chisholm might want to continue the delusion that he was a murderer? That once he had got into it so deeply, he might want to keep going with it now that he was free?'

'Dr Pochard oversaw his treatment in his final few weeks here. She was convinced he was ready to return to the community. Chisholm is well educated and showed very few signs of mental illness. His grip on reality was a lot firmer than McCrea's.'

Only someone with a very firm grip of reality could have murdered Pochard so ruthlessly, thought Herron. She asked Barker for a photograph of Chisholm and all the notes relating to his release. He rang the details through to his secretary.

'McCrea also mentioned a therapist called Dr Sinden. How can I contact him?'

Barker's voice grew tense and low. Herron sensed the importance of what the director was revealing, its crucial role in explaining what had happened on Ward G. 'Before I give you his details I have to tell you what kind of therapist Jeremy Sinden was. He was trained in the old school of psychotherapy. He had certain listening talents but he was also naive, quite unaware of the dangers his patients posed to the outside world.'

'How?'

'He believed that with enough memory recovery therapy he could completely cure his patients and they would never go back to being criminals, even if they wanted to. His theory was that all the patients on Ward G were repressing traumatic events in their past, and if he could only unlock these memories then the patient would no longer rely on mental illness as a coping method.'

'And did his therapy work?'

'Jeremy inspired hope, and his approach was humane. However, it almost always led to failure. I came to the conclusion that he had completely lost his professional bearings on the ward.' Barker was interrupted by the secretary bringing in the file on Chisholm. He hunched forward and grabbed it protectively, but Herron had already noticed the photograph of the patient on the cover and his dark haunted eyes. It was the face of the strange man she had met in the forest clearing. She flinched, feeling an underlying excitement take hold. However, Barker seemed oblivious to her reaction.

'Initially, Sinden was convinced the patients were accessing repressed memories of actual murders,' Barker went on to say. 'When it became clear that these memories must be false, he became very upset and began to worry that his theories on repressed memories might be wrong. That was when he began to work harder on recovering Chisholm and McCrea's hidden memories. Sinden had impressive powers of persuasion, and he wanted to come up with a new insight into the psychology of the criminally insane, one that would demonstrate his impressive talents. I understand that he even drove some of the patients to nearby forests to help trigger their memories. He took photos of sites that were further away and gave them to his patients. I told you earlier that the delusion of a murderer in a forest was a form of collective madness. Well, that madness grew to include Dr Sinden, which is why I had to suspend him from his work here.'

'Is it possible that McCrea internalised the psychopathic plans of Chisholm?'

'Quite possible.'

'And that in his imagination, he is following Chisholm down the same path?'

'You speak as though Chisholm is suddenly your prime suspect.'

Herron took a deep breath. 'If I'm not mistaken, Chisholm was there at the crime scene. Or at least someone who strongly resembles the photograph on the cover of his file. He told me he was troubled by his memories, and he pointed to the murder scene. He knew about the pile of stones.'

'Chisholm? But why was he in the forest?'

'When we understand that, maybe we'll know why Dr Pochard was killed in the first place.'

'Have you any ideas?'

'I have plenty of ideas, but the best thing you can do now is stop hampering this investigation and hand over everything you have on Chisholm. His history, the addresses of his relatives and any other contacts he might have with the outside world.'

'Let me assure you, Sergeant Herron, Deepwell has no interest in hampering this investigation or hiding what happened on Ward G. We want Dr Pochard's murderer brought to justice, and I promise we will do everything to assist you.'

'One other thing I will need from you and your colleagues is the details of what you were doing last Friday evening.'

Barker appeared unruffled. 'I was at a weekend-long mental health conference in Edinburgh. Dozens of people saw me there along with Dr Sinden.'

So that was two alibis he had sorted, thought Herron. She asked, 'Are you worried about anything happening to you or your colleagues?'

'I'm not especially worried.' As he spoke, his detached expression grew alert and attentive. Was it a look of fear she saw there? 'In my profession, one learns to get by with a certain amount of worry,' he added with a frown.

'What if you were to find Chisholm waiting outside your home this evening? Would you be worried then?'

'Chisholm? No, of course not.' The frown on his face relaxed. If it was fear that he showed, then it had diminished with the mention of Chisholm's name.

She changed her line of inquiry. 'Tell me what you know about Inspector Monteath. McCrea and one of the female patients mentioned him to me. They both thought I should know him.'

Barker flinched slightly. 'I can't say. Professional code of confidentiality.'

'This is a murder investigation, as I keep reminding you. Your professional commitment to secrets no longer stands.'

He hesitated and spoke slowly. 'All I can say is that he's another one of those stories that keeps circulating on Ward G. His name crops up in nearly all the patients' fantasies and delusions at some point.'

Another recurring motif, thought Herron. How many more

lay hidden in the minds of the patients? She was becoming convinced that their confessions were full of messages, signals and warnings, and that plans for the murder of Pochard had been in place for some time.

'But if two people see the same hallucination,' she said, 'then it's no longer an hallucination. It must be linked to reality in some way.'

'In the case of Monteath, each of the patients see a different detective. None of their descriptions ever matched. Which proves he is a figment of their individual imaginations.'

'But one that was passed between the patients. A group hallucination. How do you explain that?'

Barker gave a tiny shrug. 'A psychiatric ward is a fragile environment. Once one patient in the group deteriorates, then disorder spreads.'

'How did the story about Monteath start in the first place?'

'Why do you want to know?'

'A detective's curiosity, that's all.'

'The patients began mentioning him about nine years ago. At the time, we believed he was some sort of archetypal figure. His expressions and the things he said seemed to come straight out of detective films.'

'Could it be that he's some sort of imaginary confidant?'

'We explored that idea in therapy. But it kept leading to dead ends. Monteath seemed to represent a negative force, an obstacle.'

'What does this imaginary detective do or say? In their imaginations.'

'He makes a few promises in exchange for information. He tells them that he will talk to the powers in charge, and get them to grant favours. Sometimes he warns them not to speak to anyone else, that the staff at Deepwell are their enemies.'

She nodded and wondered if there were any subjects of inquiry not grounded in fantasy that she could discuss with Barker. One sprang to mind, and she thought it was a good note with which to end the interview.

'I have one final question to ask you,' she said.

Barker looked relieved and smiled.

'Who do you think killed Dr Pochard?'

His blue eyes stared at her with all the professional ice he could muster. 'I have absolutely no idea,' he said slowly and firmly. 'That's your job, not mine.'

After taking Chisholm's file, Herron asked to speak to Dr Pochard's secretary. She had important questions to ask about the murdered doctor's diary. Barker did not object and left her alone in the reception area for a few minutes. She stared into the courtyard garden at the cowed figures of the patients walking along the paths and talking to the nurses. The view seemed so controlled and pedestrian; it was as though every word and step taken had already been mapped out during therapy.

Pochard's secretary was a woman called Martha Brooke. She was middle-aged and slightly flustered. Herron could sense her discomfort immediately.

'I was her secretary for the last five years,' she explained. 'I also helped her with her private practice and her correspondence with academics and universities.'

'What was she like?'

She was silent for several moments and then she said, 'I can't tell you.'

'Why not?'

'She never revealed anything about her private life to me. I was her secretary, not her confidante.'

'But you must have learned something about her. Please, I need to know whatever you can remember.'

However, she refused to give Herron any more information. The detective pondered her reticence and her growing discomfort.

'What about her final appointment last Friday? She was due a visit from one of her patients at eight p.m.'

The secretary seemed to hold her breath. 'A patient?'

'Dr Pochard marked the slot with an "S". Whoever it was, she saw them at the same time every week, and the sessions always lasted an hour. She wrote some brief notes about how the meetings went, but nothing to identify the patient.'

'Are you absolutely sure?'

'Why would I ask you if it wasn't true?'

'Yes, why would you? But Dr Pochard never saw patients after six p.m. She was very firm about that. Even during emergencies. Whoever she saw that evening it was definitely not a patient.'

'Then who was it?'

'As I said, I didn't know that much about her personal life.'

Didn't know or didn't want to talk about what she knew, thought Herron. 'Tell me about what you do know,' she asked.

The secretary pointed to a large photograph hanging on the wall behind them. 'Try asking them,' she said. 'They were the ones closest to her.'

Herron stared up at the photograph. A group of professional-looking men and women standing next to a lake with firmly focused eyes and smiles that looked as though they were boring into the skull of the photographer. The secretary pointed out Dr Pochard with her red hair, and Dr Barker. She also pointed out Dr Sinden and Professor Eric Reichmann, with whom Dr Pochard was meant to go on a walking holiday. However, the rest were strangers to her.

'That photograph will tell you more than anyone else can

in this hospital,' said the secretary. 'Everything you need to know about Dr Pochard is in that group of people.'

'What do you mean?'

'They're the Scottish Holistic Foundation of Psychotherapists. Some of them are staff here at Deepwell. But none of them ever talk about the foundation or its members. It's against their code of conduct. Dr Pochard's entire life was based upon the foundation and its theories on psychotherapy.'

The sense of uneasiness Herron felt about Deepwell returned. She stared down the corridor at the doctors and nurses marching briskly, arms swinging, energised by the intensity of their visions, their belief in psychotherapy and in the institution of Deepwell itself, a hospital that was beginning to resemble a stage set, a structure of dubious lights and shadows.

Herron rose and told Brooke that was all for now, but that she would be in touch again.

'Who do you think did it?' asked the secretary with sombre eyes.

'I have no idea,' said Herron, 'but I'm convinced the answer lies on Ward G.'

She took a final look at the patients in the courtyard. I am hunting a murderer through the disturbed minds of these men, she thought.


Driving back from Deepwell Hospital, Carla spotted David walking along the main street of Peebles pushing a double buggy. His face was flushed from the fever and he was wearing that downturned expression that usually made him appear so aggrieved, but for some reason the look, which would normally have irritated her, made her feel more sympathetic towards him. She waved at him, but he did not see her.

He looked so outlandish, so far out of bounds from the man she had fallen in love with, the kind, amusing and impeccably dressed boyfriend, the dedicated teacher who wanted to have a family, whose main desire now seemed to be to get through the day with a minimum of tantrums and fuss. He was so far beyond what she knew of him that she felt invisible.

Several shopping bags were dangling precariously from the handles as he attempted to steer the loaded buggy over the uneven pavement. Ben looked to have succumbed to the bug, and Alice, clearly unwell too, was throwing a tantrum. Herron cringed at the sight of their child's tear-stained face, her runny nose and her disordered hair. At that moment, one of the bags slipped from the handle and spilled its contents across the pavement. A pair of wine bottles rolled into the gutter, along with some apples and several tins of tomatoes. Her stomach contracted.

As the car slowed, David stopped the buggy, but still did not look across at her. He had not noticed her concerned face in the driving seat. Instead, he stood amid the spilled groceries and wailing children, and raised his face to the sky, his arms outstretched, the drizzle wetting his cheeks and forehead. His shoulders trembled as if he were about to roar with the ferocity of a wild animal trapped in suffocating domesticity, but his mouth remained clamped shut, his eyes closed, and his brow rigid and furrowed more deeply than she had ever seen before. She could feel the enormous pressure building inside him. Her heart leaned towards him, wishing that she could protect him from the inner torment he was parading for all of Peebles to see.

However, the other pedestrians and motorists kept moving on, unaware of the tableau of fatherly misery unfolding at the side of the road. She drove on, and soon David and the buggy were a retreating image in her rear-view mirror. Not stopping was the best thing to do in the circumstances, she thought, and she made a vow not to mention the incident that evening. She sat stiffly at the driving wheel as she made her way back to the station.

# CHAPTER FOURTEEN

If there was any meeting during Dr Barker's long career at Deepwell that might be considered crucial to the survival of the institution, the one he attended that evening had to be it. Entering the room where he had assembled the members of the holistic foundation, Barker wore his sharpest professional smile, his eyes shining as though filled with a new vision for this group of psychotherapists and professionals from the wider criminology field. In reality, he was counting numbers, translating each of the figures hunched in their chairs into votes, debating who might object to his leadership bid, who might scupper the plans he had in store for the society now that Dr Llewyn had retired as leader, and Pochard, its fiercest critic, had been silenced.

He detected at once, as he searched their serious faces for the rosy glow of endorsement, a strange out-of-kilter mood that he linked to grief and shock at Pochard's violent death. He had thought of postponing the meeting, but too much time had passed already with the foundation effectively leaderless.

Some of the younger members seemed on the verge of tears. The heaviness in their faces was profound, filling the room like a block of resistance. Rain pecked at the windows and added to the sombre atmosphere. It was time to make his stand and take firm control of the group.

The foundation's existence was virtually unknown to the general public, the names and careers of the people in the room appeared in no official records, and the foundation itself was only mentioned in obscure psychiatric journals and directories. It had taken his predecessor, Dr Llewyn, almost twenty years to build the core group that Barker now planned to lead. He had waited in the wings, silently suffering the elderly psychiatrist's mistakes, watching the reputation of Deepwell slowly crumble against the increasing scepticism of the psychiatric world, its founding principles seemingly doomed. Llewyn had spent the last year looking increasingly offended at his irrelevance, a fossil cast upon a strange shore of new ideas and antipsychotic drugs, and dwindling council budgets. Nor had Llewyn managed to take adequate stock of the weaknesses within the holistic foundation, the strong emotions that lay dormant within its members, liable to grow into uncontrollable anger when ignited.

Barker decided to treat the group like he did his patients, swiftly and decisively. He opened the meeting by warning of the great dangers that lay ahead for the foundation. He said it needed to defend itself against the barrages of criticism and hostility that were to come. For too long, the group had been sunk in a state approaching catatonia. It was time to stop their self-indulgent games and the bickering between rival camps. This evening they had to elect a leader that would forge a new future for them all.

He felt a thin line of perspiration form on his forehead as

he went in deeper with his finely honed words. Their Scottish founder had retired and one of their oldest members was dead. He didn't want it to look as though he were trading on Pochard's death for his own ends, but the sooner they faced up to the new realities the better. He kept speaking in his most persuasive voice, trying to shape their response to Pochard's murder, reorganise their feelings about it, and deplete the event of its unbearable grisliness. There were balancing compensations, he told them. The group was now smaller, more intimate, and its bonds of trust could be repaired and strengthened.

He took stock of their mood and decided that what the more emotionally wrought members needed were sharp words. He was the one to deliver them.

'I don't want you to be suspicious of each other, and I don't want you breaking into open conflict,' he warned them. 'We have to set our differences aside and concentrate on the future of the foundation.'

He gave a brief lecture on how they must return to the core teachings of psychodynamic theory. As he scanned his eyes across the twelve men and women, he felt as though he were magically in touch with the great, lost forebears of their movement: Sigmund Freud, Carl Jung and Erich Fromm. Then the crucial stage of the meeting arrived. Before they could proceed, he had to deal with Dr Llewyn's sealed letter, which the former director had asked him to read out before the members cast their secret votes.

Barker almost shivered while opening it, wondering what ghostly order would come from the man who had hand-picked each one of them, transforming them through therapy and his personal supervision into devoted followers. He had been their leader and inspiration, the man who had made everyone in the group feel safe and loved – these serious men and women who were so successful in their careers but so desperately lonely in their personal lives. The man who had known every nuance and shadow of their inner worlds.

Barker had feared that Llewyn would give the group its marching orders, or vent his feelings in a stream of bitter complaints against each one of his acolytes. However, he was surprised to see that Llewyn had pushed his egotism to one side. The letter contained a single sentence.

I have no personal interest in whomever you elect as your new director.

Barker felt a burst of adrenalin as he relayed the message to the group. The mood in the room changed. He thanked them for listening and asked if anyone wished to propose another candidate to contest the leadership. When no alternatives were offered, the voting slips were handed round, marked and then counted. There were several abstentions, but a majority of the members had voted for Barker.

However, there were no congratulations forthcoming from the group.

Laura Dunnock was the first to speak. 'Now that you have been elected as director, will you share with us what is being covered up at Deepwell, and in particular on Ward G?'

'Covered up?' He managed a smile. 'Why do you think anything is being covered up?'

'You've known about these so-called patient confessions for months, but the police were only informed this week after I told Dr Llewyn about McCrea's confession.'

'Confidential matters involving patients cannot be discussed.'

'We've shared personal secrets with each other. We all know that anything said in this room is confidential.'

'Because these are matters relating to Deepwell Hospital, not the foundation.'

'Before Dr Pochard was killed, she sent me an email. It contains some shocking facts about Ward G and the treatment programme there.'

Barker used his most professional mask to hide his surprise. Whatever happened, he had to go on playing the role of Llewyn's natural successor, impervious to any criticism that might come from within the group. 'I'm curious,' he said. 'Why did Dr Pochard decide to send you this email in the first place?'

Her expression froze at the question. 'I presume she thought I was trustworthy, and not connected to the therapies on Ward G.'

Barker showed his dissatisfaction at her answer. 'But why you and not anyone else in the group?'

'Because I shared some concerns with her in the past.'

'Were you planning to undermine the staff on Ward G?' Barker's tone was polite but implacable.

'God no, that's ridiculous. Jane was distraught at the idea that the foundation and Deepwell might have failed the patients.'

'And she talked to you about her concerns?'

'No. I tried ringing her on her phone, but she never answered. I thought I would speak to her at work, but I never got the chance.'

Dunnock grew quiet, and Barker allowed the pause to develop. Eventually, she spoke. 'I just want to know, are you prepared to do what it takes to act on Jane's concerns and save the reputation of the foundation?'

'I think I can safely answer yes,' he said, smiling wryly.

'What would happen if I were to show the email to the police or the press?'

His smile turned cold and unhappy. 'If you are determined to find out what is going on I will arrange a special meeting with you. In the meantime, I trust you will be kind enough to show me the email.'

'One meeting will not be enough, but it will do for a start. As for the email, I'll show it to you after the meeting.'

Barker sighed. He wanted to tell the group that if anyone was going to reveal the truth about the confessions on Ward G, it was going to be him, in his own time and in his own way, when the current furore had settled down. Anger rose in his chest at the thought of Dunnock poking her nose where it did not belong. Nobody said anything for a long while. There was nothing to suggest in their faces if it was silent resistance or acceptance of his decision.

One of the women began talking about Dr Pochard and her hopes of writing a book about her experiences as a therapist. Barker watched as the tears rolled down her face. What was the point in sitting any longer with a group gripped by the forces of negativity, these emotionally flawed therapists who had lost their father figure in Llewyn, and now had nothing to hold onto but their own mad selves? They expected him to take Llewyn's place and lead them in the struggle to change the world of forensic psychiatry, as well as ease their own neuroses. Tomorrow, he would draft a document that would suspend the society's activities, but first he had to conclude the meeting.

He called the group to order, but the members ignored him, whispering in little groups, their voices indignant. None of them noticed his growing vexation. Dunnock was engaged in several conversations at once, with several members trying to get a word in edgeways. Hard to believe that, minutes ago, he had them completely in his control and had negotiated the most important role in his career. He raised his voice but no one heard him. He sat frozen in his seat. It unnerved him, the intensity in the room, the pained looks on their faces, their rising voices. Llewyn retired, Pochard murdered, and now it was as if he no longer counted. He had become a shadow plunged in darkness, part of the drama that was unfolding within the group. He heard patients' names on their lips, Chisholm and McCrea, and others from Ward G, and the criticism of the strange therapies conducted on the ward. He flinched at hearing the phrase 'borderline therapeutic inter-ventions', and then someone accused Deepwell of allowing 'a monster to spring to life'.

No one noticed as Barker rose and left the room with a look of fear on his face, as though he had just seen the doomed landscape of Judgement Day rolling towards him.

# CHAPTER FIFTEEN

Before, it had never occurred to Carla that running a house-hold might be a cure for her frustrations as a detective, the nagging sense of impotence she felt when confronting the handiwork of a murderer, and that there might be a reward, rather than stress and more frustration, in tending to sick children.

That night, she spent the hours of darkness checking their temperatures, filling hot water bottles for the cold and shivering, and iced drinks for the feverish. Alice's temperature settled a little under the regimen of paracetamol, but Ben and David's did not back off at all. She gave in to his feeble requests for a hot whisky, and then went back to the camp bed in Ben's room, guarding him as his breathing strained in his sleep. She had stripped the sheets from his bed and put on a small fan, but he remained wretched, his small cramped body sweating profusely.

Oddly, the presence of illness made her house feel more like a home, and brought out emotions in her she had not felt since the first weeks after delivering Ben, dissolving the tensions between her and David, rounding the sharp corners, until all that remained was the stark essence of her family, the very nucleus of her existence. It no longer mattered what would happen to her tomorrow at work. Her mind ceased roaming the forest by the loch like a restless beast.

A strange hush settled upon the house, interrupted only by the sounds of the children moving in their sleep. She kept slipping into a shallow slumber, and then snapping awake. Just before dawn, she heard the yelping of a fox in the back garden, a creature that had adapted itself to survive on the fringes of modern life. She felt it call to a similar half-animal instinct inside her, a sense of tribal solidarity, the will to protect her family at all costs, the will that played hide-and-seek with her detective's life, but that now rose up, intense and uninhibited. The instinct felt so strong she believed it would make her soar, and remove any obstacles in her way. She must never forget this, she told herself, never lose sight of this, no matter what the dawn brought.

In the morning, she checked that David was fit enough to look after the children. He gave her a gloomy look from his crumpled pillow, his eyes, enlarged by illness, floating up from her pyjamas to her face and then grimly floating down again with the knowledge she was heading back to work.

She spoke gently. 'I've left out drinks and a bottle of paracetamol for the children. Will you see that they get them?'

He nodded. 'Good to see someone's full of beans.'

She gave him a quick kiss on his forehead, and then she showered and dressed herself with the blinds still down. She visited the children one more time, bending down to hug them as they lay sleeping, pressing their cool faces against the white silk of her blouse. She grabbed a quick breakfast of toast and coffee, and drove to work with a trance-like feeling of elation and extreme exhaustion.

Police officers weren't allowed to park in front of the building that had previously served as Peebles' quadrangular poorhouse but had been refurbished to house the council offices and, as an afterthought, the town's police station. That privilege was reserved for the elected representatives, who strutted about like a breed apart, most of whom Herron could now recognise due to their frequent comings and goings. Usually, she didn't mind the imposition. She quite enjoyed parking at the side and walking under the mature cherry trees that lined the circuitous route to the building's cream stone front. Like so many of the old buildings in Peebles, it seemed to emit its own light. Perhaps it was the colour of the stone, which contrasted so sharply with the nearby granite terraces, especially on rainy, dark days.

She had been stationed here for six months, and no longer felt like a complete outsider. She had stopped staring with her detached stranger's gaze at the orderly drift of shoppers and hiking-clad tourists, who all seemed much older than her, the gently moving traffic, and the solid stone houses, irreproachable and dull. She was only an hour's drive from Edinburgh, where a neighbour could be killed without you ever knowing about it, but she might as well have been in another part of the world.

However, everything had changed this morning as she hastened under the trees. With a murder investigation under way, the police station now had the air of a backwater venue preparing to host the big star of the criminal world, a gruesome murderer at large. It was the police officers and detectives who dashed in and out of the building, too caught up in their own drama to notice the curious looks of the council staff, who must have been wondering how long it would take to have the town restored to its conventional routines and legality. In fact, the council leaders were already putting pressure on the team to have the killer caught before the walking season took off. They expected even the most psychopathic murderer to comply with the same strict standards that governed the rest of life in Peebles. They were used to the high points of the month being the council meetings and the latest charity drives by the chamber of commerce. The forests and river walks of the Tweed valley were meant to be safe and comforting escapes, a world away from the bewildering territory of murder scenes. This was, after all, the town that marketed itself everywhere as 'Peebles for Pleasure', and the last thing it wanted was for an unsuspecting visitor to be nauseated by a bloody trail on a hiking trail.

Herron stepped into the incident room and saw Morton already working at one of the desks. He regarded her with a look of concerned watchfulness. 'Are you all right?' he asked.

'Apart from spending the night getting friendly with a flu virus I couldn't be better.'

He reported that the murder investigation was advancing on two fronts. Officers were still searching Pochard's home for clues. In the meantime, the two of them would progress the search for the man with the missing finger, whom they now suspected to be Billy Chisholm.

She straightened her skirt and stepped out of her role as mother to a sick household. The morning light looked foggy and unclear, and she felt a heavy tingling travel down her head into her neck and shoulders, as though a pain-killing medication was wearing off. The sense of elation mixed with tiredness now resembled a hangover, one of those that lingered all day, like a hatchet planted in the back of the skull.

A meeting of the investigative team had been scheduled for ten o'clock that morning, but just as she was gathering her notes to join the rest of the officers, a call came through from the front desk. According to the receptionist, a woman had walked in through the front doors saying she wanted to report a missing person.

'Can no one else handle it?' asked Herron.

'She wants to speak to a female detective. Says it's urgent.'

Herron stared at her male colleagues trooping in through the doors of the main meeting room, and decided that whatever was spoken at the start of the meeting would not be as urgent as a missing person. 'I'll be down in a second,' she said.

The woman was waiting in one of the interview suites. She stood in an agitated manner, looking uncomfortable in the surroundings.

'I'm worried about my neighbour,' she explained. 'She lives alone, but two nights ago, she had a row with someone, her boyfriend I think, and I haven't seen her since.'

Herron beckoned her to take a seat. 'Who's your neighbour?'

'Laura Dunnock.'

Herron thought for a moment. The name was familiar.

'Does she work at Deepwell Hospital?'

'Yes. I called the hospital this morning, but no one has seen her.'

Herron remembered that Dunnock was the therapist who had first reported McCrea's confession. She started making notes, and in the silence, the woman began to talk freely.

'I'm not nosy. I certainly don't consider myself that way. It's just she had an argument with an odd-looking man and I'm worried about her.'

'Odd, how?'

'He was much older for a start.' She paused as if weighing up how much more she could say without sounding judgemental. 'I heard him shouting at her.'

'Had you seen him before?'

'Only his back when he climbed the stairs to her flat. Ms Dunnock is always very discreet about her private life, and I'd never intrude by asking questions about her callers.'

Most of us do not believe that our private lives are the business of our neighbours, thought Herron. She imagined that Dunnock was the type of woman who opted for discretion even when there was no need to be secretive.

'The way he left her flat wasn't reassuring at all,' continued the woman. 'So the next morning, I went to see was she all right.'

'What do you mean?'

'He looked capable of doing something... violent. Which was why I checked her door. It was unlocked. I thought something must have happened to her so I went inside. But there was no sign of her. This morning I went up again and found the door still unlocked. That was when I decided to call her work.'

'Can you describe her caller?'

'He looked so angry and he came down the stairs with such force that I shivered and avoided his gaze.'

'But what did he look like?'

'All I can remember was his dark look of anger.'

'Was he short, tall, fat, thin?'

She glanced at Herron apologetically, and made a further effort. 'He had greying hair. A medium build. He was the only man I ever saw go up to her flat and they seemed an unlikely pair.'

'How do you know they were a pair?'

She appeared to weigh up how much to tell Herron without compromising herself. 'Well, sometimes I was able to hear their voices through the ceiling. Their tone suggested they had known each other a long time, and not superficially.'

'We'll definitely check it out,' said Herron. 'There's probably a simple explanation for her absence. There normally is.' Deep down, however, she felt a sense of dread. She thanked the woman and said she would be in touch. She logged Dunnock as a missing person and filled out a report. Then she hurried upstairs and walked into the middle of the meeting.

Afterwards, she could not remember if she had excused herself or explained what she had been doing. The case meetings were conducted according to such a fixed agenda that everyone turned to look at her in surprise when she interrupted Chief Inspector Bates. In a breathless voice, Herron told the room that the investigation would now have to include the disappearance of the Deepwell therapist, Laura Dunnock.

# CHAPTER SIXTEEN

Nobody said anything for a while. Herron's announcement seemed to have sucked the air out of the room. She felt her face grow hot, reminded suddenly of her junior status in front of officers like Morton and the chief inspector. She thought they were ignoring her announcement, their blank faces showing an utter lack of urgency or tension. She could hear her heart beating. Then she realised that the pressure in the room was so intense it prevented everyone from thinking clearly and articulating an appropriate response. A murmur broke out among the team, and then Morton spoke in a sharp, clear voice.

'Deepwell is where the lines of investigation meet,' he said. 'Two strands and now perhaps a third.' He took his time to formulate his thoughts, trying to be as thorough as possible. 'Patient Alistair McCrea confesses to murdering Dr Pochard in a forest, even though he was on a secure ward at the time of her death. Then there is the man with the missing finger who we believe to be Billy Chisholm, a recently released patient, who also happened to confess to murdering a woman in a forest.

Now the therapist, Laura Dunnock, has been reported missing. Memories, especially traumatic ones, figure in the professional practice of both Pochard and Dunnock, yet we don't know how important they are to the murderer. But this is the most significant similarity from an investigative point of view, as both McCrea and Chisholm seem troubled by memories that may or may not be figments of their imagination.'

The team took a while to digest the detective's comments. Something was missing, thought Herron. They still did not have a clear motive.

'We have two sets of confessions,' she said, 'but we still don't know exactly why Pochard was killed, or why Dunnock should go missing. I don't think the usual motives for murder apply here.'

'Pochard wasn't killed,' said Morton. 'That is too simple a term. She was butchered. We still don't know exactly how she died or where the rest of her body is.'

'It's clear we're dealing with a madman,' said Bates. 'A madman who managed to convince the psychiatrists at Deepwell that he was sane enough to leave.'

It seemed almost too terrible to imagine, Pochard signing her own death warrant the day she agreed to Chisholm's release from Deepwell. A man who had pulled the wool over her eyes and those of her colleagues. Herron recalled her fleeting conversation with Chisholm in the forest. A madman? Perhaps, but not a methodical and calculating madman. He had seemed distressed and confused. She could not help worrying that the delusion he shared with McCrea had been brought into being on Ward G to prepare the ground for Pochard's murder, and that somewhere in the forest, a killer with hooded eyes watched over the scene, like a puppet-master pulling the strings.

Somewhere on Ward G lay the answers, she thought, which put the murder squad at a terrible disadvantage, since the hospital was in the delicate position of controlling the flow of information in order to protect its reputation. She thought of the mysterious Dr Sinden and the subtle figure of Dr Barker, who refused to give anything away, and of Ward G itself, its silent corridors, the neutral colours of its walls and the watchful expressions of the staff.

'The question is where to start looking for Chisholm?' said Shaw.

'Until we get a positive lead from the public we are relying on the cooperation of Deepwell,' replied Morton. 'An institution that might be facing its biggest ever crisis. Chisholm is our main suspect, but we have to keep an open mind.'

The team discussed lines of inquiry in the hope that they might lead to better ideas. The pauses between suggestions lengthened. The forensic team gave a verbal tour of the forest clearing. They had been up to their knees in mud and rain, and the search for clues had been painstaking but fruitless. They had found no signs of a struggle or spatters of blood, which suggested the murder had happened elsewhere. Similarly, Pochard's house had shown no signs of forced entry or struggle. Nor were there any traces of blood. The only thing they had found that might be of interest was a piece of a woman's painted fingernail lodged in the side of one of the leather chairs in Pochard's consulting room. Tests showed the nail belonged to Pochard.

Shaw and Rodgers had interviewed all the patients that Pochard had seen that day, but none of them had reported anything strange or unusual. The only one they could not trace was the eight o'clock appointment that had been marked with an 'S'. Pochard had made extensive notes on the previous patients but few for 'S', who in all probability was the last person to have seen the psychotherapist alive – but who was 'S'?

Herron mentioned that Pochard's secretary claimed the psychotherapist never saw patients after six, yet 'S' had always been given an appointment in the late evenings.

'A special patient, then,' said Morton. 'One she sees only outside of normal working hours.'

'Perhaps they had a busy job and wanted the meetings kept confidential,' said Bates.

Herron pointed out how the previous notes on 'S' were always kept to a minimum. Just a line or two on how well or badly the session went. Morton asked Shaw and Rodgers to double their efforts to find out the identity of this mysterious patient. He also ordered a search of Dunnock's flat, and contact to be made with her relatives, if she had any, in case she had gone to stay with them. Meanwhile, he would speak to Dr Barker about her disappearance. Herron said she would interview Dr Sinden to see if he could throw any light on what had been happening on Ward G.

Finally, Bates concluded the meeting and organised a time for the next one.

While her colleagues were getting coffee and lunch, Carla slipped home to check on David and the children. The inside of the house was bathed in the same low glow and silence she had left it in that morning, the same smells of sleep and sickness, the same frowning looks on her children's faces, her little nest safe and intact in spite of her abrupt departure at dawn. Again, she felt the tug at the core of her being, the pleasant sense of weight and rootedness, as she crept from bed to bed, listening to her children's breathing. She was a happy trespasser, her domestic world suddenly precious to her. Alice briefly opened her eyes and seemed glad to see her. Her blue eyes were clear and she looked at Carla without blinking, as though not entirely sure if it was a dream.

David moved his head on the pillow when she entered their bedroom. His dark hair stood out against the sweaty pallor of his face. She could sense his discomfort and awkwardness at being laid up in bed.

'My morning's been completely wasted,' he complained. 'Haven't been able to do a single thing.'

She tried to be as brief and efficient as possible, asking him questions, most of which he ignored or mumbled at in reply. Yes, he had given the children a dose of paracetamol and made sure they had enough water to drink. No, none of their temperatures had spiked. He said he did not like being ill and alone with the children. He looked at her and blinked as though her face shone with a piercing light.

She got some soup from the fridge, heated it in the microwave and brought it up to him, and then she made the children some toast.

'I'll cook you a proper meal tonight,' she promised him.

'That's fine,' he replied. 'You go back to work and enjoy yourself chasing bad people.'

When she closed the front door behind her and hurried back to her car, she felt as though she were sealing off the hushed little chamber of her family life.

# CHAPTER SEVENTEEN

The door opened and a pale, sleepless-looking face greeted Herron. She recognised Dr Jeremy Sinden from the photographs in the forest. However, his arrogant expression had been replaced by the humiliated look of a doctor in disrepute. Herron introduced herself and he said, 'You'd better come in. I've been waiting for someone like you to call.'

He invited her into his kitchen. She could feel the wariness in his gaze. He behaved politely but was clearly nervous of the interview. She began by asking him about his therapeutic work on Ward G and the false confessions made by his patients.

Sinden's first line of defence was to refer to his clinical qualifications, the papers he had published on the effects of suppressed memories and the groundbreaking research work he had carried out at Deepwell. Before he arrived on Ward G, the hospital had no interest in curing its patients, he told her. It was focused on giving men like Chisholm and McCrea a secure and decent institutional life, and if they ever referred to disturbing memories or dreams, they were given powerful drugs and simply ignored.

'However, I wanted to change all that,' he said. 'I wanted to reach out to these patients and release them from their memories and disturbing thoughts. I was convinced their mental illness had its roots in their pasts. At the very least, I wanted to make their lives more bearable.'

'Tell me about Billy Chisholm.'

According to Sinden, Chisholm had arrived at Deepwell about five years ago after being convicted of staging a bank robbery that was doomed to failure. Chisholm had gone along with it in order to end a bad relationship with a woman he had met in Aberdeen. He had no friends and his family had completely disowned him.

'At the beginning, Dr Barker eagerly supported my therapeutic work,' said Sinden. 'I was flattered by his interest and decided to go deeper into the patients' fantasies and dreams in order to extract their most painful memories. Everyone was enthusiastic about it. We all felt as though Ward G was on the brink of a new dawn. A more enlightened approach.'

Herron showed him the photographs of the forest trail. 'Is this what you mean by a more enlightened approach?'

'Where did you find these?'

'They were retrieved from a fire in Dr Pochard's garden.'

One of the pictures showed Sinden standing with a waterfall in the background, gazing at Alistair McCrea who was being helped along a path by two nurses. The sun had lit up Sinden's face, and a flash of something proud and heroic shone in his eyes. He stared glumly at the picture. 'I thought the patients on Ward G were going to represent the high point of my professional career,' he explained, looking defiantly at Herron. She could see the shame in his eyes. He had risked his professional reputation, the respect of his colleagues and his job in order to prove his theories on traumatic memories, forcing his patients to hunt in the undergrowth of forests while he stood by, glassy-eyed with ambition and self-belief.

'I tried to prove that, if not actual serial killers, these men possessed serial killer personalities, and subject to certain emotional triggers might be coerced into committing murder,' he said. 'To help them cope with the trauma of remembering these shocking events I had to increase their medication to very high levels. After they made their confessions, I recommended to Dr Barker that they should never be released. Instead, they needed even closer supervision on Ward G and an increase in their treatments. However, Barker discounted my research completely, and warned me that I should never try to publish my findings. He told me the hospital faced the dilemma of explaining my research methods and justifying them. He said that what had been a professional embarrassment for me would turn into a minor scandal for the hospital.'

'What was Dr Pochard's role in Chisholm's treatment?'

'She took over his case from me. She gradually weaned him off his antipsychotic medication and recommended his release back into the community. She accused me of mistreating my patients, and took over the care of the other patients on Ward G. She began reducing their medication, too. Then she lodged a complaint about my practice with the Borders council.'

The events on Ward G no longer seemed so strange to Herron. Who could blame the patients for going along with Sinden's theories and his unusual forms of therapy? Briefly, everyone had been happy on the ward, sharing the same delusion that Sinden's therapy was working.

Sinden said he had clung on for months to the hope that his theories were correct, even though he began to realise his patients could not have committed the crimes they were confessing. He had held on to his job in spite of the growing criticism of his colleagues. He told Barker that he would not give up or resign his post, and would go on no matter how loud the accusations of malpractice and self-delusion.

'I was used to professional rivalry, even hatred from my colleagues,' he said. 'Psychiatric institutions like Deepwell aren't monoliths dominated by one particular form of therapy. There are different currents, varying approaches, opposing models of practice.'

He frowned at the detective. She saw a flicker of his arrogance in his eyes, their dominating gaze, hinting that he had a secret power over sanity and madness, and knew the symptoms and causes of all mental disturbances, if not their cure. He began to breathe harshly, and she saw that he had the eyes of a bully.

'I was misled by my theories, but none of my patients came to any harm. No one was hurt. But I had to endure the worst possible punishment, suspension from my work, and my colleagues feeling superior. These past few months have been the worst of my career.'

A detective would be out on their ears if they tried anything Sinden had done, thought Herron. It was akin to planting false evidence, misleading witnesses, helping them fabricate a story, all to prove a hypothesis that would advance a career and achieve renown amid one's peers. A detective would be sacked and sent to jail, rather than suspended, and no questions asked.

'I realised that I'd gambled my entire reputation on a delusion,' he said. 'I thought I'd found a murderer on Ward G, a deeply disturbed individual who would prove my theories were correct. But the figure of a murderer was doubled and multiplied and suddenly I had no idea what I was dealing with. It was like finding myself surrounded by mirrors in which the fantasies of my patients kept appearing and disappearing, and the murderer was always out of reach.'

Herron wondered who had arranged the mirrors: the patients or Sinden himself? Or was there another controlling intelligence hiding in the midst of the patients, waiting to transform the forest clearing into a murder scene?

'By the way, Laura Dunnock has disappeared,' she said. 'She hasn't turned up for work at Deepwell.'

'Impossible. I saw her at a meeting the other night.'

'What sort of meeting?'

He gave her a wary look. 'A meeting of our professional society.'

'The Holistic Foundation of Psychotherapists?'

Sinden nodded.

'Did you notice anything unusual about her?'

'Nothing. She was her usual self. The only thing out of the ordinary was that she arrived late.'

'How long have you been a member of the foundation?'

'About six years.'

'How did you join?'

'I was invited.'

'Who are the other members?'

'I can't talk about them.' Sinden maintained his defeated grimace, but something defiant had appeared in his eyes.

'Why? Has someone forbidden you to?'

When Sinden remained silent, Herron considered threatening to bring him down to the police station and subjecting him to a harsher style of interrogation.

'Is it true that membership of the society is a strict secret?'

'No, but its membership is not a part of your investigation.'

'Has anyone ever left the foundation or been expelled from it?'

'Not that I know of.'

'Surely there must have been someone who disagreed with the group or felt unhappy within it. Someone who didn't feel as loyal as you do.'

'Everyone is loyal to the society.'

'Everyone?'

'Why do you want to know? Obviously, there are minor differences between the members, professional disagreements from time to time. It's human nature.'

'What do you think of the way Dr Pochard raised her concerns, bypassing Dr Barker?'

'It's not my place to comment... officially.'

'But on a personal level, how did you react?'

'I thought she had overstepped her mark. Her main criticism was aimed at Deepwell as an institution and the way it was being run. She believed I should never have been allowed to pursue my theories on Ward G. She said I had gone astray. That I had inspired and facilitated these delusions in my patients. That I had turned these grey shadows of men into murderers and psychopaths.'

'Did Pochard have any enemies?'

'Not that I'm aware of.'

'But she had ruffled feathers?'

'Yes. She claimed we had become members of a secret sect. She said the foundation was flawed because it believed in one approach and blocked out any outside influences or criticisms.'

'And how did the foundation react?'

'Barker gave her a strong rebuke for going behind his back and lodging a complaint with the council.' A gloating tone of satisfaction crept into his voice. 'He threatened her with disciplinary measures, even dismissal from the foundation, but she kept complaining away to the authorities, to anyone who would listen, in spite of the reprimand.'

'And now she's dead. Murdered.'

'Yes, and Chisholm did it,' he said with aggression. 'My initial interpretations have turned out to be correct.'

'How can you be sure?'

'What is there not to be sure about?'

'A motive, for a start.'

'You're suggesting she was killed for rational reasons.' He seemed upset by the illogic of her thinking. He shifted his weight in the seat and breathed harder.

She thought there was something rehearsed about his reaction; it was all too contrived. The thin sour smell of his sweat wafted in the air. She could tell that he was annoyed, distracted even. She was reminded of her first impression, how wariness and desperation seeped from his eyes.

'The fact there might be a perfectly rational motive for killing Dr Pochard has annoyed you,' she said.

'I'm not annoyed,' he replied, a little too loudly.

'Do you think that Chisholm is in control of what he is doing?'

'I don't know what's going through his mind. I'm not his therapist.'

'But for a long time you were. You must have an idea of what he is thinking.'

'If he's stressed, I know there is only one escape route open to him.'

'What?'

'His fantasies. You've read his notes, I take it. I'm sure you understand the dangerous implications.' His voice lowered slightly and he smiled. 'Perhaps Chisholm will vindicate me in the end.'

Herron decided to call the interview to an end for now. Sinden had given her enough to think about, mainly in relation to the holistic foundation, and she would get back to him soon enough. She sensed there was a lot more to the foundation than what he had told her, but she had to proceed cautiously. She didn't want to scare its members off completely.

'No more interviews with the police,' he told her at his front door. 'I never want to speak about these things again.'

# CHAPTER EIGHTEEN

In open defiance of the duty manual's strict advice regarding the professional appearance of police officers, Harry Morton's face was one consisting chiefly of hair, unkempt hair drifting in strands of grey and black across his features, hair clinging to the matt of his overgrown beard, and his bushy eyebrows, hair twirling around his mouth even when he spoke. A face that accumulated hair, hiding the sharpness and intelligence of his eyes.

Herron had seen photographs of him as a young officer, and he looked much the same back then, tall and serious in a long coat, his straggling hair and beard framing a gaunt but handsome face with a wild look in his eyes. She had heard the stories that he was a recovering alcoholic, hence his addiction to roll-up cigarettes and coffee. Rumour had it that on one occasion he had been found drunk and fast asleep close to the scene of a housebreaking, but had denied any involvement in the crime.

This evening, his curls were kinked against his rumpled

shirt collar and his tie undone, making him resemble an untidy schoolboy. She had noticed an increasing air of disorder descend upon him since the investigation opened and wondered if he had taken to drinking alcohol again.

Without thinking, she said, 'Can't you find someone to tidy you up?' She had never considered his domestic situation before and when he grunted, she thought she might have overstepped the mark.

He leaned towards her with his hair nuzzling his haggard cheeks. His thick beard made it look as though his lips were snarling. She had to stare deep into his face before she saw the twinkle in his eyes. 'When we find the killer,' he said, 'I promise I'll celebrate by visiting the barber.'

Herron was beginning to realise that on a murder investigation team, she could be explicit with her colleagues. As daring or offensive as she liked. Their working relationships were not the sort in which trust was gained by slow degrees over months and years. A pregnant pause arose. She wondered if now was the perfect time to switch from discussing the investigation to asking about his personal life. Should she follow her natural instinct and go on? The moments ticked by and neither of them spoke. She was overcome with the worry she might say something foolish and annoy him. With his increasingly dishevelled appearance, Morton was behaving as though he had no life or future beyond the murder investigation – and so was she, it dawned upon her.

The investigation team had spent the day chasing down leads to Billy Chisholm, interviewing staff at Deepwell and his estranged relatives for any clues as to the former patient's whereabouts. A separate patrol had spent the day combing the forest around the murder scene without turning up any trace of him either. Later, Herron and Morton had talked to neighbours of Dunnock and examined her flat without getting any closer to solving the mystery of her disappearance. They had checked her answering machine and listened to her optician saying her new glasses were ready, then her mother had called to reschedule a meeting that weekend, and finally there was Dr Barker's gruff voice urging Dunnock to pick up. His last call had been made on the evening Dunnock had her row with the male caller. They checked with her neighbours and lingered at her flat, Morton growing more reticent and worried, smoking his rolled-up cigarettes and staring pensively ahead.

Now, back at the station, he slumped in his chair and half-closed his eyes while Herron recapitulated their findings so far, including her interview with Sinden in an effort to shine some clarity on the investigation. Morton had said very little, and she sighed. She read through her interview notes with McCrea, until she came to his description of the forest clearing. She searched for further clues as to what might be going through Chisholm's mind, but found nothing. She sighed again, her frustration mounting. She wished that Morton would give her a little guidance or at least act as a sounding board for her ideas.

Finally, Morton leaned forward and stared at her. 'You're a good detective, Carla. I think we make a good team.'

'But you say almost nothing to me.'

'It's better to listen rather than talk,' he said. 'Most of the time it's better to keep quiet and listen, especially in this job.'

His comment about her detective work surprised her. She had thought he was going through the motions with her, doing his duty in having her, a junior detective, at his side, but shunning her with his silences, refusing to show any real interest in her as a person. In spite of their odd exchange of banter, she had felt a set of blockages existed between them as colleagues.

'I've never felt that,' she said.

'OK, let's talk then,' said Morton. 'Tell me what's on your mind.'

'For a start, I always get an odd impression when I visit Deepwell.'

'What sort of impression?'

'That the building itself is hiding something.'

'Deepwell is an institution. It exists as a separate state from the rest of society. There's always something an outsider is not supposed to see.'

'It's just a vague feeling I get,' she said.

'Complex investigations depend on vague feelings. Often the breakthrough comes out of hunches and vague suspicions, the sense of discomfort we get when we enter a room or meet someone for the first time. In this way, our feelings grope their way forwards, invisible to our thinking, little by little, until one day the solution falls into our lap.'

She was surprised by how suddenly Morton was able to cast his defences aside, and attune himself to her thoughts and feelings. His face, usually so world-weary and hardened, was warm and sincere, the change even encompassing his eyes, which were now piercing and alive.

'A lot has changed since I became a detective,' he said. 'The field of forensics and technology has transformed murder investigations. However, my emotional response to a crime scene has never changed. When I approach one, I feel like an intruder, or a fraud. The question it asks me is, "Who the hell do you think you are, tramping in here with your big detective shoes?" A police officer has to earn the right to be there.'

'How?'

'It's something that comes with experience. Nowadays we have the field of forensic analysis, the whole scene mapped out for us by different gadgets. But if you can't stand back and read the entire crime scene intuitively, then it will never open itself to you, and you'll be unmasked as an amateur. A murder scene like the one we are confronting will pass judgement on every one of us, and the consequences for our careers could be serious.'

She understood the implications of what he was saying. Like almost all of her generation, she had spent most of her life reading and studying, educated at least to university graduate level. But what if her training, her university degree, all the baggage of her education was only of benefit to a certain point, and beyond that, it became a hindrance? Somehow, the physical and emotional intoxication of pregnancy and then parenthood had altered the way her mind approached new challenges. More and more she found herself thinking and acting from the depths of her being. This was why she respected detectives like Morton, officers who had worked their way up through the ranks without a university degree. If he gave her some advice, it was something fresh and original, all his, and certainly new to her.

'That scene in the forest,' said Morton with a strange confidence in his voice and a glow of his eyes, 'it looks into a different and more dangerous world than the one you and I belong to. The killer sees the world in a darker, barely human way. You have to earn the right to be invited into that world. Only then will you uncover its secrets.'

'What if it never opens up to me? What if I never work out what happened to Dr Pochard?'

He seemed to lose patience slightly, but it may just have been weariness. Their shift should have ended hours ago.

'Then you will just have to admit failure, stop deceiving yourself, and accept your position. That you are an ordinary police officer with an ordinary life, destined to keep searching for meaning and fulfilment in the everyday world around you.'

There was a hovering threat in Morton's words that made her feel her age and lack of experience, a young woman intimidated by the mysteries of life and death.

'When we visit the murder scene I want you imagine you are wading into deep water,' he said. 'Just let go your thoughts and relax into it.'

She could see in the dim glow of his eyes the experience of witnessing countless crime scenes. It reminded her of how encumbered she was, how futile her attempts to balance her work and family. Morton did not give a damn about his own health or anyone else's, and because of that, he could go further than she could. His commitment required an element of self-destruction. How else could he put so much of himself into his job?

'What should I do in the meantime?'

'Keep digging.' His eyes returned to their hidden stillness, half-obscured by his hair. 'You're going to be fine. Don't even think about making a breakthrough at this stage.'

She thought she had found an opening with him, and in spite of his body language, she pressed on with more questions. 'What do you think about Deepwell? Do you believe there's a conspiracy there?'

'When an institution has to defend its reputation there is always a conspiracy.'

'Who's behind it?'

'At this level, for the conspiracy to succeed, practically everyone will have to be involved in it.' Morton's voice grew deeper and more serious, but his eyes remained hidden from view. 'Places like Deepwell can become dangerous and unhealthy for patients and staff. Removed from society, at odds with public opinion, with too many professionals protecting their careers in too small an occupational space. Eventually, the careers of people like Barker and Sinden become entangled and the more they strain against each other, the tighter the knots become. They become a professional contradiction, more dependent and chained to the institution than the inmates themselves.'

'How do we break the conspiracy?'

'Each staff member will automatically cover up for the other, defending themselves collectively from any outside threat. What we need to do is convince one of them that their interests are best served by denouncing the others.'

'But how?'

'By a mixture of cajolery and threats.' He turned towards her. His eyes met hers, so dark and dangerous-looking, she almost started. 'And if that doesn't work we will have to set a trap.'

# CHAPTER NINETEEN

When Carla returned home that evening, she noticed a different car parked outside her house. She hesitated, wondering whose it could be. The silhouette of a woman appeared briefly at the living room window. Carla opened the front door cautiously and stood listening. She heard nothing. The hallway was in darkness but she did not switch on the light. Somehow, the atmosphere within the house had changed.

It was a heavy footstep she heard in the kitchen, making its way to the bathroom by the back door. The door closed and the bolt clicked into place. Furtively, as though she were the intruder, Carla slipped into the kitchen and waited. The bolt clicked free and the door opened. The shadow of a small, overweight woman appeared, and then she stepped into view. Carla's alarm was replaced by a sense of betrayal and faint disappointment. No feral woman had slipped into her house to steal her husband. The person standing before her was her mother-in-law, Bernadette Herron.

'Oh, it's you,' said Carla.

'Are you all right, hen?' replied Mrs Herron.

'What are you doing here?'

'I know it's no business of mine,' Mrs Herron began evasively. 'But David rang me this morning. He had a raging temperature and said he couldn't cope on his own. He's fast asleep now and the children are all grand. They've had their medicine and their fevers are down.' She had the air of a captain who had taken control of a drifting ship, and already plotted a new course, in spite of the uncertain weather conditions. 'David asked me to stay a night or two. Until he's back on his feet.'

Mrs Herron had prepared a meal of lamb stew and set the table in the kitchen. She had even hunted out the condiment jars. In the early days of Carla's relationship with David, love rivals her own age had been bad enough, but the love of this Glasgow mother for her only son had been Carla's real terror. Communication of any kind with her had always been awkward and hard-won, and now she felt the woman's emotional strength, the solid confidence of her body, a woman who never seemed to relax, even in her own terrace home, always at the centre of things, directing her own household and that of her daughters, who lived nearby.

Carla stuck a spoon in the stew and began to assemble a portion for herself, ejecting some of the fattier pieces of meat. David had not mentioned this as his solution to their domestic problems. What right did he have to invite his mother into the heart of their home like this? The consequences for their domestic routine were serious. Much more than excluding her, the invitation had passed judgement upon her role as a mother and a wife, condemning her to life on a lower plane. It made her feel diminished in the place where she should feel most confident and relaxed. The hurt of that realisation hit her. However, there was only one way of dealing with the situation, and that was to stay afloat, to maintain some sense of dignity and accept it for what it was, a temporary arrangement that would ensure her children were not left alone with a sick husband or an inexperienced childminder. In the meantime, she would find fulfilment and meaning in her work.

'Thank you, Bernadette,' she said. 'David and I really appreciate you coming down at such short notice. You're a godsend.'

Still standing, Carla tried some of the food, and her shoulders relaxed a little. Perhaps this was for the best, until the children got better, or the murder investigation concluded and she could take some time off work. She sat down to eat, and Mrs Herron went upstairs to check on the children.

The confident way in which her mother-in-law strode from room to room and across the landing irked Carla again. Mrs Herron had taken control of the serious business of looking after sick children, needed by her son, trusted by him beyond doubt or scrutiny. Carla heard her read a story to Alice in her soft Glasgow accent, and then tuck her in. After eating, she went upstairs to check on Ben and they bumped into each other on the landing.

'Good night, hen,' said Mrs Herron. It disturbed Carla a little, the way the look of compassion had slipped suddenly from her mother-in-law's face.

David stirred when she crept into bed. She knew that if she woke him fully they would spend the night arguing and she did not have the energy for that. She remembered Morton's saying about words being the very devil, and dragged herself to the edge of sleep with gritted teeth.

*

The next morning, Carla and Mrs Herron were up together. 'Ring me if the children or David get worse, or you need anything,' said Carla, writing her number down on a piece of paper and handing it to her mother-in-law.

Without looking at it, the older woman let it flutter to the table. 'Of course I will, dear,' she said.

Before leaving, Carla glanced into the kitchen and saw that the piece of paper was no longer on the table. She found it in the bin, dumped there with the breakfast scraps, and her face reddened in anger. She picked it up, brushed it down, and placed it back on the table.

She drove off at speed. For months now, she had wanted to show her true face to the world as a police detective, rather than a harried mother-of-two and wife. Why then did she feel this wave of sorrow wash through her at the thought of her mother-in-law looking after her children? Perhaps she was not a true detective, after all. Morton was, with his shrewd silences and calm reasoning. But not her, with the tugging weight of her family and all her ordinary worries, her home life of nappies, toddler tantrums and a disgruntled husband. She drove into the car park of the police station, wondering what Morton had seen in her to believe she was capable of leading the murder investigation.

# CHAPTER TWENTY

A visitor was waiting for Herron at the front desk, and when she went into the reception, she realised immediately who he must be. A tall, elderly man with shining eyes and a smile on his slightly twisted mouth, speaking to the receptionist in a soft German accent. A suitcase and a smaller carry bag stood beside him. It was Professor Eric Reichmann.

'I didn't mean to turn up without warning,' he explained. 'But my flight got in earlier than expected.'

Herron had never met a professor of psychotherapy before, but she thought Reichmann looked too relaxed to be the founder of a therapy school, and the guardian of Sigmund Freud and Carl Jung's ideas on psychodynamic thought processes and behaviour. In the interview room, he opened up immediately, and began describing his relationship with Dr Pochard. As well as being a dear friend of hers, Reichmann was the director of the International Holistic Foundation and had helped the Scottish therapists set up their own society.

'I was due to come over and join Jane on a walking holiday

in the Trossachs,' he explained. 'We were both looking forward to it.'

As well as giving the impression of complete honesty, he also seemed curious about what was going through Herron's mind, leaning forward and watching her with his clever eyes as he spoke, striving to understand what wasn't being expressed in her questions. Not because he had an ulterior motive, she sensed, but because this was his natural response to all human interaction: openness and curiosity.

'What kind of therapist was Dr Pochard?' asked Herron.

'Beautifully balanced,' he replied immediately. 'Kind but firm. Practical and yet full of hope for her patients. Her powers of insight shone through her entire being.'

'And as a person?'

'She was a very private person. She never allowed anyone to get close to her.'

'What about her family?'

'She had a sister in Edinburgh, I believe. But she wasn't in regular touch with any of her relatives. Her patients were her children, her own family. Better than most families because she got to choose its members. From what I understand her patients reciprocated.' He hesitated, choosing his words carefully. 'Recently, however, Jane told me that the loneliness she felt in her personal life was enormous. She was entering a critical time in her life. She was about to end a relationship with a man who had meant a lot to her.'

'Not a patient then?'

'No, definitely not.'

A thought shaped in her mind. Could this be the mysterious person marked 'S' in her diary? Laura Dunnock had had an argument with a man on the night she disappeared. Might there have been some sort of love triangle operating secretly between the two women? 'Could the man have been a colleague at Deepwell?' she asked.

He smiled slightly. 'Whatever her feelings towards her colleagues were, I cannot say for sure, but it definitely wasn't love. She told me about the moves the staff at Deepwell were making against her after she lodged a serious complaint about what was happening on Ward G. They wanted her to resign from her post. She had several bruising meetings with Dr Barker. He accused her of trying to destroy the reputation of the hospital.'

'How did she react?'

'Dr Barker's response came as a huge surprise to her. She had to endure being criticised in front of her colleagues. She told me she suddenly saw his schizoid side. You were either in or out with him. If you didn't toe the line and accept his decisions then you were frozen out.'

'When was the last time you spoke to her?'

'She rang me on Thursday night.'

Herron raised her eyebrows. 'What about?'

'She wanted to wish my wife and me a happy wedding anniversary. I was surprised. She'd never done that before. I realised immediately there must be some other reason she called.'

'Why? Did she sound worried?'

'To tell you the truth, it was a strange conversation.' Reichmann frowned. 'She wanted to say more, but not on the phone. I pressed her and she said it was something personal.'

Reichmann seemed pained by Pochard's mysterious manner and how it might have reflected upon him as an open and benevolent man, determined not to keep any secrets from the detective. 'I tried to chat to her about general things, the weather in Scotland, our holiday plans, the latest papers on psychodynamics, but she wouldn't be drawn.'

'Dr Pochard had an appointment marked for eight o'clock

on the Friday night before she died. If the patient turned up, he or she was probably the last person to see her alive.'

'Who was the patient?' asked Reichmann.

'We don't know. He or she was marked in her diary with an "S". Did she ever discuss her patients with you?'

'No. The seal of confidentiality forbids that. But she would have discussed them with her clinical supervisor.'

'And who was that?'

He flinched at the directness of her question. 'Most likely one of her colleagues at Deepwell. I know it used to be Dr Llewyn, but he's retired now.' He flashed an almost embarrassed smile. 'You know that sometimes the supervisor is the puppet-master and the practising psychotherapist the mere puppet.'

A thought struck her. 'Who was Dr Sinden's supervisor?'

'That's what I'm trying to find out as part of my inquiry.'

'What inquiry?'

Reichmann took a deep breath. 'The foundation never discusses its internal operations, but I'm prepared to make an exception in this case, because you probably know too much already.'

'Go ahead.'

'Dr Pochard made a formal complaint to me about the behaviour of one of the foundation's members. The implication could not have been more serious. I had no option but to begin a full investigation with a commitment to handing my verdict over to the practice licensing authorities.'

'And what was your verdict?'

'The inquiry will be long and slow. By the time it concludes, the verdict will be irrelevant.' The grim look on his face intensified.

'What do you mean irrelevant?'

'Irrelevant for Dr Sinden. He is suspended from Deepwell,

the place to which he had committed his professional life. He has been ostracised and scapegoated by his colleagues who are wary of being contaminated by a professional pariah. The damage to his reputation is already permanent and severe.'

'But what did you think about the way he treated the most disturbed patients on Ward G?'

'It was a professional catastrophe. When a patient of his committed suicide he blamed his colleagues and accused them of not digging deep enough into the patient's repressed memories. He accused Jane of personal weakness, of being neurotic and flawed. When Jane tried to lift the lid on his failed therapies, it started a war. By the time she contacted me, the situation had got completely out of control.'

'Was the foundation sympathetic to Sinden's approach, his belief that he could cure psychosis by digging up buried memories?'

He gave a start. 'Of course not. The foundation's approach to so-called repressed memories is clear. Decades of research into memory has not produced any evidence that people are able to repress traumatic events. In fact, the opposite is true. Memories of terrible events are more vivid and longer-lasting than other memories.' He was about to continue, but then he smiled. 'I don't know how aware you are of the latest theories on memory, or how much you want to know?'

'Take it that I don't know anything. Please enlighten me.'

'We are still discovering how wonderfully creative and adaptive our minds are, but also how treacherously wrong our memories can be,' he said. 'Research shows that about thirty per cent of us can be induced to believe in traumatic events that are completely made up, but which feel as emotionally true as real traumas. Scientists have devised a theory to explain this phenomenon, called retrieval induced forgetting. Simply put, it states that the process of remembering is also a process of forgetting. Instead of consolidating a memory every time we recall it, and thus strengthening its accuracy, we are actually recreating the memory from scratch to be stored again. So we throw away the old memory and copy a new version, which is then stored in its place.' He tapped his temple, and smiled, checking that she was following him. 'Unfortunately, the theory has serious ramifications for the therapeutic process because it suggests that every time a past event is recalled, it is vulnerable to distortion. In fact, during therapy, inaccurate information can be introduced by the therapist when discussing the past, and then incorporated into the patient's memory.'

'In other words,' said Herron, 'their memories can be hijacked or misled to plant false memories.'

'Or rather memories recovered during therapy are likely to have been created by the therapeutic process itself. We now suspect that patients undergoing intensive therapy, while being treated with benzodiazepines, are constantly floating between reality and fantasy. They have a poor or damaged awareness and knowledge of their own memory, and find it difficult to distinguish between things they imagined and those they really observed or participated in.'

'Why then did Sinden persist with his therapies?'

'Unfortunately, it appears that he did not care for the latest scientific research.'

'But he's a trained professional working as part of a team. I thought psychiatry was a research-based study.'

'No,' he replied, giving her a tired smile. 'Primarily, it's a battleground. Open warfare waged between different schools who launch critical attacks on each other. There are those who persist in believing that repressed memories exist, and those who don't.'

She thought of the patients on Ward G, the hopelessness in their faces, and the confessions that were not their own. 'When a therapist plants a false memory in a patient, how do you get rid of it?'

'You don't. Especially if it's a traumatic memory. Once you've slipped poison into a well, you can never get rid of it.'

He paused and Herron could sense his exhaustion, as though the notion of false memories was capable of haunting him, of shattering reputations and ruining lives. She asked him how long he was staying in Scotland.

'Two weeks. I'm going to hire a car and drive up to the Trossachs. No phones or internet connections. Just trees and peace. Nobody will be able to get hold of me and I can walk wherever I want. No limits.'

He's dreaming, thought Herron. There was no escape for Reichmann now that he and his foundation were part of a murder investigation.

He shook her hand as if to say goodbye.

'I'll be in touch with you again,' said Herron. 'You'll have to leave me a contact number.'

Reichmann stiffened slightly but agreed. Before leaving, he asked for a favour in return. 'I'd like to spend a few minutes alone in Jane's consulting room,' he said. 'She described it to me so often in her letters, especially the vista of trees she could see from her balcony.'

He seemed completely innocent of the ramifications of his request. 'I can't authorise that,' she said. 'It's a crime scene.'

'You can search me when I come out. I'll not touch anything. All I ask is a private moment or two in the room where she did most of her listening.' He saw her seriousness but smiled, as if he were asking her to indulge the sentimental whim of an old friend.

'That might be the case, but I could not possibly—'

'I don't think you understand. I'm in mourning for a dear friend and colleague. Just a moment, that's all I ask. I want to take in her view of the forest.'

'Unless you have something specific to help the investigation I can't let you near there.'

He glanced at her as if about to make a trade. 'If I see her room, I might remember more, something she said that could be important.' He waited several moments for her response. 'I only want something very simple. To listen to the silence of her beloved forest.'

'OK, Professor Reichmann. You can see her room, but I'll have to be with you at all times. And you can't touch a thing.'

# CHAPTER TWENTY-ONE

Herron drove Reichmann to Dr Pochard's house in the forest. The psychotherapist had never visited her home before; their meetings had usually taken place at his lakeside home in Switzerland. The road meandered along the bottom of a lonely river valley dotted with sheep, and then it began to climb through the pine trees. Reichmann sensed the change in the landscape and stared through his passenger window, his twisted mouth slightly open, his face expressionless. The road was completely immersed in the forest's shadow, the trees forming a high rampart against the wind and sun, the same fixed view of pine trunks and densely needled branches travelling alongside them, like a single image stuck in a broken projector.

'You know that Jung believed the forest was an archetype,' said Reichmann as the car laboured up a steep turn. 'That it exists in our collective unconscious.'

Herron kept her concentration on the narrow road. She knew Pochard's house was not far away, yet it seemed inaccessible amid the encroaching trees.

'Look at all these trees rising up to the sky,' said the professor, 'trying to connect us to heaven and the sun. Yet nothing can compete with a forest for signalling our darkest, most earthly fears.' He turned to her and spoke more softly. 'What do you feel, Sergeant Herron? Do the forests give you a sense of terror or ecstasy?'

She shrugged and frowned, staring at the road ahead. She glanced at Reichmann and saw that he was smiling at her in a friendly, inviting way, but his eyes looked perplexed by her lack of interest, disappointed even that she was not prepared to share his enthusiasm for their surroundings.

Through the side window, the view of trees unspooled, glimmering with sunlight refracted through the pine needles. She remembered the track through the forest leading to the stone chamber, and Pochard's eyes staring up at her. She felt a physical sensation, a tightness in her throat at the thought of returning to the forest's strange depths.

'Jane told me that the forest calmed and inspired her,' said Reichmann. He took a measure of Herron's silence. 'What was the scene in the forest like?' he asked.

She knew that he was referring to the murder scene, but she could not express her feelings. She kept watching the road, impatient to get to her destination. For a while, she thought they were lost, and then the road curved and she saw a chimney pot rising above the treetops. She turned up a gravelled lane and found the house, its front turned discreetly away from the road, its windows blank and empty. Already an air of dereliction hung over the building, which was still surrounded by police tape. The clapboard walls on the north side were green with algae. Ivy had crept along the guttering and poked through cracks in the eaves.

Herron and Reichmann got out of the car and simultaneously

turned to take in the view. There was a slight breeze wafting up from the valley, and the pine trees should have been moving, but they were completely still, adding to the eerie mood of the place. Further up the valley hung a plume of smoke that seemed to have lost its direction, floating almost at a standstill.

They went straight upstairs to Pochard's consulting room. Herron expected Reichmann to glide over to the French doors leading to the balcony, but he seemed more interested in the interior of the room, scanning the pair of leather seats, and between them, the small coffee table with the box of tissues and the pot plant.

'It's strange,' said Reichmann. 'I feel she is so close, sitting right there in her leather chair.'

Herron saw that he was talking about the larger of the seats. However, the forensics team had found Pochard's fingernail down the back of the smaller one. What did that signify?

'This is her room,' he said. 'She is near. I can't believe I'll never see her again.'

Reichmann seemed so present in the room, so willing to share his thoughts and feelings, so determined there should be no shadows in his delivery. However, Herron tried to tune in to what was behind his words. What was he not saying? She did not know what he was hiding, only that it was probably bound up with the reputation of the foundation. And because it represented a professional threat, the professor was both charming and intense, performing in front of her with all the authority of a man who had spent a lifetime neutralising such threats.

Reichmann opened the French doors and stepped out onto the balcony. She joined him and stared at the view. She had the sense that standing there with the forest stretching all around them she should be able to hear everything in the secret depths of the valley, but there was not a single sound. She felt her hair stand on end, and wished for a signal to reach her, but none came.

'Now I understand why Jane worked here,' he said. 'The forest throws you back upon yourself. By threatening you with absorption in its total quietness, it makes self-expression a necessity.'

She nodded and thought she understood. The quietness of the forest seemed so mysterious and abundant. Already it had summoned up a cascade of images, sweeping her memory back to the forest clearing and waterfall.

'Do you think the murderer was a patient of hers?' she asked.

'I don't know. I don't like admitting my ignorance. Patients start out in poor emotional states, and there's always a tendency to relapse. More than likely some of them had dangerous histories and spent time in secure mental units.'

Herron asked him again about the cryptic 'S' in Pochard's diary, and the lack of her usual patient commentary. 'Why would she have kept S's identity a secret?'

Again, he looked unhappy to be unsure of himself. He stared at the empty leather seats. 'Perhaps the client wanted to remain anonymous. He or she might have some important role in the community.'

Eight o'clock on Friday evening, thought Herron. The moment of intrusion by a stranger, a dark noise against the silence of the forest, a shadow in the world of a respected psychotherapist who usually kept meticulous notes about her clients.

'This inquiry you're holding,' she asked. 'Have the staff at Deepwell cooperated so far?'

'Up to a point. But they won't give me the name of Sinden's supervisor. I'm convinced that Sinden was not acting alone in mounting these strange memory experiments. He was relatively inexperienced. There would have been special precautions, procedures put in place to prevent mistakes. He must have had high-level support from within the clinical management team at Deepwell.'

'You mean another psychotherapist collaborated with Sinden?'

'More than collaborated. I believed Sinden was directed and controlled by someone who is doing everything they can to cover their traces.' He stared meaningfully at Herron.

'You want me to help you find out who this person is?' she asked.

'Yes.'

'In other words, you have no proof that they exist at all.'

'We will have proof. Once you have concluded your murder investigation.' His voice had grown flat, lacking any theatrical twist. 'Dr Barker is no fool. As soon as I announced the inquiry, he understood that it wasn't Sinden I was after, but his supervisor and the management at Deepwell. He has been very clever. I suspect he has promised Sinden his old job back in return for his complicity.'

'What's to stop Deepwell closing ranks completely now that Pochard is dead? Most of her notes have been burnt. What if she was the only one prepared to speak out?'

'I have more evidence of clinical malpractice at Deepwell, apart from what Dr Pochard was prepared to reveal.' Reichmann's eyes glowed. 'Evidence I have been collecting for a long time. Jane was going to provide the final proof I needed.'

'What is this other evidence?'

Reichmann smiled. 'You will have to wait, Sergeant Herron, until I have prepared my notes. Be patient and then you will see.'

A gust of wind picked up and rustled the branches of the nearby trees. Reichmann seemed to relax as the physical presence of the trees drew closer, interrupting their conversation and halting Herron's scrutiny.

# CHAPTER TWENTY-TWO

He woke in a strange house and, at first, could not remember where he was. From the darkness, he could tell that it was night outside. Relief flooded through him. Dreaded daylight, the weight of all that light and the knowing eyes following his movements was enough to drive him deeper into insanity.

Walking with the slowness of a sleepwalker, he stumbled against a table and knocked over a bottle that rolled along the tiled floor. In spite of the unfamiliar surroundings, he managed to find his plastic tray of tablets in the fridge, his tranquillisers laid out in their little compartments according to the time of day and dose. He fumbled several of the capsules into his mouth. Now he just needed to find his therapist and talk to him. He had no friends in the outside world, and what family he had left had long grown sick of his drug-taking and crazed behaviour.

For years, his fellow inmates on Ward G had been his only company, but they were just as disturbed as he was, fantasists and attention-seekers, and none of them had exactly been sympathetic company. No, his only hope of escape from near total loneliness had been his trusted therapist. He wished that he were here with him now, asking him those gentle questions, gripping his restless mind in the trance of his overwhelming understanding. He remembered the flooding sense of relief at being able to reveal his innermost thoughts to a truly great listener, a trained professional who could sit for hours, a whole lifetime if necessary, tuning himself to the tone of his troubled soul. Not a day had passed since leaving Deepwell that he had not thought of the man. Often, his tall figure appeared to him, on the shadowy threshold between his waking and dreaming, listening to his words, reminding him of the therapeutic contract he had yet to fulfil.

He tried to let the quiet of the house envelop him, the peace of its warm shadows gather him in, but a sense of tension rose in his body. His therapist's plan was under way. Already, he had completed the first part and now he was somewhere in the middle with one more murder to commit. But was he where he should be? Had he somehow stepped out of the tunnel his mind was meant to be travelling along?

He checked all the doors in the log cabin, apart from the one that had been locked shut. He wondered where it led. He worried that he had strayed from the plan he had been rehearsing in his mind for the last six months. He stood in the hall by the mirror. There was no way to clear the sense of confusion in his mind.

The minutes passed. Slowly the tablets took effect, and he felt the tunnel open before him again. He grew convinced that his doctor was waiting behind the locked door. He could hear fidgeting, a chair scraping the floor, faint sounds as though whoever made them was trying not to be overheard. He pressed down the handle, but the door did not budge. He banged the door, demanding that it be opened, but the furtive sounds within abruptly ceased. The locked room marked him out as an outsider in a strange house, a lonely eavesdropper, a crazy fantasist who was trying to intrude upon someone else's story. He tried to stifle his rage, and rested his forehead against the wood of the door. His understanding of what was happening to him kept flickering on and off like a faulty light bulb. When the drugs wore off, his mind would be eclipsed into darkness once again. Determined now, he walked into the kitchen and found a screwdriver in one of the drawers. He marched back to the door and with a practised movement wrenched the lock loose.

As soon as he entered the room, it became clear to him that his therapist had not yet arrived. Instead, he identified the woman tied to a chair in the centre of the room, recognised her voice as he heard her scream, a desperate uninhibited shriek that rippled through his entire body, and then changed in pitch to the raw huskiness of someone who'd been left alone for days.

Her name was Laura Dunnock, and he knew with clarity that she was his next victim.

# CHAPTER TWENTY·THREE

When Carla got home, she found David sitting by the TV with a beer. She gave him a quick kiss on his cheek. Looking up she saw her mother-in-law standing in the kitchen wearing a pair of oven gloves. She was watching Carla with the staring look of someone practised in the silent art of reproach. A freshly baked lasagne was sitting on the table and the children were already in bed, even though it was only seven o'clock.

'How are the children?' asked Carla.

'They're right as rain,' said David.

'Then why are they in bed so early?'

'Because. Now give me another kiss.' He expelled a belch and excused himself. She realised it was not his first beer of the evening.

'Not with your mother watching,' she said under her breath.

Upstairs, she found the children fast asleep with open story-books next to their beds. She stumbled a little as she bent to kiss Alice's composed face. A new domestic world was taking shape around her, softer lights, tidier rooms, smells of soap and air fresheners, quiet children. It all contrasted so sharply with the way things had been before Mrs Herron's arrival.

When she returned downstairs, her mother-in-law had retired to her room to watch a soap opera. David had served out the lasagne and was wagging a bottle of wine at her.

'To domestic bliss,' he said, filling two large glasses.

She took a large gulp and thought, it's *her* domestic bliss, not ours. 'What would you do if I gave up my job and stayed at home?' she asked.

'What?' But he wasn't fully listening. He was keeping one eye on the football match on TV.

It did not matter. She had not really meant it. What was the point in risking an argument when there was a witness residing in a room nearby, one who would surely take sides?

'Rough day?' he asked with his glass raised to his lips.

'The usual. When this investigation is over, I'm going to take some annual leave.'

'Good.'

A goal was scored on TV and his eyes lit up. It had been ages since she'd seen him so relaxed. Over the wine, they discussed possible holiday destinations, places that were child friendly. They even toyed with the idea of taking the children to Disney World. Afterwards, they cleared the table and loaded the dishwasher. She was not used to drinking and felt the warmth of the wine course through her veins, instilling a sense of liberation, which was enhanced rather than inhibited by the thought of her domestic rival watching TV in the spare room. She concluded that there were benefits to having her mother-in-law staying under the same roof, at least until things calmed down at work. Mrs Herron was fulfilling what mattered most to her – the maternal wish to look after her son and grandchildren – and she was getting on with her career. Nobody was using or taking advantage of anybody.

When they had finished the wine, she drifted to the computer in the study. She stared at the screensaver, a photograph of Alice and Ben, without thinking about anything. She heard David stumble towards bed. He was drunk and would be asleep in minutes. She went to her briefcase and took out the copies of the photographs from Pochard's house. She stared at them and told herself she had to work out the other locations, especially the one with a log cabin in the background. Where were they and what did they mean? The body of water glinting through the branches, the thickets of brambles and overgrown paths that led absolutely nowhere except into the mind of a killer. She studied the hopeless looks on McCrea's face, the patient with the stray eyes and long white eyelashes, looking in different directions in each of the photographs; the excited gaze of Sinden, always fixed on McCrea, and in the background, an older man, another psychotherapist, she thought, his tall figure wrapped in shadows. She wished he would step into the open, that for just one shot he would turn his face fully towards the camera. She could not decide if the photographs were clues or red herrings, and her uncertainty made her impatient.

She moved the mouse of the computer and clicked on the button for Google Earth. The landscape of the Scottish borders lay before her once again. She felt in control, swooping over its forests and hills, far above the pine needles and dripping heather. She followed the lines of paths and rivers, the imprint of old foundations and field works showing through the hillsides. After a few screens, the houses grew sparse and the terrain more rugged. The landscape lost the sheen of civilisation, the bright roads and clusters of buildings. She searched the vast swathes of forests, the ridges and swirls of the trees reminding her of water ebbing over sand.

She zoomed into a valley full of darkness, and then a glitter of sharp silver appeared on screen, sunlight on a remote loch. She scrolled faster, towards the water. The loch seemed to have a face, eyes like islands and inlets that resembled a nose and mouth. However, there were no signs of what might be a log cabin around its edges, so she scrolled towards the border, making zigzag sweeps across the terrain. She focused in and moved along paths that might have been deer tracks. None of them were continuous, the moor seeming to swallow their traces. Burly mountains formed on the screen, little clouds hanging over their peaks. Patch by patch, she pushed through the purple heather and bogland. She saw the remnants of tumbledown bothies, which might also have been random deposits of rocks. She hovered over ravines and dead alleys of stones that looked to be several miles long. Then she navigated back to the lower lying forests. She scrolled over the blocks of green and brown, the forests and hillsides where her instinct told her Chisholm might be hiding Laura Dunnock. She chose a suitable-looking loch and scanned its fringes, but could find no sign of a cabin that might resemble the one in the photographs.

She moved out and found another loch. There was some sort of industrial building at one end of it, surrounded by heavy machinery. What could it be? She zoomed closer. A large concrete embankment closed off one end of the loch. A reservoir, she thought. It looked too exposed, the trees too sparse, to be the one she was hunting for. She travelled north again, and the trees grew denser. She came to a pine forest darker than the others, sucking in all the colour and light even when she zoomed in as close as she could. Everything on the screen looked as black as night. A sudden chill gripped her. She leaned closer, peering at the darkness that lay waiting for her.

She scrolled some more, but the images began to freeze on the screen, the forests blurring into each other. Exhausted, she switched off the computer and went to bed.

'You're back,' mumbled David. 'I thought you'd done one of your disappearing tricks again.'

'No. Just googling possible murder sites.'

She slipped in beside him, her mind fixated on what he had just said. Searching for Pochard's killer *had* become her disappearing act, she realised. She settled into sleep with the strange feeling that she was rising above the border hills, like a lost soul or a star, reaching through miles of fathomless space. She roamed the corridors of darkness, the shadows between the trees, and the spaces between the stars, until there was no more light and nothing more to be discovered or remembered, her thoughts burning themselves out one by one, with only a final image remaining, the murderer's door locked day and night, and then that vanished, too.

# CHAPTER TWENTY-FOUR

If anything, Sinden looked more sleepless and worn-out when he opened the door for Herron the following morning. The darkness around his eyes gave him a frightened, haunted look. He explained to the detective that being stuck at home every day had not agreed with him, and that he was dreading the day he would have to return to Deepwell.

Herron had not appeared on his doorstep to provide sympathy. She pushed on into the hallway, no longer so concerned about disturbing him. 'I have some important questions to ask you,' she warned. 'Your refusal to answer them could obstruct an important murder investigation.'

'Fire away, if you must,' he replied.

'Who was your supervisor on Ward G?'

Sinden braced himself, but did not reply. She was growing used to silences now, and she allowed a very long gap to develop in the interview. He is not going to tell me, she realised as the moments ticked by and Sinden withdrew deeper into his thoughts. She tried a different front. 'What do you know about the disappearance of Laura Dunnock?'

'I don't know anything about that.'

'What about your colleagues? What do they have to say?'

'I've no idea.'

'So you haven't spoken to any of them. Not to Dr Barker or even your supervisor? Not once in the past week?'

He shook his head.

'Tell me about the holistic foundation,' she asked. 'What does it do? What are its principles? How is it different from other psychotherapy groups?'

He glanced at her furtively. 'I'm not at liberty to talk about those things.' The shadow of the foundation seemed to lurk over him.

'Look, I've already talked to Professor Reichmann,' she said. 'He says the foundation and your supervisor are the subjects of an investigation.'

He looked at her in surprise. 'What is he investigating?'

'He knows that the group is hiding something. He says that he has been compiling evidence of its malpractice for some time.'

Sinden's eyes widened but he remained silent. He stared past her and out the window. She was going to have to use subtler means to change his attitude and force the truth out of him. She asked could they sit down together and when they had settled into chairs in his kitchen, she said in a softer voice, 'May I ask you a personal question, Dr Sinden?'

'Go ahead.'

'What made you want to become a psychotherapist in the first place?'

He gazed at her with his slightly haunted eyes, and then, slowly, he began speaking. He said that after he qualified from medical school his personal life had felt like a complete mess.

'I wanted to know where I had gone wrong in my relationships,' he explained, 'and so I decided to see a psychotherapist. I thought the reasons lay in my childhood and in my difficult relationship with my parents. There was no one else I could turn to, and so I became a patient of Dr Robert Llewyn, who was the director of the hospital at that time.' He clasped his hands upon his knees. 'Robert helped me escape from loneliness and the sense of being completely directionless in my life.'

'How?'

'I hadn't decided on psychotherapy as a career until I came to see him. He fixed things for me, made sure I completed the correct courses, and then he examined me on psychodynamic practice. I was still in therapy with him, but I was also his student, and disciple. I felt so privileged.'

'You mean your entire career as a therapist was born out of being one of Dr Llewyn's patients?'

'Yes. I was in therapy for over a year when I asked him to teach me. He produced a sheet of paper from a drawer. On it was a list of names, all patients of his, whom he was also training. He invited me to join their study group. Over time, the group became the holistic foundation.'

'Who else was on the list?'

'Dr Pochard and Barker, and also Laura Dunnock.'

'You mean they were all patients of his?'

'Yes. Normally it's a hanging offence for a clinical supervisor to be also one's personal therapist. But since Dr Pochard and Barker had followed the same path, I thought, why not? Dr Llewyn flew in the face of conventions and rules. He was brave and controversial.'

That did the trick, she thought, wetting her lips with her tongue. Finally, Sinden had revealed the name of his supervisor, Dr Llewyn.

'And during your therapy sessions with Dr Llewyn, you also discussed your patients?'

'Robert helped me understand their mental conditions. He showed me the way forward by linking my feelings towards them with events and relationships in my own childhood. His analyses were always impressively sharp.'

'So your treatment plans emerged while in therapy?'

'In principle, all his patients who were also therapists had to discuss their treatment plans.' Sinden explained how hard it was to work intensively with patients on Ward G. Without firm guidance, a therapist might grow confused and lose their way.

'How could you be so sure that his guidance wasn't flawed?'

'Robert had worked for such a massively long time in the field. Instinctively, he knew the right approach to take. Other therapists placed their absolute trust in him, as well. He kept telling me that I was breaking new ground, that I was an expert in the field, going in more deeply than anyone else.'

'Your theory that some of the patients on Ward G were repressing terrible memories such as murder, whose idea was that?'

He grew uncertain for a moment. 'It was an idea that came from me.'

'During therapy with Dr Llewyn?'

'Yes. I knew that it was the approach I needed to follow. I could sense that my patients were suffering from traumas that had not yet been mapped out, and Robert understood that.'

'How many of them had ever hinted at being murderers?'

'None of them.'

'Why didn't you tell me earlier about Dr Llewyn's role as your supervisor?'

'I wanted to protect his good name. My treatment plan for Ward G was branded a failure because I had ignored the latest research on false memories, but it was my fault, not his. Robert suggested that I had not worked intensively enough on my own problems, that the therapy had failed because of my own weaknesses. He said I lacked drive, that I didn't have enough passion to do what had to be done to vindicate our therapeutic vision. He stopped my therapy for several months and I had to be content with seeing another one of the foundation members.'

It was evident to Herron just how much Llewyn had meant to Sinden. He had been his therapist, his teacher, and his father figure. In spite of his arrogance, there was a childlike simplicity about Sinden, and Herron was appalled at the image of him sweeping through the corridors of Ward G, the near-blind treating the blind, attaching the most grotesque interpretations to the patients' illnesses. And Dr Llewyn had been behind it all, working in secret on Sinden's mental state, expanding his confidence, dominating him completely, and all the while treating his patients like specimens in a jar.

Sinden gave her a weary smile. 'The only way to cure patients is to make interpretations. That's what Robert always said.'

'Have you spoken to him?'

'Not recently. He's retired now from Deepwell and the foundation.'

'Do you know where I can find him?'

'I've tried myself. But he's not at home and won't answer his phone.'

'Would you think it right for his friends to hide him, to protect him from the law and not cooperate with the police?'

'Of course not.'

'What if Dr Llewyn were working hand in hand with Chisholm? What if he were behind Pochard's murder and the disappearance of Laura Dunnock?'

'Impossible.' Sinden had lost his sense of weakness and confusion. He seemed energised. 'You have no idea,' he said, leaning towards her, his eyes glowing. 'You have no idea what it was like being Robert's patient. If you had any inkling you would be clamouring to be one yourself.'

'Apart from Dr Pochard, was there anyone in the society not dedicated to Dr Llewyn and his theories?'

'Like I told you, everyone is loyal to the society and its leader.'

'Everyone?'

She said it in such a disbelieving voice that Sinden stared at her.

'Well, almost everyone,' he replied. Without uttering a word of explanation he left the room. She looked at the door and waited. After a while, she began to wonder if he had slipped out of the house in order to escape further questioning. She would have gone in search for him, but then she heard, from much deeper within the house, drawers being opened and shut, and the scraping sound of heavy objects being pulled out of dark corners. At last, Sinden appeared. There was a look of satisfaction on his face when he placed a photograph on the table beside her.

'The society has strict rules of confidentiality,' he explained. 'And I can't break them by revealing the names of any of its members. However, I can show you this. It was taken a few years back.'

Herron looked at the photograph, and immediately recognised the serious figure of Derek Cavanagh, the father of Alice's playschool friend, standing next to the equally serious figures of Pochard, Barker, Sinden and a few others.

'That's Derek Cavanagh, isn't it?' she said.

He seemed intrigued that she knew him. 'You've crossed paths?'

'I can't say. Is he a member of the holistic society?'

'Was.'

'Expelled?'

Sinden laughed. 'Cavanagh would deny that as if his life depended on it.'

'What were the circumstances?'

He leaned back and gave her question some thought. 'I can only speak in general terms. You see, the society has a professional mindset, a fixed belief system.'

'Like a sect?'

'I wouldn't go that far. But it has to sift out those who would launch critical attacks from within, or reject the guidance of the society's leader.'

'Would an expelled member have difficulty afterwards working in the psychiatric field?'

'I think they would struggle. Doors in that field would be closed to them.'

'What about the emotional repercussions?' She wondered how difficult it would have been for Cavanagh to detach himself from such a cult-like community.

'In the case of Cavanagh, he was probably unbalanced from the start. His contributions at meetings were uninteresting. My colleagues regarded him as a mildly boring narcissist, a sociopath.'

She nodded and filed away the information for further investigation. She had just one more question for him. 'Are there any staff at Deepwell who weren't under Dr Llewyn's influence?'

He shrugged. 'We belonged to the one family.'

'The foundation?'

'Yes.'

# CHAPTER TWENTY-FIVE

Silence and privacy. Nothing can be unearthed from the human mind without the two of them, and now, for the first time in his life, he had both in abundance. He walked from room to room in the log cabin, carefully avoiding Laura Dunnock, who was still tied to her chair in the back room.

He picked up books from the shelves, the heavy tomes on psychotherapy, and flicked through the pages, but did not bother to read them. He sat in a chair and stared at the trees outside. There was no television or internet connection in the cabin. He was completely cut off from the rest of the world, and the place felt blessedly peaceful, but still he could not shake off the inner voices and thoughts. His therapist had told him to accept and get used to them, and then perhaps the feeling of being watched and haunted might disappear. As for Dunnock, she had been quiet for hours, adding to the restful mood that he kept trying to enjoy but could not. He had entered into a state of nervous anticipation. He felt glad that the oppressive mood would soon end. It was almost over. Tonight was the appointed time for the second murder.

Fantasies belong to more people than their creators. Once a disturbing dream has been told, it's anyone's to share, and his had become common currency on Ward G, twisted and changed in the minds of his fellow patients and the doctors who tried to listen in and analyse every word. He was no longer sure if it was his fantasy, and not someone else's, that he was committing the murders secretly for another person and waiting for their approval.

He wondered why his therapist had not come. He had tried ringing him but there was no answer. Why had he heard nothing from him? Was he expected to do everything on his own? He needed the doctor to help him map out the issues at play in the room with the prisoner, to scan the emotions and problematic areas, to look inside his head, search for answers and make the right decisions.

He rose from the chair and walked into the prisoner's room. He saw that she was wearing her professional face, again. Staff at Deepwell were good at learning how not to look shocked or afraid. He studied the contrived indifference in her eyes as she gazed at him, trying to shift in the chair, rolling its coasters on the floor, her shoes skidding on the wooden boards.

Her expressionless face watched him without blinking, her shoulders writhing as she worked on loosening the ropes around her hands. He could guess all the hard work going on inside her head, sizing up her choices, pondering the limited means of escape, trying to anticipate what he might do next. He admired her courage, her decision to put caution behind and go for an all-out struggle against the chair. He wondered what questions she would fire at him to distract his attention if he removed the cloth gag from her mouth. What period of your childhood are you enacting? Can you see a little boy? How old is he? What happened to him?

She lost control of the struggle against the ropes. The chair rolled across the floor and bumped against the wall, knocking an object from her grasp. He stood up, walked several steps and snatched it from the floor. A broken pen that she had been clutching secretly as a weapon. Something swelled inside him. He felt outside time, removed from his body, in some sort of trance state, a hovering witness to the crime that was soon to be committed, foreseeing everything that would unfold. He had an instant memory of how Dunnock would die. An image from a photograph came to him, a setting his therapist had organised.

Slowly he came back to the surface, as though rising from the depths of a dream. He decided it was time to change the cloths that gagged her. They were soaking wet.

'Soon it will be time,' he told her.

'When?' She was breathless.

'In a matter of hours.'

She gave a little sob.

'First, I'm going to confess to the act of murder. Not because I'm seeking your understanding or forgiveness – it's too late for that, now – but because I have to remember exactly how it is meant to happen. It's possible that I may have misremembered it or misunderstood what I must do.'

Slowly, he grew in confidence. Now that he had a witness to his telling, his memories rose up, imagery and words surfacing in his mind, the details growing in importance. The best therapy was a form of thinking aloud, the way it helped the speaker to construct a narrative out of random thoughts, remote memories and fantasies. He wanted her to see the scene that lay hidden in his memory, to see the action from the very start.

'What are you planning to do?' she asked, her voice trembling.

He frowned. It was not meant to be an interrogation, and he did not want to be wearied by questions. In principle, she should behave as a therapist should, neither afraid nor distrustful of what he might reveal.

'Please,' he said. 'Don't interrupt me. I haven't remembered everything yet, and there is a chance I may not have to do anything to you at all.'

He pulled his chair closer. 'I don't want you to ask another question unless it is absolutely necessary. If I want you to comment, I will tell you. All I want is for you to listen to me and help me remember. You must respect that.'

She did not answer.

'I'm worried about forgetting something, you see. But, somehow, the prospect of remembering frightens me more than not remembering.'

'Dr Pochard thought you were cured.'

'It was a bluff, I'm afraid. All those years of therapy on Ward G smartened me up, made me sly. I learned to say what was expected of me. The truth is I'm the most dangerous man ever released from that loony bin.'

And the most lonely, too, he wanted to add. The rest of the staff at Deepwell, including Dr Pochard, had been unwilling to take on the burden of his loneliness. Everyone except his therapist had baulked at assuaging the void inside his heart, the emptiness that constantly threatened to consume him from the inside. He waited now with hope for the return of his therapist, the man who had treated him with infinite patience and listened while he talked, the man who had been strong enough to resist the pressure of his peers, but at the same time could behave mercilessly when the need arose.

# CHAPTER TWENTY-SIX

Morton's face was set in a frowning mask as he paced around Dr Pochard's house, not uttering a single word and avoiding eye contact with Herron, who had already grown resigned to this fresh bout of silence. She had the sense that his taciturn moods were loaded up carefully in advance like gunshot in a double-barrelled rifle. Once one charge was expended, another lay sitting in wait, ready to be unleashed on the unsuspecting world.

They entered the consulting room together and listened. Herron felt the extreme quietness of the house haunt her, as if the murderer had removed every single sound, every creak and sigh from the floorboards and walls. Her senses were tuned to almost breaking point. She glanced at Morton and saw that he was sitting on one of the leather chairs with his head hidden in his large hands, concentrating deeply. She tried to reach out mentally to him, but he got up and walked away.

'Would you rather be on your own?' she asked.

'No. I just need space to think.'

This morning Morton reminded her of a tomcat that had spent the night being mauled by other cats. His hair was more unkempt than usual, and his raincoat badly creased. Did he ever stop working, and what on earth was his personal life like? He was always at the station first thing in the morning, and usually the last to leave. Rarely did he take part in officer banter. He had developed the trick of slipping beneath the surface of conversations and sinking out of sight. In fact, he was a complete stranger to her in almost every regard, a tall detective with lank hair and a long raincoat, whose curt answers and reticence somehow gave her greater confidence in her instincts and sharpened her mind, but on another level frustrated and irritated her beyond belief. They had grown to know each other in the shadows of the crime scene, but nowhere else. Their lives were a complete mystery to each other. She wondered if there was a future to their strange working relationship, and if, when the investigation concluded, they would go their separate ways and any connection between them disappear completely.

'What was Professor Reichmann looking for?' asked Morton.

'Something he thought would be here but wasn't.'

They walked around the house again and stared at the rooms for several minutes.

She tried to start a conversation with him about Reichmann, but he refused to be drawn and instead mumbled, 'Time to draw upon the most important skills of a detective.'

'What are those?'

'Patience and watchfulness.'

It was a disconcerting experience working a crime scene with Morton. She felt comfortable in his presence yet incapable of saying anything meaningful. She followed him around, staring at what he was staring at, trying to work out the real reason for Reichmann's visit.

'Something *is* amiss,' said Morton eventually.

'What?'

'Just a vague notion. Do you feel it? Something has been changed or moved.'

They stood still, breathing softly. The silence felt unique. It seemed to start at a single point, Dr Pochard's large leather chairs the epicentre, and from there it emanated outwards, fanning into all the rooms.

Morton marched towards the French doors. He loosened his tie and stared out at the pine forest. The police officer guarding the house was moving at the edge of the trees. He appeared to be searching for something amid the brambles and nettles. Morton stood for several minutes letting the vista take effect on him. She could tell he was thinking about something crucial to the investigation, but she had no idea what it was.

Eventually, she could bear it no longer.

'What are you thinking about?'

'Two things.'

'What things?'

'One of them has nothing to do with you or this investigation.'

'And the other.'

'It strikes me that this case is about people who are unable to draw the line between their own fantasies, wishful thinking and reality.'

She assumed he meant Chisholm and McCrea, but he began talking about the staff at Deepwell.

'I've looked into Barker's background. He appears obsessed with awards and commendations. For himself and Deepwell. There doesn't seem to be an honour for which he is not willing to grovel. He even gets himself invited on radio programmes and news stations as a psychological expert into the criminal mind. His office is plastered with certificates and photographs of him mingling with the great and powerful. I can just imagine him strutting around the place when he thinks he's alone.'

From Morton's reflection in the window, Herron could see he was grinning to himself, a wolfish grimace framed by his long hair.

'I find his personality lacking in something,' said Morton. 'Like a lot of other bosses I've met in my time.'

It was true, she thought. Responsibility and power attracted a certain type of person.

Morton kept speaking with his back to her as though he was talking to himself. 'Quite often, they are vain, self-promoting egotists trying to hide the fact that they are frauds. But with Barker the vanity seems more extreme, more restless. I think he is as deranged as some of his patients. Without a single speck of self-doubt in him.'

'Sounds like one of those personality disorders,' she said. While they were on the subject, she told him about her interview with Sinden. She had found him an unusual psychotherapist. For one thing, he seemed a lot more vulnerable and lonely than the ones she had met before. He also appeared to have an irrational belief in his own powers to reform criminal behaviour.

'He really thought he was curing the patients on Ward G?' said Morton. He turned and looked at her. For the first time that morning, he appeared interested in what she had to say.

'I think he's a committed therapist. But there's also an element of self-delusion about him. He believed in his theories even when the evidence was mounting against him.'

'Another fantasist, then. How does he feel about Pochard's murder and the disappearance of Dunnock?'

'He seemed anxious, but I got the impression it wasn't his biggest concern.'

'Did you notice anything else about him?'

'Like what?'

'What we've been talking about before. Vanity, self-promotion, wishful thinking about one's own talents.'

'You mean is he like Barker?'

Morton nodded.

'No. I think he is just one of those people who are vulnerable to cults. I don't think he's able to withdraw himself emotionally from the foundation.'

Morton stepped away from the window and lowered his head. He walked around the room without looking at her. 'It's been more than a week since Pochard was murdered. And we're no closer to finding Chisholm or Laura Dunnock.'

She didn't reply. In the circumstances, what could she say?

'The pressure is rising,' he said, his voice almost cracking. 'We're getting closer and closer to having another dead body on our hands. Do you feel it?' He squatted by the chairs and examined them. Then he walked slowly in a circle. He spoke in a low voice that welled up from deep within his chest. 'Let us presume that sometime on Friday evening the murderer appears here at Pochard's house. She is about to see her last patient of the day, or perhaps has already seen him or her. Either she invites her killer in or he somehow slips in without disturbing anything.'

'You say "he". I presume you're talking about Chisholm?'

'For the sake of argument, yes. Let's say he attacks her and transports her body without leaving anything incriminating behind except a broken fingernail in one of the leather seats. After taking such great care, I can't get my head round what he does next.'

'What?'

'Placing the head in the stone cairn. Usually you move a body part to hide it, but in this instance, the intention was the opposite. There must be some logical reason why Chisholm took such great care to cover his tracks but then went to the considerable effort of removing her head, depositing it in the middle of a forest, and then hanging round so that a passer-by might find him.'

'Not to mention losing his finger in the process.'

'Exactly. I can't understand how his frame of mind shifted.'

'A psychotherapist might say that in his derangement, Chisholm was compelled to act out his fantasies.'

'And yet he remembered all the details of the pseudo-confession in the middle of this attack of madness.'

Herron thought about the forest clearing but could no longer see it clearly. Her trips through the forests around Peebles, Pochard's photographs of rocks and trees and over-grown tracks, the confessions of the patients on Ward G had trapped her mind in an endless loop, turning the murder scene into a recurring dream, all muddled up in time and overex-posed, full of the blinding light of repeated revelations, more light than she could bear, but what was it she still could not see?

'To me, the scene in the forest is too concise,' said Morton. 'It matches too many details from the confessions. Yet there are no signs of struggle or violence in this house, nor clues that might lead us to the murderer, except the figure of Chisholm himself, standing in the darkness like some sort of sinister signpost.'

Or someone trying to remember a dream, thought Herron. 'What struck me when I saw him was his uncertainty,' she said. 'I got the sense that he couldn't see clearly, that he was peering at a scene that might have been real or invented.'

'Did he say anything that sounded odd?'

'He kept mumbling to himself about taking a trip down memory lane. He said he was just watching.'

'Just watching. But he did not know what he had watched. That's for the detective to work out. To see what the person who left the head in the cairn wants us to see. Solve this and the case will be closed.'

'The person? Not Chisholm but someone else?'

'Yes. The person who went to the effort of leaving the head there.'

Neither of them spoke for a while. They were trying to uncover a secret presence in the crime scene, another person, a guiding intelligence. Herron wanted to tell him her suspicions about Llewyn but she held back. 'What conclusions can we draw, if it's possible to make any sensible conclusions?' she asked.

'The head was left in the cairn to communicate something to us. That Deepwell had failed to cure Chisholm and that Sinden was correct in his assessment and Pochard disastrously wrong.'

'But Sinden could not have been directly involved in the murder. He was at a mental health conference in Edinburgh. Dozens of people saw him there along with Dr Barker.'

'Who else could have done it, then?' said Morton. 'Someone else connected to Ward G and familiar with the patients' confessions.'

Herron took a deep breath, knowing that their conversation had reached a crucial point. 'I managed to find out something else from Sinden,' she said. 'Dr Llewyn was his therapist and supervisor. In fact, all the therapists at Deepwell were being treated by Llewyn.'

Morton turned and stared at her with a look of intense

concentration. 'This is an interesting development. It means that the idea of a conspiracy is starting to hang together.'

'You think it's Llewyn?' she said.

'I don't know. All we know for certain is that Sinden and Barker have rock solid alibis that will stand up in court. If they were behind Pochard's murder, then they must have had some sort of accomplice.' Morton turned and stared at the leather chairs. 'This may be a fatal mistake, but let's forget about Chisholm for the time being. We don't know the entire terrain but we can see that Pochard, Dunnock, Sinden and Barker are all connected to Llewyn. I think it's time I tracked him down and checked his alibi.' He glided across the room like a leopard in search of prey. Before disappearing through the door, he turned round and said to her, almost as an afterthought, 'Well done, Carla, we're on to something. Keep focusing on the foundation. This society of psychotherapists might well be hiding a bloody psychopath. Holistic therapy, I'll be damned.'

# CHAPTER TWENTY-SEVEN

Driving back to the station at speed, Herron devoted her mind to pondering what was missing from Pochard's house. An important piece of evidence should have been there, but was not. Some sort of clue was being withheld from her and Morton, and possibly Reichmann, too. The thought nagged at her so much that she almost crashed into a red post van at the bottom of the valley. She had to steer onto the grass verge to avoid the vehicle, the car rocking over mounds of grass and pitching her roughly in her seat. She caught a glimpse of the driver, waving a reprimanding finger at her, and then he sped on.

She watched the van disappear in her rear-view mirror, and broke into a cold sweat at the thought of how close she had come to a collision. Then her brow furrowed at the thought of the van visiting the lonely farmhouses along the valley. It struck her that the daily post was something she had not thought about in relation to Dr Pochard's house. The mat at her front door had been completely empty. Not even a trace of junk mail. Yet on the day they had broken in, there had been an assortment of letters jamming the bottom of the front door. What had happened to Pochard's post in the meantime? There had been no mention of it in the forensic reports so why had it been removed? Perhaps it had never arrived in the first place and had been redirected elsewhere? She realised she could not solve the mystery without first checking at the local sorting office.

After she had shown her police ID, the post office manager explained that all of Dr Pochard's letters had been redirected to Deepwell Hospital, care of Dr Barker. It struck Herron as strange that she had not been informed of the arrangement. Perhaps Morton had set it up, and forgotten to tell her. But why allow Deepwell access to Pochard's post, some of which might have been confidential?

'Who authorised this?' she asked.

'The detective in charge of the investigation.'

'Detective Inspector Harry Morton?'

'I don't think that was his name.'

'Did he have long hair and a beard?'

'No. Quite the opposite. He was bald and clean-shaven.'

'Was his name Detective Chief Inspector Bates?'

'That was more like it.'

'I'd like to see any post that has not already been delivered.'

The manager went into the sorting office and soon returned with a bundle of letters. She told him she would deliver the post to Deepwell personally. He hesitated, but seeing the determined look in her face, he handed over the letters. Among the sheaf were circulars from pharmacological companies and a subscription notice to a psychotherapy journal. There was one envelope with Pochard's address handwritten on the front, and postmarked from Switzerland. She waited until she was sitting in her car before she opened it. She knew immediately who had sent it – Professor Eric Reichmann.

DEAR JANE,

I am sorry to hear of the setbacks you have had in your supervision and therapy with our esteemed colleague Robert. I fear that I should have arranged to come over and visit you sooner, but I have been so busy lately. Every day there is a new demand to treat a patient or supervise a new therapist. Just this week, I have been dealing with lawyers who are demanding that I discuss a patient's notes and details of his disturbing dreams as though they were nothing more than a teenager's secret diary. They do not understand that confidentiality is our watchword and the basis of our profession, which brings me to this troubling request of yours to investigate Dr Llewyn's role at Deepwell.

I am disappointed to hear that his mistakes have shaken you enough to reflect on where the society as a whole is going. The failures on Ward G should not affect your faith in our holistic methods of treatment, although I do concede they will have serious consequences for your professional relationship with Robert.

Sometimes, we therapists listen more to ourselves and our egotistical needs than to the patient. You have every right to expect him to listen to your concerns and consider them carefully rather than accuse you of back-stabbing.

None of us is above criticism, especially from such an experienced practitioner as yourself. I thoroughly understand your desire to end his supervision of your practice and patients, and to stop undergoing therapy as his patient.

You asked me if anyone has registered a complaint against Llewyn in the past, and in particular if any documentation suggesting a conspiracy at Deepwell to protect his name exists. Unfortunately, I cannot supply the answer to these requests in writing. Rest assured, you are not the only one to have looked critically at the foundation's role at Deepwell. Scepticism has infected the group before, with several members withdrawing their membership.

However, I urge you not to talk to anyone else about your misgivings until I have investigated them thoroughly. The consequences might be disastrous for the society as a whole. Even assuming that you are correct in all your fears there are bound to be contrary arguments presented by Llewyn and his colleagues. Nothing is ever as clear as it first seems, not in the world of forensic psychiatry, and it would be better if tempers were allowed to cool. You won't be walking away from a fight. You'll be saving your ammunition for another day.

The treatment of Billy Chisholm might appear to be the low point of Deepwell's history, but with careful thought and analysis, and in your wise care, his case may yet turn out to be the high point of your professional career, and give you the recognition you have craved for so long.

So I ask you to suspend your lonely pursuit of the truth. Withdraw your cavalry from the charge, at least until I can visit you in person, and in the meantime, go back to what you have always been, a loyal and gifted member of our foundation, who always has the best interests of her patients at heart. Ask yourself, will your patients be best served by dragging this alleged scandal into the light, or are you in danger of exposing their vulnerabilities to society in general, as well as dragging down the honourable reputations of therapists who believed they were advancing their profession in the most difficult of circumstances?

Yours sincerely,

ERIC.

P.S. I trust you will keep the trays you have recovered from Ward G under lock and key! Or at least away from prying eyes.

The first question that struck her was what were the trays Reichmann had mentioned at the end of the letter? And why had Pochard taken them from Ward G? Were they evidence of some sort of malpractice? Also, it seemed to Herron that Reichmann had as good as admitted that Pochard's misgivings had been shared by other therapists. She sensed the professor's desperation to keep a lid on the problems at Deepwell, and a dread in making the visit to Scotland and in dealing conclusively with Pochard's complaints. Had there been a measure of relief in Reichmann's cheery arrival at the police station? Was he at heart a coward, or was he also involved in the conspiracy to protect Deepwell's reputation at all costs?

She picked up the phone and dialled Reichmann's number. Perhaps it was time to goad the professor into holding a proper investigation, she thought. However, when she rang him, his mobile kept cutting out.

'Where are you?' she shouted in an effort to make herself heard.

'In a glen overlooking Loch Lomond. Far away from consulting rooms...' He sounded almost giddy with joy. She heard a few indistinct words about walks and barriers and a wide-open sky, and then his voice became clear again. 'Has anything happened?'

'Yes. Something has come up.'

He told her he would walk back up to the road where the mobile reception might be better, and then the signal cut out.

Half an hour later, he called to say he had found a little tea-shop. 'I'm doing a walking tour around the loch,' he explained.

'The views here are so peaceful and dramatic. I've been staring at the loch for ages and it does nothing, absolutely nothing but lie there full of its own mystery.' He laughed. 'Sometimes it feels more disturbing than sitting with a patient who is in deep psychosis.'

'So a psychotherapist keeps listening, even on holiday.'

'Always. What have you found?'

'Your letter in reply to Dr Pochard's request for help.'

Reichmann paused. 'Where did you find it?'

It was clear from the shift in his voice that the letter was important. She suspected that Reichmann had been desperately looking for it on the morning of his arrival in Scotland.

'At the sorting office. It was about to be sent to Deepwell Hospital but I intercepted it. What information were you bringing Dr Pochard? What was it you could not write in the letter?'

'I'm not able to give you those details.'

'Then that makes you worse than Dr Barker. He values the reputation of his hospital above his patients, but you're an academic putting his theories above all else. Dr Pochard turned to you for guidance and support but what did she get? Why are you over here now?'

'To pay my respects to Jane. And hunt out members of the foundation not following the orthodox models.'

'And what have you found?'

'Very little.'

'How can that be? Dr Sinden's experimentation was untested and dangerous. Patients got worse and more dependent on drugs, not better.'

'I don't want to hear anything more about Ward G. I find it so tedious and depressing. Psychotherapy is not a blunt instrument to treat incurable inmates on a psychiatric ward.

It is a subjective approach based on intellectual dialogue and empathy. It belongs to the arts not the sciences. Dr Sinden's attempts to reach an understanding of his patients' psychoses were commendable, if naive. Their false memories felt completely real once they were formed and established. The foundation will take no action against him.'

'I am determined to get to the bottom of what was going on at Deepwell,' she replied, 'whatever the vested interests of the foundation. I expect your cooperation with my inquiries, and if this is not forthcoming I will have to use my powers as a police officer to compel your assistance.'

'You don't have to threaten me. I'm in a very difficult position here, and you have to understand that. All you can focus on is a dead body and a missing woman. I have to consider the future of a foundation that aims to alleviate the mental suffering of thousands of patients.'

'Sinden told me that Dr Llewyn was his supervisor. What is your opinion of Llewyn?'

'He is a gifted therapist.'

'What do you mean by that?'

'He is absolutely focused and concentrates with his entire being on what his patients tell him. He sees and understands them in new ways.'

'Does everyone in the foundation think so positively of him?'

'Of course he has had his critics from time to time, but the current members support him.'

'And what about his patients and those of Sinden's? As his supervisor, Llewyn would have been responsible for patients like Chisholm and McCrea.'

'I am sure they respect him, too. I have heard countless stories of patients recovering because of his interventions.'

'But Dr Pochard did not agree.'

'Evidently not.'

'What form did his interventions take?'

'He uncovered painful memories that he believed lay at the heart of the patients' mental illnesses.'

'How?'

'Through dreams, free associations, listening to the patients' fantasies and delusions, and encouraging them to let their minds wander.'

'Did the process involve the use of high doses of tranquillisers and psychoactive drugs?'

'There is little point discussing Llewyn's methods with someone untrained in psychiatry. To the untrained eye, his use of medication during therapy sessions might seem hard to comprehend.'

'Do you think that Sinden and Llewyn might have unintentionally turned the patients on Ward G into drug addicts?'

'No comment.'

'Who do you think killed Dr Pochard?'

'Isn't it clear that Chisholm is the murderer? He had been harbouring this dreadful fantasy for years, even sharing it with his fellow patients. He managed to hide his psychosis and persuade Pochard to release him back into the community. These are the facts, or are they too simplistic for you?'

'What if Pochard was murdered to protect the reputation of Llewyn and his colleagues? What if Chisholm were somehow manipulated by someone with secrets to hide?'

'Nonsense. Why would you think such a thing?'

But his words faltered and Herron sensed his voice slipping into a void of doubt, as unfathomable as the loch he was staring out onto.

'OK,' said Reichmann. 'For argument's sake, I'll pretend there is a possibility that what you are saying might be true.

Tell me, how did you draw such a conclusion?' His voice had recovered its benevolent authority. 'Where did you get this wild idea? What clues have you gathered? Tell me everything you know so that I can decide if your conclusion is rational or not.'

'You didn't tell me that Llewyn was still Pochard's supervisor.'

'I thought you only needed the name of Sinden's supervisor.'

Suddenly she had a disturbing idea. If she had not been on the phone to Reichmann, she would have shouted it down the corridors of the police station. However, it would be a professional disaster if she were mistaken. To prove that her hypothesis was not badly wrong, she needed Reichmann to give the right answers to two questions.

'How often did Llewyn and Pochard meet for therapy?'

'It depends on the intensity of the process. It might have been once a fortnight or once a week even.'

'And who would have kept notes of the meetings?'

'That would have been the responsibility of the therapist, Dr Llewyn.'

'Not Dr Pochard?'

'No.'

They were the replies she had been hoping to get. For the first time in the investigation, she thought there was a possibility of putting the murderer behind bars.

'What were the trays you mentioned at the end of your letter?'

'I have nothing more to say.'

'You told Pochard to keep them in a safe place, away from prying eyes.'

'You may think these items are important in your investigation, but nothing could be further from the truth.'

'In a murder investigation like this, I can't overlook a single detail. I want you to end your walking holiday and attend an interview at the police station tomorrow at eleven a.m. I need to know exactly what these trays were used for on Ward G.'

However, there was no reply from Reichmann. She realised the line had already cut out.

# CHAPTER TWENTY-EIGHT

Deepwell Hospital, thought Herron as she walked up to the granite building escorted by the security guard, looked weary, as though it had been up all night, protecting its shadows.

She had booked another interview with Dr Barker and Alistair McCrea, and was hoping to get answers to the questions that had been raised by Reichmann's letter. However, she could feel the heaviness return as soon as Barker's secretary came out to meet her. She heard the uneasiness in the woman's voice as she explained that the medical director had been called away on an urgent meeting and would not be able to see her this morning.

Herron asked when Barker would be free, and the secretary hesitated. A cold smile tightened around her mouth. 'I think you should check with your chief inspector and arrange another time through him,' she said.

Herron wondered why the secretary had mentioned the chief inspector but let it pass. She explained that she urgently needed to speak to McCrea. The secretary warned there would be a slight delay, but that one of the nurses from Ward G would be with her soon. The uneasiness did not leave the secretary's voice nor did the expression on her face change.

The delay was longer than Herron expected. She was kept waiting for an hour in the corridor outside the music room. She walked up to the double doors leading to Ward G and stared through the window of reinforced glass. She allowed her senses to sweep through the building like a radar. A mood of mystery had settled over the ward, the moments of light and clarity growing more fleeting. She saw the blank, open-mouthed face of a patient watching her from a side room, the back of a nurse disappearing around a corner, a large white clock counting down the minutes, the bright tie of a doctor swishing behind a door, but the overwhelming impression was one of deepening shadow.

Eventually, a male nurse appeared and told her there had been an incident involving McCrea. Staff were busy trying to resolve the situation, he explained, and then he left her to her own devices again. A short time later, she heard McCrea's ghostly tenor voice shouting from behind the locked doors. She could feel through the floor the steps of people running. When she looked through the windows, she saw two nurses hauling away McCrea, who had a bleeding nose. That was the moment she realised she was on the threshold of a world she knew nothing about and had no control over. She banged on the door and shouted, but no one appeared to hear her protests. She marched back down to reception and demanded to speak to Barker, or whoever was in charge. She wanted to register a complaint about the nurses' treatment of McCrea.

The nurse in charge of the ward came out and told the detective that staff had placed McCrea in a secure room. He had started an altercation with another patient and had been removed from the ward for his own safety and that of his fellow patients.

Herron demanded to speak to McCrea, but the nurse refused.

'I want to speak to the other patients on Ward G. Anyone who might have witnessed what happened to Alistair.'

The nurse raised her eyebrows and thrust her chin forwards, both hostile reflexes. 'I can't allow that.'

'Why not?'

'Dr Barker's orders. The patients on Ward G are undergoing intensive therapy right now, and it's important not to disturb them.'

'I only need to ask a few simple questions.'

The nurse pressed her lips together. 'My instructions are that they must be protected from any unnecessary interrogations conducted by you or your colleagues. Unless you have evidence they have committed a crime.'

'So Dr Barker is refusing me access to the ward?'

'He is worried that your style of questioning will undermine the therapeutic relationships staff have built up over many years with the patients. We have a duty of care to these vulnerable men and women and we have to fulfil that duty. Surely you understand that?' The way the nurse stared at Herron, her fixed expression, the tone she used in explaining the refusal, and the seriousness of her frown, were all professional techniques to deter her. 'Now, if I can be of any other assistance, Sergeant Herron?' The nurse smiled at her, but she did not mean it. Her polite offer was more a challenge than an invitation to help.

On her way out, Herron glanced at the photograph of the holistic foundation members hanging on the wall. The expressions of the psychotherapists seemed to watch her with a cold intent, as though their experiment was well under way and could no longer be stopped, their subjects isolated and shut away behind glass, beyond help from the outside world.

There was no sign of Morton back at the station, and Herron had to make do with a quick briefing with Shaw and Rodgers.

They had interviewed the other residents in Chisholm's half-way house but none of them had been inclined to help the investigation or offer any valuable information. They had knocked on the door of the closest neighbouring house several times, but no one had answered, even though they suspected the owner, a man called Jack Murray, was hiding inside.

'That's about as far as we got,' said Rodgers.

'Strange that none of Chisholm's neighbours have a clue what happened to him,' said Herron.

'We managed to get a few vague reports,' said Shaw. 'An unfamiliar car seen on the day he disappeared, but nothing definite. Most of his fellow residents either drink heavily or are on some sort of medication. Their memories are too blurred to give us a clear lead.'

'What about the neighbour who kept hiding from you?'

There was a silence, and then Rodgers sniffed loudly. 'What do you want to know?'

'Perhaps he might open the door to me?'

'You're welcome to try,' said Shaw.

'If you think it's a priority,' added Rodgers.

She detected a note of contempt in his voice, which annoyed her. 'Why would interviewing the neighbour of our prime suspect not be a priority? He might be hiding from police because he knows something or has a guilty conscience.'

'I didn't mean to offend you,' said Rodgers.

'No offence taken,' she said, picking up her keys. 'I'll let you know how I get on.'


Several times, she knocked the door of Murray's house on the main street of Innerleithen but got no reply. However, she had the impression that Murray was at home. She rapped the windows, unwilling to give up. Eventually, the door opened slowly.

She introduced herself to Murray as a police detective, and his eyes scanned hers, full of guilty suspicion.

'What do you want?'

'I'm trying to find Billy Chisholm.'

'I'm busy right now.'

'This is important, Mr Murray.'

Again, she saw a look in his eyes, probing and uncertain, almost reproachful. However, he must have realised that now he had opened his door, his caller was not going to be deterred. He looked down at the doorstep and allowed her in. 'This is to do with the murder of that psychiatrist, isn't it?'

'Billy was a patient of Dr Pochard's. Naturally, we want to speak to him.'

'The whole thing sounds so terrible.' He gave her a submissive glance and led her into a tiny living room. 'I don't know Billy that well. The men who stay next door tend to be secretive and lonely. But Billy would stop for a chat now and again.'

'Can you remember your last conversation with him? Anything unusual that he said or did?'

'It was about a week ago. He told me he was going to meet a detective inspector. Someone called Monteath.'

She froze. Her mind had been focused on the questions she needed to ask but now they were cast into disarray.

'What name did you say?'

'Monteath.' He had registered her look of surprise. 'Is the name important?'

'No, not at all. I just wanted to check.'

'It seemed odd at the time that he was meeting a detective, but then I heard he had a troubled past.'

'What about Dr Pochard, did he ever mention her?'

'No, all he wanted to talk about were forest paths and waterfalls. Then he would mention this man Monteath.'

'What exactly did he say?'

'He complained that even though he had left Deepwell, he couldn't shake off this detective. He said that all the patients there were flies in his web.'

'What else did he say?'

'I can't remember every conversation that we had.'

'You don't have to. Just tell me the bits about Monteath.'

'I can't think of anything else specifically.' He looked at her with curiosity. 'I take it you can't discuss your colleague or his work?'

'My colleague? Who are you talking about?'

'Inspector Monteath.'

'Who said Monteath was a colleague of mine?'

'I just assumed.' His face reddened. He seemed bothered by the sharpness of her questions.

'All I need to know is did you ever see this Inspector Monteath, or have any reason to believe he might be real, and not a symptom of Billy's mental illness?' She tried to keep the tension from rising in her voice.

His eyes grew disturbed and a grim expression formed on his face. 'I never doubted Monteath's existence. Billy sounded so convincing, and I'm not easily fooled.'

'It's not a crime to believe in someone else's delusion.'

'I never questioned what Billy told me. He seemed so

consistent.' His eyes looked down and then they came up again. 'I thought I saw him with Monteath one evening. I was in my car, about to leave, when I looked in my rear-view mirror and saw Billy walking out of his flat with an older man.'

'What did he look like?'

'It was twilight and they were both silhouetted. When Billy saw I was in my car, he made to go back into the flat, but the other man made him keep walking. I remember thinking that must be Monteath.'

'Tell me everything you can remember about him.'

His brow furrowed and there was a look of doubt in his eyes. 'He was tall, late middle age. The collars of his coat were turned up. He walked in a purposeful way. Definitely, an old school policeman, I thought. He seemed in control.'

So in control, he could rearrange reality and the thoughts inside Chisholm's head, thought Herron. It seemed she was unable to follow a lead in this case without hitting some form of delusion or a figment of the imagination. However, she felt that in the spreading expanse of the investigation, it was through these teasing fragments that reality might be revealed. Even lies and fantasies contained little granules of the truth, and she had to investigate each one in order not to miss a valuable clue. She had to keep digging.

Murray gave an apologetic grimace. 'To tell you the truth, I was wary of Billy's companion. I'm not that keen on police detectives at the best of times, and Billy had made Monteath seem so sinister.' He glanced at her and added quickly, 'Not that I have anything to hide.'

'I'm sure you don't,' said Herron. She smiled to reassure him, but Murray appeared to have clammed up. She recovered her gentler tone and began crossing off the questions she had planned to ask.

'Did Billy ever mention any plans or places he was intending to visit?'

'No.'

'What about people he was in contact with?'

'No one, apart from the detective.'

'Did he mention any grudges? Had anyone upset him badly?'

'No.'

'Did he mention any other doctors at Deepwell?'

Murray shook his head.

'What about a log cabin in a forest? Near a loch. Did he ever talk about that?'

'Possibly. He talked about forests a lot but I never thought to pay attention. I didn't think it would be important. Anyway, I've told you everything I can remember.'

Herron thanked him for taking the time to talk to her, and told him he had been very helpful. She got up, preparing to leave.

'There was something else about Billy's companion,' said Murray. 'It's nothing really, but he kept turning round as though he were checking was anyone else watching him.'

'Thank you,' she said. 'That's helpful too.'

He walked her out to the front door, and at the last minute said, 'I take it you don't know any Inspector Monteath.'

'Not professionally.'

'Does he exist at all?'

'Your guess is as good as mine.'

'If he doesn't exist, then how can this conversation be helpful to your investigation? An imaginary detective can't play any meaningful part in a murder plot, can he?'

She walked off without answering him.

★

The streets of Innerleithen were quiet, and her feet and brain welcomed the walk back to her car. She would have gladly kept walking to the edge of the village, emptying her brain, and pitting her muscles against the hills that formed a backdrop to the rows of houses. Walking was the best way to tackle a mental block, but she was already late and needed to get back to the station. Her pace slowed as she approached her car, wishing that her feet could ignore what her mind was up to, find the right path and allow her thoughts to sort themselves out.

Her first thought when she saw the envelope tucked under her windscreen wiper was that she had been given a parking ticket. She looked up sharply, hoping to catch sight of Innerleithen's only traffic warden. She thought she saw a figure hurrying between the cars at the bottom of the street. She could not determine if it was male or female. All she saw was a shape, a shadow merging and blending with other shadows, the darkness of old beech trees and granite houses.

She ripped open the envelope and read the handwritten note inside. It wasn't a ticket, but something quite different. She read the note again, and stared at it. Surely she must be imagining it? But there was no doubt about it. The sinister-sounding words printed in block capitals beginning with the name, Inspector Monteath.

I am Inspector Monteath, but that is not my real name. My real name is a secret. I am the detective who makes up clues just like those poor patients locked up in the dark. Perhaps I am real and perhaps I am not, sitting here in my log cabin by the loch. It does me good to think up clues in the dark, but sooner or later I will run out of time, and then what will happen to little Miss Dunnock?

Her breathing grew shallow and her fingers trembled. The bastard has left me a trail. He knows about the photographs and confessions. Perhaps he even selected which ones to leave behind in Pochard's back garden. She tried ringing Morton, but there was no answer. She sat in her car and read the note again. Something did not feel right. Her breathing grew steadier. Why had the message been left for her and not the investigation team, and how did the writer know she was in Innerleithen? There were two interpretations running through her mind. She sensed the vulnerability of her position as a female detective in a male-dominated police station. She considered the possibility that one of her colleagues was playing a prank upon her. They might even be acting in league to gull her and derail her attempts to prove herself. In which case, she decided to keep the note to herself for the time being. She would have to watch the rest of the team like a hawk from now on. If one of them had written the note as a prank, they would eventually give themselves away. This was her first interpretation; the second was that if the note was genuine, then someone was using her, someone connected to the murder who knew what she was thinking, and also the car she drove.

She started up the engine and drove off quickly. A false message from a real detective, or a real message from a false detective. How could she tell the one from the other? If the note was a clue, then who exactly was leading her? Perhaps Monteath was a red herring planted to make her lose sight of the real investigation. She should be hunting a killer and a crime scene, not getting lost in the delusions of Deepwell's patients. This was still her investigation, she reminded herself. It was time to stop letting herself be dragged passively along by the decisions and obstacles posed by others. The staff at Deepwell and its patients, even her colleagues and chief inspector, they all seemed in her imagination to be accomplices to the general confusion.

The murderer could perform disappearing tricks and cover his tracks, but there was one thing he couldn't hide. He was as physically real as she.

When Herron returned to the station, the incident room was empty, and there was still no sign of Morton. At the computer desk next to hers, she saw the pinched profile and hunched shoulders of Shaw. She examined him out of the corner of her eye. Like the other officers based at Peebles, he behaved a little warily around her, and tended to treat his computer screen or his phone as a more rewarding and reassuring form of company. He was somewhere in his forties, with the bearing of a man trying to keep the lid on a troubled personal life. However, work at the station, the mundane details of its paperwork and briefings seemed to provide him with enough comfort to wear a slightly amused smile most of the time. This evening, he was busy at his computer, flicking through files, steering his mouse around its pad like a toy car.

The last thing she wanted to mention was the message from Monteath, in case he thought she had fallen for a prank. Still, she felt the need to probe his thoughts. She said hello, and he replied with a sigh, without looking away from his screen. When she lingered at her desk without sitting down, he looked up.

'Have you ever come across confessions as strange as the Deepwell ones before?' she asked him. 'Confessions made before the crime occurs?'

'I wouldn't know,' he said blankly, and then he gave the question some more consideration. 'I mean, the person would have to convince their confidant that the confession was genuine in order to have it reported to the police in the first place. People make all sorts of mad claims, especially in places like Deepwell, but they convince no one.'

'What about cases where the listener, say a psychiatrist, is told the confession but only informs the police when the crime or something unusual comes to light afterwards.'

'I'm sure you could find cases like that.'

'Where?'

'The best place would be the patient files at Deepwell.'

'But they keep erecting barriers, and Barker is avoiding me. What am I supposed to do?'

Shaw leaned forward and rubbed his nose. 'I think you should be pushing Morton harder. If you're searching for a way into Deepwell, he's the one to show you the way. He should know it by now.'

'What do you mean?'

He opened a file on his computer and began tapping away on his keyboard. He seemed reluctant to say anything more.

Herron pushed further. 'Any time I ask Morton about what he knows about Deepwell, he goes quiet.'

Shaw smiled sympathetically. 'His silences do get monotonous.'

'I spend a lot of time listening to the coffee pot and the air conditioning whenever he's around.'

He laughed. 'Sometimes, I think Harry's silence is greater than God's.'

'But you think he knows more about Deepwell than he's letting on?'

He rubbed his nose again. 'I'm not in a position to comment on rumours. I'm not leading this investigation, so it's not up to me.'

What investigation? she wanted to say. And what rumours?

'So what's he keeping from me? How do I get him to talk to me?'

Shaw flinched. 'I don't know,' he said. 'If Harry won't help you then I suppose it's up to our dear leader.'

'What do you mean?'

'If you need a door kicked open at Deepwell, Bates is the one to ask. As far as I can see no one has ever dared to do that at the hospital before.'

She walked towards the door, glancing at his computer screen. He was scanning through the duty inspector reports from the night before, a dull litany of road traffic offences and vandalism. An officer who knew his place, and didn't push against the boundaries. She stepped into the corridor and began to pace up and down. The silence of an institution and the silence of her colleague. Were the two somehow linked? Or was she getting too hung up on these matters?

The door to the chief inspector's office lay slightly ajar, and she knocked a couple of times, before poking her head into the room. However, there was no sign of the DCI, apart from his jacket, which had been slung over his chair.

She stepped back into the corridor, and bumped into his secretary.

The woman smiled at her. 'Can I help you?'

'The chief inspector, where is he?'

The secretary went to get his appointment diary and after a minute came back with Constable Rodgers in tow. He smiled at her, too. 'The boss had to go to an emergency meeting in Galashiels,' said Rodgers. 'He won't be back till late evening.'

'But he's left his jacket behind.'

'Must have been in a hurry. Is it something urgent?'

'I need to talk to him about Deepwell. Is there any way I can contact him?'

'Other than barging in on his meeting, no. Can anyone else help?'

'No thanks.' She walked back down the corridor with leaden steps.

That evening, the sound of Bates's voice echoing down the corridor roused her from the confusion of her notes. The DCI could not avoid her for ever, she thought, as she knocked on his door.

Bates asked her what was up, and she said straight out, 'I need complete access to all the patient files on Ward G.'

'Barker has already made concessions. He's given you the relevant notes on McCrea and Chisholm. If you ask for anything more, I really am going to lose my temper.'

It was a warning, however, she had no choice but to ignore it. She wasn't going to be put off any more and her voice rose. 'Maybe the murderer is Chisholm but that doesn't let Deepwell off the hook, especially if they're covering up some sort of malpractice. They must think we're a bunch of plodding idiots.'

'As will the public, if we don't pin down Chisholm.'

'I believe Deepwell are covering up something more sinister—'

He interrupted before she could mention her suspicions about the figure of Inspector Monteath. 'Listen, Herron, you were sent to Deepwell in the first place to check out a crazy confession that didn't seem to have any bearing on reality, let alone a proper police investigation.' Seeing that she was about to speak again, he leaned forward, his eyes bulging. 'You might think you're a golden girl in some people's eyes, but the only reason Morton dragged you into this investigation was because he couldn't face up to his demons at Deepwell.'

'What demons?' she said. Was Morton somehow compromised by a past connection to the hospital?

'If Morton hasn't mentioned them, then clearly he doesn't think you need to know his private details, and I respect his judgement.'

'If these private details are linked to Deepwell, then they are private no longer. We're detectives investigating a murder and we can't keep secrets from each other. Morton may not like the idea of sharing his private life, but in the circumstances he has no choice. You have to tell me, did he get some kind of help there?'

'You mean psychiatric help?'

'Yes.'

'I can't say.'

She wanted to drag Bates and Morton down to the interview suite and subject the pair to a thorough questioning. That would make her life much easier. She was about to press for more information but Bates glared at her, and then his eyes flicked to the door behind her. She turned round. She hadn't been aware of him, but Morton was standing there. She had no idea how long he'd been there, and how much of the conversation he'd heard. He was breathing heavily and staring at her, his eyes deathly still. She brushed past him and into the corridor.

She stopped at a row of photographs on the wall outside Bates's office. They showed the station's detectives and police officers at various special events over the years. She stood for a moment, staring at one in particular. It was of Morton standing next to a superintendent, who was handing over some sort of certificate or award. Morton's face looked as empty as the open grave, while the superintendent wore a beaming grin. As covertly as possible, she took out her phone and took a picture of it. She knew she was crossing an invisible line, extending her inquiries into the personal life of a colleague, but it was time to probe Morton's reticence.

Out of the corner of her eye, she noticed a figure making his way along the corridor. She pocketed the phone and swung away from the photographs. She was relieved to see that it was Shaw, and that he was on his own.

'What's up?' he asked, eyeing the phone in her pocket.

'Nothing much,' she replied.

'Any luck with Bates?' he whispered.

'None whatsoever.'

He gave her a glum but sympathetic look. 'It might surprise you but I know exactly how you feel.'

A new possibility of an ally opened up before her. 'If you're at a loose end, you could do something for me,' she said.

'What is it?' he asked cautiously.

She asked him to contact the staff at Deepwell he had interviewed earlier, and tell them the police were looking for a man calling himself Inspector Monteath.

'Why?'

She gave him a thorough description of what she had learned of Monteath's movements, and he listened carefully.

'What do you think we're going to discover? Aren't there better leads to follow?'

'I think this Inspector Monteath, whoever he is, is playing a game of hide and seek with me.'

Shaw gave her a disbelieving look.

'I think he knows I'm searching for him,' she said. 'He's hiding somewhere but he wants me to keep looking.'

With the air of someone playing along with a charade,

Shaw said, 'And to keep the game going, he has to be sure you're still playing?'

'Exactly.'

'But what if he doesn't exist?'

She gave him a straight look. 'He does exist.'

'How are you so sure? All the patient notes suggest he's a delusion.'

'Because he's leading me on a trail. The same one he laid for Billy Chisholm.'

It all seemed too much for Shaw. He pulled a face. 'I think the whole thing is a fantasy.'

'But we have to try everything. Our investigation meetings are getting shorter and shorter. We're running out of time and leads.' She stared him in the eye. She saw a slight look of surrender there and worked on it. 'I know you think this is a wild goose chase, but we're detectives and sometimes we have to follow our craziest hunches. Some of the people you interviewed might have held something back on purpose, or without even knowing about it.' She kept staring at his eyes and knew that she was winning him over. The look of surrender gave way to submission.

'OK, then,' he said.

Her victory was confirmed. If only she had realised earlier that a little emotional force and prolonged eye contact would do the trick.

'What shall I ask them?' he said.

'Ask them about Inspector Monteath. It's a straight yes or no question. Either he exists or doesn't. Check also what links Morton might have with Deepwell. If they mention confidentiality, tell them we're trying to stop a murderer.'

When Shaw left, Bates's door at the bottom of the corridor opened and closed, offering Herron a glimpse of Morton's shadowy figure, standing and staring at her like a cold-eyed sentry. What secrets are you guarding? was the question ringing in her mind as she hurried down the corridor.

She drove to Deepwell at speed. She needed to find out more about Monteath, and it had to be as soon as possible. At the reception desk, she asked to speak to Dr Barker about urgent matters, but her powers of persuasion fell short, and the receptionist told her that the psychiatrist was busy. However, she was permitted to sit in the waiting room in case Barker was able to free up some time in his diary.

After a few minutes, she placed a call to the reception desk from her mobile phone. While the receptionist was busy answering it, she slipped out of the waiting room and down one of the corridors. Some nurses were ahead of her, and she stepped in behind them as they made their way through the security doors. She knew she was not supposed to be in this part of the hospital. At any moment, a door might lock behind her and she would have to call staff for help. She worked on the principle that if she exuded enough confidence, she could make any door open for her. Without a challenging word, staff and patients stepped aside for her. She strode down a long, quiet corridor and came to a locked door. Above it a small red lamp flashed; the doors were hooked to an alarm system. If there had been a staff member around, she would have ordered them to open the door, but there was nobody in sight. She pushed against the doors but they didn't budge. She waited, expecting security guards and sirens at any moment. However, nothing happened. The corridor beyond the doors was full of shadows and quiet as a cemetery. Her sense of urgency grew. She walked back down the corridor and found an emergency exit. She pushed down the bar, and stepped into the courtyard garden, holding the door ajar.

A group of patients were planting rows of seedlings, bending in unison as if to an inner metronome. One of the patients looked up at her. It was Mary, the woman with the scarred arms. She gave Herron a vague smile, as if in recognition. Herron beckoned and the woman approached, her smile fading slightly.

'Have you seen Inspector Monteath recently?' said Herron.

Mary's smile vanished. 'I don't know,' she replied.

'Don't know what?'

She seemed unsure about Herron's question, yet serene, as though the repetitive gardening duties were working their effect today. Her features turned dark and heavy.

'A few days ago you told me you had a clue for him.'

She looked Herron in the eye. 'I still don't know what you're talking about.'

'You told me Monteath drops by whenever Dr Barker leaves. Is that because he wants to avoid Barker?' Herron's attention was completely concentrated on her face, waiting for a signal to leak out. 'What questions does he ask you? Did he ever show you any ID to prove who he was?'

Again, Mary didn't respond.

'I was here a few days ago. You asked me about him. Do you remember?'

She shook her head. 'I don't know what you're talking about.'

'I'm trying to find Inspector Monteath. Outside. In the real world.' On an impulse, she showed Mary the photograph of Morton on her phone. She had no real evidence that Morton was Monteath, nor that he posed a risk. It was just her hunch. 'Do you recognise this man?' Herron tried to hide the tension in her voice. 'Is this Inspector Monteath?'

Mary's eyes darted about. Her mind is wandering, thought Herron, I need to keep her focused. She showed her the other photographs she had taken, copies of the pictures depicting Sinden's excursions into the forests. Mary's brows knitted in puzzlement.

'What do you see here, Mary?'

She looked at Herron with a vacant gaze.

So many delusions piled upon each other by patients and psychiatrists working together to form a thick foggy layer through which a murderer might slip, unnoticed, and vanish. 'It's the story of a murder,' said Herron, trying to help her along. 'The one Inspector Monteath tried to recreate on Ward G. You know about it, don't you?'

'I never spoke to the boys on Ward G. They're all completely crazy in there.'

In spite of the denial, Herron could sense the patient's muscles tensing up. Only her eyes moved, scanning the corridor behind the detective.

'I know there's more to Monteath,' said Herron. 'More than everyone is letting on.'

Mary chewed her lip.

'Did the doctors warn you not to speak about Monteath?'

She chewed again.

'Why can't you talk about him?'

'Because the doctors are helping me control my delusions.'

'They're not helping you. They're trying to stop you talking. They're covering up something bad on Ward G.'

Mary's face grew pale. My questions are scaring her, thought Herron. Is it me she's scared of, or something else?

'I can't talk about Monteath,' said Mary. 'You shouldn't talk about him either, else they'll lock you up, too.'

The other patients had stopped planting. They watched

Herron, gauging her mood, like children who could sense tension in the air and were listening out for danger.

'You must tell me what you know about Monteath.' Herron's voice rose again. 'A woman's life might be in danger because of him.'

'Doesn't matter what you say or do. I can't talk about him.' Mary sounded rational and precise in her words. This time it was Herron who felt desperate for verification, and slightly out of control, as though Monteath was her delusion now.

The other patients dropped their plants, and drew closer. She felt as though she was hitting another brick wall. She did not know if Monteath was completely irrelevant to the investigation or whether he held the entire truth about the conspiracy at Deepwell. If he was an imaginary detective, why did he leave so many traces? Why did he crop up in so many of the patients' stories, why did she keep finding traces of his presence? The faces of the patients stared at her. She could see the madness peering out of their eyes, reacting to the madness in her, her agitation and desperation. In asking these questions about Monteath, she had entered their world.

'I can give you my mobile number,' said Herron. 'In case you see Monteath again.'

'You're crazy,' said Mary, her voice rising. She backed away. 'Someone call the doctors. This bitch is crazy and she won't leave me alone.'

An alarm began to sound. She would get no further in her search for the mysterious Monteath. She turned and slipped back through the emergency exit. She passed a pair of pensive-looking nurses hurrying towards the courtyard garden. She exited through the door they had left half open, and slipped out the front door without anyone noticing her.

# CHAPTER TWENTY-NINE

The atmosphere of the briefing meeting the next morning was charged from the outset. The murder investigation, which had progressed without a clear sense of direction, now felt hollow at the centre and full of ragged edges. Detective Chief Inspector Bates walked in and glared at the assembled officers, who were all on edge, including Herron. Morton was more subdued than normal, plunged into an even deeper silence, watching Herron and the boss carefully, as though he sensed that something was up.

'Is this the full team?' demanded Bates.

Morton shook his head. He explained that a group of officers were doing door-to-door inquiries on the streets near where Chisholm had been living.

'OK, let's run through what we have so far,' said Bates. He took out a large pad and started to write.

Rodgers and Shaw began by saying that Pochard's private life seemed to have been boring in the extreme. Her main social contacts had been through the holistic foundation, but its meetings were confidential and shrouded in secrecy. None of the psychotherapists at Deepwell were prepared to talk about the group. However, the officers had found a former therapist who had briefly been a member about ten years ago, a man called John Carson. He had undergone a painful divorce and had sought counselling from Dr Llewyn. He had tried for more than a year to join the foundation but Llewyn had told him there was a long waiting list.

When Carson started to bring up disturbing memories of his childhood, Llewyn took the unusual step of inviting him to join the foundation in spite of the lengthy waiting list. From the start, Carson noticed that the other members led solitary lives and were emotionally dependent upon Dr Llewyn. There were clearly defined roles and levels of influence within the group, but, overall, everyone seemed immensely supportive of each other. Some of the members were from professions outside the psychiatric and medical worlds, and they all encouraged him to talk about his memories and dreams, which they then interpreted.

However, Carson soon realised that something unpleasant was going on beneath the surface. The stronger members of the group displayed an arrogance and coldness that he thought he would never see in highly trained psychotherapists. They would force members to dredge up traumatic experiences from their childhood and repeat them until a repressed memory had been revealed. The disturbing thing was that some of the members would fabricate a story of abuse just to be validated by the group and answer the yearning of the leading therapists. It had scared him, what he witnessed, the way people's memories could be shaped by a group, and all independent thought and judgement cast aside. Those who brought up uninteresting or mildly upsetting memories were cruelly ignored. In his case, he had felt the need to unburden himself of terrible things he had dreamed or fantasised about, but never actually experienced. After about a year, he stopped going to the society meetings because he was not prepared to endure talking about false memories any longer or be caught up in the mad processes of the group. As well as Llewyn, the lead therapists in the group were Barker and Pochard. Carson's departure appeared to have a negative effect on his career as a therapist, and he had been unable to find any work in that field afterwards.

'Sounds like a cult,' said Bates. 'But what does it have to do with Pochard's murder? I think we need to stick to the relevant facts.'

Herron summarised her meeting with Dr Sinden, which reinforced the findings so far about Llewyn and the foundation. She talked about her attempts to shine a light on what was going on at Deepwell, and her frustration at the resistance of Dr Barker and Professor Reichmann. Then she took a deep breath and mentioned the mysterious figure of Inspector Monteath.

Morton gave her a warning look, but she went on. She summarised what she had gleaned about him from the patient notes and Murray's possible sighting.

'My instinct tells me there is more to Monteath than a shared delusion,' she said.

'Who do you think he is, then?' said Bates, barely suppressing the mockery in his voice. 'An accomplice of the killer or a perfectly normal detective working somewhere in the Borders?'

Bates's tone brought her up short. The truth was that he could be anybody at all.

Morton spoke. 'I've already checked the databases and the only Inspector Monteath on the records lived in Aberdeen and died fifteen years ago.'

Herron was surprised by Morton's intervention, but tried not to show it.

'There is of course the other possibility,' said Bates. 'That Monteath is a complete red herring.'

'Of course,' she said.

'I'm sure you see what I'm getting at, don't you? You seem to be creating something out of the patients' testimonies that fits with your suspicions about Deepwell. But this is not the real world. These are not real leads.'

'It's true that we're dealing with unreliable accounts but Pochard was investigating them before she was murdered.'

'Then by all means, give their confessions some credence. But be careful. They are full of traps. From what I understand, these patients have great experience making fools of professionals, especially those desperate to advance careers and humour their fantasies.'

She bit her lip. Was that last comment a jibe at her? 'Can't you see that Deepwell are covering up something?' she said.

'There may well be a conspiracy of silence but the reason may not be as sinister as you think. Perhaps they are just trying to protect their reputation and good name. You need more evidence, more proof that this Monteath figure exists before we start launching a search for him. Or wasting more time with hours of useless speculation.'

Afterwards, no one spoke.

Bates waited until the mood had reached a concentrated level. Then, speaking in a low voice, he said he welcomed intelligent and carefully planned investigative work from his detectives. However, the directions the team had taken were futile and stupid. His voice grew gruff and annoyed. He wanted everyone to give more careful attention to their attitudes towards Deepwell and the staff who worked there, in particular the director, Dr Barker. 'I want everyone in this room to treat him with courtesy,' he said with a warning note in his voice. 'He has complained to me about the manner of some of the officers on this team.'

'We treat everyone with courtesy,' said Morton. 'Dr Barker is no different from any other suspect in the investigation.'

Bates rapped the table with his knuckles. 'I will not countenance any attempt to tarnish the reputation of a highly respected psychiatrist who has worked tirelessly to address the mental health problems of the criminal population, and has always cooperated with police inquiries in the past. I want the entire team to give very careful thought to what I am saying. Only return to the investigation when you are sure you understand my order.'

The room grew quiet. Morton stared at a remote corner of the room.

'What do you suggest we do about Deepwell, then?' asked Shaw, breaking the awkward silence.

'I want you to drop your investigation into the holistic foundation and the professional rivalries that may or may not have existed between staff. There's no point making a fuss, not now when it's clear the murderer is Chisholm.'

Morton spoke up again. 'When were you speaking to Dr Barker?'

'Yesterday morning.' Bates's cheeks coloured in anger. 'Why should that matter?'

'Sergeant Herron was meant to meet him yesterday, but he cancelled at the last minute. Now it seems he met you instead.'

'What are you suggesting?'

'How many of your investigations as SIO relied on expert testimony from Barker and his colleagues at Deepwell?'

'That's got nothing to do with anything.'

'Why are you so quick to interfere on Barker's behalf and criticise the direction we are taking? Deepwell is not on trial here, but that doesn't mean individual members of its staff and their practice are above suspicion.'

It was clear to Herron that Bates was hiding something, and Morton was the only one in the room willing to expose it. He knew and understood. In his silent and watchful way, he could be dangerous.

'There's something else I have to ask you,' said Morton.

Bates was brisk and ignored the question but Morton interrupted again.

'I need to know why you arranged for Pochard's post to be sent to Deepwell. Why did you not tell anyone else about this?'

Bates grunted in surprise. 'Dr Pochard's work included some sensitive and urgent cases linked to Deepwell. Letting her colleagues look after her post was the professional thing to do.'

'I would say it was inappropriate, at best. Not least because you didn't inform anyone else. There should be no secrets within an investigation.'

'Nor should anyone intimidate a highly respected psychiatrist,' said Bates.

'I don't think anyone has intimidated Dr Barker,' said Morton. 'I would say it's the other way round. The entire set-up at Deepwell seems to be based upon controlling vulnerable patients and protecting the institution's reputation at all costs. Besides, Sergeant Herron and I have always treated Barker with respect and stuck to his requests.'

'I don't mean Herron and you personally. I mean what you're inadvertently doing. Deepwell relies on council funding. It looks after patients who would otherwise be causing havoc on the streets, or languishing in jail. OK, it may have mismanaged Chisholm's treatment, but we can't allow its reputation to slide down the pipes because of one mistake.'

'I agree,' said Morton, 'but I also think everyone involved in this investigation should be communicating back to the team what they are doing and who exactly they are talking to. Including you, sir.'

'I must say it's rich being lectured by you of all people on the importance of communication.' Bates had risen to his feet. His body language and tone were not overtly menacing but Herron felt the tension roll across the room like a dangerous wave. Bates remained standing, staring at Morton, his face reddening.

By contrast, Morton leaned back in his seat, relaxed yet alert. Before, he had behaved as though he was barely listening to Bates, sitting deep inside himself, his eyes hidden behind his tangled hair, staring out from the depths of his lair.

'My reticence is no excuse for a chief inspector to behave in this way,' said Morton.

'I won't have a subordinate attack me like this in front of the rest of the team,' growled Bates. 'That's the strange thing about you, Morton. You behave as if you never made a mistake. You feel no responsibility whenever an investigation turns into a monumental mess.'

'Are you referring to this case or cases in the past? Cases where you were the SIO?'

'Listen, Morton, you were a good detective once, but now you're a total fucking flop. You've lost your nerve and imagination. I never understood why you weren't demoted after they found you drunk at that housebreaking.' His eyes shifted about the room. 'And now you're taking the entire team down with you. Look at the state of you all. There's Shaw. Ever since his wife left him, he's been falling apart in front of everyone. And I see that Constable Rodgers managed to come in on time today, the first time in months, and he even managed to shave off that straggly beard he's been nurturing. Something extraordinary must have happened to him last night.' He paused. There was no sound in the room apart from the rasp of Bates's heavy breathing. 'You think I don't notice these things.'

Nobody said anything. It was as if the air had been sucked from them. In the vacuum, Bates's voice grew louder and more dominant.

'And what about our new graduate recruit? What have you got to say for yourself?'

Herron looked up and saw to her alarm that Bates was staring at her.

'Top of the class at Edinburgh, isn't that right, Herron?'

'I wasn't the top exactly, sir.' She tried to appear confident but her voice sounded hollow.

'Whatever – the college said you were an academic wonder girl. They thought the sun shone out of your arse. Are you going to let your career follow the same course as your colleagues?'

'Which course is that, sir?' asked Morton.

'Straight down the fucking drain.' The DCI thumped his hand on the desk for emphasis. 'I come into this office every morning and see my officers sitting around with cups of coffee and tea, whinging about staff cuts and long hours, and every conceivable and inconceivable obstacle in your working lives. It's not a question of lack of insight or brains. It's just that you don't want to see the bloody obvious. And when a case like this comes along, you'd rather investigate the institution and invent explanations and excuses for what happened, rather than hunt down the wretched individual who is clearly to blame.'

By now, the DCI's voice was half-strangled by his anger, which seemed beyond his control. 'I have a bad feeling about this case. It's going to turn into a wreck that will pull us all down.' He glared at his staff. 'Here I am, trapped on a sinking ship with a crew of failures. Not the usual run-of-the-mill failures you meet in the police force, mind you. You lot are far beyond the fucking pale.'

Morton seemed impervious to Bates's outburst. He rose from his seat and pushed it neatly under his desk. Then he flicked his thick hair back from his face and walked out of the room. It was not the usual absent look that Herron saw there. Instead, he appeared cheerful, his gaze level, pleasantly upbeat. His eyes caught hers and for a second she saw the steely glint of his determination. She realised that no matter how withdrawn and reticent he might appear to her personally, in front of an audience he possessed the charisma of an actor about to step into the spotlight.

Bates stood up and leaned upon the desk as if to regain his balance. He put away his notepad and slowly returned to the cranky authority of a man obsessed with paperwork and procedure.

'I want you all to think about what I've said, and write a report outlining your plan of action, including any obstacles that are preventing you from finding Chisholm, and special requests for assistance. I'll do my best to make sure you get the resources you need.'

He glanced at the officers one more time before leaving. 'And if any of you don't feel up to following my orders, put that on record, too. I haven't ruled out bringing in a fresh set of detectives to take over this case.'

After he left, Herron wondered how much of his outburst had been planned and how much had been due to his loss of temper. Morton had hinted at the truth. There was a lot more to Deepwell than any of them knew, and all the paperwork that Bates was requesting seemed to be more than an adjunct to the investigation. It felt like a smokescreen, a security measure.

The team dispersed and Herron walked out in search of Morton, but there was no sign of him and his car was gone from the car park. Instead, she found Rodgers hunched over a cigarette and looking exhausted. He straightened up on seeing her approach. She wondered if he was brooding upon the DCI's humiliating words.

However, his voice sounded strong and sure of itself. He even flashed a grin. 'Forget about what that bastard said in there,' he told her. 'Bates really means the opposite. He desperately needs us to be failures and losers. The last thing he wants is a crew of successful detectives biting at his heels, exposing his failures and weaknesses as a police chief.'

She had never heard him speak of the DCI with so much amused detachment.

'He's obsessed by the insecurity of his role and everything he does and says is geared to alleviating that insecurity,' added Rodgers. 'That shouting match was just his weekly therapy session.'

She raised her eyebrows. 'What do you mean, his therapy session?'

'It's just an expression.'

She felt annoyed at Rodgers' light-hearted interpretation of Bates's behaviour, and the way he was treating such a bullying tirade. It made her question why he and his colleagues tolerated such bad behaviour in the first place.

'I don't mean to play down what happened in there,' said Rodgers. 'He said some hurtful things. He's made a career out of telling his officers what failures they are.'

'Not just hurtful. He's interfering in the investigation, under-mining our leads. Surely that's more demoralising than any personal insults?'

It was impossible to tell from Rodgers' detached expression if he was troubled by Bates's attempt to barge in on the investigation. He seemed the embodiment of inaction, and the blankness of his expression depressed her further. Where was Morton? she wondered. He had swept out of the station, full of his moody and secret presence, leaving her with this bunch of failures, blind and faltering in his wake.

She thought of the pine trees encroaching upon Pochard's home, the entire forest rippling with a sense of dark and unlimited knowing, and Morton striding beneath them.

# CHAPTER THIRTY

Past her terrace house, where her mother-in-law would undoubtedly be making one of her legendary stews; through the park, oblivious to the young children and their mothers in the late afternoon sun; along Malvern Street and back to the house where she had taken Alice to the four year old's party. All the while, Herron was busy formulating questions in her head. When the door opened, she was disappointed to see that it was not Derek Cavanagh, but his wife.

She directed Herron to the back garden where her husband was tending to his hives and nestboxes. The beams of sunlight were thick with bees and motes of dust, and a figure with a black mask and white gown was stalking through bushes of yellow roses. A venomous cloud hung over his head. She waved and shouted a greeting. He removed his protective headgear and gloves, and recognised her immediately.

'Ah, Carla, investigating the mystery of the missing red shoe, I presume?'

She apologised for interrupting him, and the delay in collecting the shoe.

'Before I get you the shoe, I want to introduce you to my new patients,' he said with a good-natured smile. 'When I left psychotherapy I had a lot of free time on my hands. And then I discovered the wonderful world of bees, the perfect insects to surround oneself with. They spend their lives afloat on a sea of colour and scents.' He pointed to the swarm and named the types of bees and the flowers from which they were collecting nectar.

He beckoned her closer, waving at an opened hive as though he were the host of a party with thousands of buzzing guests. 'Aren't they beautiful?' He was looking straight at her, his eyes glinting in the sunlight, and his wedding ring flashing on his right hand.

Massed together in the hive, the bees looked bigger, more colourful and deadly than any she had seen before. Cavanagh puffed smoke over the hive and the bees blundered away from him. She thought that beekeeping must be a kind of sport for men like Cavanagh, a game of man versus dangerous insect life.

'There's something else I have to ask you,' she said.

'Fire away.'

'You trained as a psychotherapist. You had a consulting room in your home. Why did you change and take up lecturing at the university?'

'I seem to recall you asking me that question before.'

'I'm more interested in your answer now.'

'My reasons aren't that interesting. Professionally, I don't practise any more, but in my heart I still do.'

'I presume you're familiar with the investigation into Dr Pochard's murder. She worked at Deepwell.'

She watched him carefully, wondering if he would reveal his membership of the foundation. His face grew deadly serious. 'I knew Dr Pochard and I've been following the news stories. You've launched a manhunt for an ex-patient of hers.' He replaced the lid on the hive. 'A psychiatric hospital for the criminally insane doesn't need a scandal like that.'

'I'm trying to find out more about the Scottish branch of the Holistic Foundation, and their treatment of patients including the main suspect in the investigation. But they're not exactly cooperating with me. As a former therapist, I thought you might know something about them.'

'They're nothing but a bunch of ideological idiots,' said Cavanagh with a contemptuous shake of his head.

'You know them?'

'Know them? I belonged to that accursed group for several years.' He visibly struggled with his feelings for a moment. 'I could see it was an accident waiting to happen. Some of the people running it should have been locked up with their patients.'

Herron suppressed a smile. At last, a suitably indiscreet psychotherapist, she had thought she would never find one.

'In my opinion, its director, Dr Llewyn, was a fantasist and a deeply flawed individual. A man with dangerous longings and ambitions.'

'What do you mean by dangerous?'

'His therapy room was a battleground. An arena of intellectual warfare. He tried to change the minds of any of his acolytes or patients who did not agree with his theories. He nagged me for years, telling me I had most likely been abused as a child or a witness to some horrible domestic crime.'

'And had you?'

Cavanagh half-sighed, half-groaned. 'If I had I would have

surely remembered it. Besides I had been undergoing therapy for years, and this had never come up before. But Llewyn kept saying things like, "You will have been exposed to some abuse and that is why we must not stop until we have recovered it." I tried to end the therapy several times, but he was determined to pursue this analysis of his.'

'What did he have to base it upon?'

'Nothing more than a recurring dream I keep having. Of me in my bedroom as a child listening to a creaking sound from the bottom drawer of a chest. When the noise gets so loud that I can't bear it, I jump out of bed and open the drawer, and then a huge gorilla leaps out.' Cavanagh laughed. 'I kept telling Llewyn that I grew up in a loving if not overtly tactile family, but he didn't believe me. He was like a dog with a big juicy bone.'

'So you left the society?'

'I saw the way the other therapists swarmed around him, and it made me uncomfortable. They were dependent and needy, and they placed Llewyn upon a pedestal. They were like children desperate to do anything to please their father. At times, I suspected they might be dreaming up stories and presenting their patients in a certain light to satisfy his theories.' Cavanagh's face grew red. 'After I left, I learned that Llewyn was trying to destroy my career, saying I was a failure as a psychotherapist and risked harming my patients.'

'And the other members of the group stuck with Llewyn?'

'Yes. I hear he has retired recently. Apparently, he's working on a book about his life's work, his successes at Deepwell, trying to safeguard his legacy to the psychotherapeutic world.'

'Who were the other members of the group? Do you remember anyone who might have wanted to keep their identity a secret?'

'They were mostly staff at Deepwell. I've tried to put that part of my life behind me and I don't think of them very often. Any time I get bored of teaching and looking after my bees I think of Deepwell and the holistic society, and immediately I feel better about my decision to leave.'

She told Cavanagh about McCrea and Chisholm's confessions, and warned him that he would have to keep the details confidential until the investigation had concluded. She was keen to hear his expert opinion on the behaviour of the patients on Ward G.

Cavanagh turned back to his bees and appeared to have ignored her request. 'I wasn't joking earlier when I said the bees were my new patients. Thanks to them, I believe I've advanced the professional study of memory. Do you want to hear my findings?'

'If it's relevant to what happened on Ward G, I'm all ears.'

Cavanagh allowed the bees to crawl over the backs of his hands, and encouraged Herron to do the same. 'Don't worry, they won't sting you. This particular type of bee is known officially as *Bombus terrestris*.' There was a hint of pride in his voice. 'It has an enhanced memory for the colours and patterns of specific flowers. Also, it has an unusual capacity to remember multiple things at once. In short, it's the Einstein of the bee world.' He held the bees aloft with a look of reverence. 'However, it's surprisingly easy to trick *Bombus terrestris* and implant false memories in its exceptional bee memory.' His eyes brightened as he explained how in one corner of the garden he had two different types of flower, both containing delicious nectar. One with red and white rings and the other with bright yellow petals. He had presented the bees to the flowers, and then, a few days later, took them to another garden where they were given a choice of three flowers, one with red and white rings, one with yellow petals, and a new flower, one with a combination of yellow and red rings. Surprisingly, many of the bees displayed a preference for the new yellow and red flower, even though they had never encountered it before. They had created a false merged memory, one strong enough to supplant their actual memories and control their behaviour.

'And you believe that this type of error is not unique to bees?'

'Far from it. You have to consider this if you're interviewing the patients on Ward G. Memories can be mixed up and muddled in humans, too, especially in vulnerable men and women.'

Herron thought of the patients shuffling along the corridors of Ward G, hoarding their delusions and the babble of their dreams, making and remaking their memories into something more seductive for their therapists, their consciousness somehow inhabiting a communal realm like these bees. She wondered if the psychotherapists at Deepwell occupied the same lofty perspective as Cavanagh did over his insects. Barker had kept his eye on everything and knew a lot of information about Ward G, but had decided to reveal as little as possible. She watched the bees humming with life, even under the anaesthetising effect of Cavanagh's smoke, the mass of their bodies vibrating with a common awareness. From where did they draw this urge to share their memories? Was it the flowers gleaming in the afternoon sunlight, filling the air with their scent?

'I've just one more question for you,' she said. 'Ever hear of a detective called Monteath?'

'Not sure,' he replied. A few seconds passed. 'I remember Llewyn mentioning a detective who was a patient of his. But I can't recall his name.'

'If the name comes back to you, please call me immediately.'

'Of course.'

Cavanagh puffed smoke over the bees once more and they

grew more drugged in their movements, flying around with a disconcerting slowness. Some of them lay like little statues on his shoulders and arms, utterly still, or twitching as though they were busy dreaming about fantastical yellow and red flowers. One bee had tried to escape the smoke. It struggled towards a patch of nearby flowers, clumsy in flight, and then it dropped into a clump of nettles, missing its target by several yards. She wondered if Llewyn was the beekeeper, and not Barker, in this image she had constructed of Ward G; a fanatical man, hiding behind his professional persona, who had called on his drones to feed his rage for revenge.

She left Cavanagh with his bees gathered around him like a protective cloak, and ran up to the house to fetch her daughter's missing shoe.

# CHAPTER THIRTY-ONE

Morton had told the team he was still trying to track down Dr Llewyn, but he left no details of where he was going or when he would be back. The only clue Carla had to what he was thinking lay on a crumpled piece of paper on his desk. A series of crudely drawn circles joined by a thin spider's web of lines with Llewyn's name in the centre. For some reason, he seemed to be avoiding contact with Carla and the other members of the investigation team. The entire day passed without her getting the chance to share the details of her interview with Cavanagh or progress the investigation a single step further. She rang Morton's number repeatedly but his phone went straight to an answer message.

'Why are men so secretive?' she asked David as they settled down with a bottle of wine that evening. It was an attempt to snag his interest so that he would listen to her. However, it failed. He just put down his glass of wine and gave her a pained, thoughtful look, like a man wondering what he was being blamed for now. 'Why ask a question like that when I'm trying to relax before bed?'

It was the same most evenings. Sparks flew whenever she tried to start a conversation. Now, with his mother-in-law present in the house, they were forced to keep a lid on their arguments, which she reckoned was a positive but temporary improvement in their relationship.

It had been so different when Alice was a baby. She had been the centre of their lives, their sole fixed point. They had spent their evenings sitting exhausted together and drinking tea or a glass of wine, going over the minutest and dullest details of their day, the claustrophobic routine of changing nappies and feeding, the precious little moments of communication with their infant daughter that transported them with delight, even in the retelling.

Perhaps there was a note of blame in her voice when she talked about work, a hint of aggression. Was she unconsciously annoyed with him for staying, while she had to leave, and pursue her fledgling career?

'I'm talking about Harry Morton. He's driving me mad at the moment. I can't help thinking he's hiding a dangerous secret.'

David rolled his eyes and poured some more wine.

'To be honest, it's been more like working with an answering machine than a real person. Most of the time all I get is a blank look that says, sorry the person you are calling is not available right now.'

'Sounds like a positive working relationship between a man and a woman to me.'

'But we're colleagues. How are we going to make a breakthrough if he doesn't share his thoughts with me?'

'Perhaps he's depressed. Or going through some sort of midlife crisis.'

'That's my point. I wouldn't know if he was. I suspect he is because he looks so sad at times. But I get the impression his mind is working away, weighing up clues, pondering decisions. But an hour or two will go by and he won't have uttered a single word to me.'

'You're beginning to sound like his wife.'

'I'm not his wife. I'm his work partner.'

'Talking won't help with people like Morton. You can't reach inside people who are naturally reticent by gabbling away.'

'But I need to get beyond these gloomy moods of his to the truth.'

David sighed. 'What if there's nothing beyond the moods? What if his silence is the end? For some men, reticence is the better part of their personalities. It's a protective thing.'

'Protective against what?'

'The nosiness of other people.' He smiled but when he saw the look on her face, he said, 'I'm only poking fun.'

He offered to get more wine, but instead she went up to the study. She moved about quietly. Mrs Herron was ensconced in the spare room and she did not want to disturb her. She closed the study door behind her and leaned against it as though the room was the only sanctuary she had left in the house. How had she ended up with another woman in her home, a woman she did not trust, who might be doing things behind her back to turn Ben and Alice against her? It was as though her family life had become a play, one in which she had been thrust into a spectator's seat, sitting in darkness, while her husband and her mother-in-law happily got on with their dutiful roles. She gave a sigh that was like an admission of defeat. It felt as though the only way out of her domestic anxieties was, perversely, to throw herself more deeply into the investigation.

She stared at the copies she had taken of the photographs from Pochard's house, searching for evidence of Dr Llewyn's presence. She scrutinised the faces of the psychotherapists assembled together in the middle of the isolated forests. Were they emerging from the shadows of the trees, or about to recede into them? What were the pictures trying to tell her? There was a sense of premeditation in the settings and poses, some sort of therapeutic intent in the group shots that had bound together the fates of Chisholm and McCrea with Pochard, Sinden and now Dr Llewyn. She saw in McCrea's pained look the ordeal of one patient's therapy amid the rigours of a group of professionals pushing their practice to the very limits. Or was she just inventing a context? After all, it was just a set of photographs. What conclusive evidence could it provide in the murder investigation?

In one of the photographs, she managed to pick out the figure of Llewyn, standing at the side of the group, almost lost in shadow, hovering in the background. Behind him, she could make out the shape of a log cabin and a glinting body of water. Was he the mysterious intelligence operating behind the scenes and controlling the behaviour of Chisholm? She felt certain that he had been Pochard's final visitor of the day of her murder, the one whose name had not been entered on her patients' diary apart from the letter S, and who had left behind no trace of his identity. In the home territory of her consulting room, Pochard had been the patient not the therapist, and she had probably been sitting in the smaller of the leather seats, not her usual chair.

If she was on the right track, and Morton could be trusted, it would only be a short while before he hunted down Llewyn and brought him in for questioning. She paced around the study. She had to stop herself checking online for the latest news, feeling that something momentous was going to happen, realising that she was a part of something important and as yet unknown, that would make headline news tomorrow. All Morton had to do was ask Llewyn a few questions, check some details, confirm a suspicion or two, and the entire investigation would be over. She felt a cold excitement mount. She willed Morton to call with news of the final breakthrough.

The sound of it buzzing into life had never seemed so loud, its gleaming face so bright as when Morton's name flashed up. She pressed it to her ear. His voice said something indistinct and drifted. She realised he was mumbling to someone else. She strained to listen, picturing his tall figure deep in conversation with another person. Who was it? Llewyn or a police colleague? There was a pause and then his voice grew sharper.

'Carla, I'm coming back to the station, now,' was all he said before the line went dead.

Before she slipped out the front door, Carla glanced back and saw the figure of Mrs Herron standing on the stairs, still as a totem pole, watching her with a frown. Normally, she found it hard to work out what mood her mother-in-law was in, but tonight, there was something insolent about the way she maintained her gaze. Up until now, she had shown no sign of having passed any judgement upon Carla and her working life. The flush in Mrs Herron's small face and the distortion of her frown signalled the end of that phase of her residency.

# CHAPTER THIRTY-TWO

Morton was already at the station when Herron arrived. He was in the incident room, staring at the tall windows, looking perplexed. When he noticed she was beside him, he gave a nod, but the gesture was devoid of any warmth.

'What happened with Llewyn?'

Morton cleared his throat. 'Dr Llewyn appears to have vanished.'

'What?'

'No one has seen him for the past week. One of his neighbours heard a car start in the middle of the night last Tuesday. Thinks it might have been Llewyn. His car hasn't been spotted since.'

'So he used his car to do a runner?'

Morton nodded. 'It's too much of a coincidence that he goes missing the same week a colleague is murdered and another goes missing.'

'Should we launch a manhunt then?'

'No. Too soon for that. There are no forensics linking

Llewyn to either Pochard's or Dunnock's house, or the crime scene in the forest, for that matter. We have to keep making inquiries.'

'What sort of inquiries? And with whom? Who else is there at Deepwell to speak to us?'

Morton shrugged and dug some sheets out of a drawer. She opened her mouth to ask another question, but he swivelled round in his chair and turned his back towards her.

'I'm going to write up my notes. I think you should do the same or else go home.'

Was that all he had to share? she wondered. What was he holding back about Deepwell and his past? However, try as she might, she was unable to extract anything else from him. He confined himself to answering the questions she put to him with one-word answers, and whenever he looked at her through his long hair, it was as if she wasn't there. A half-hour went by quickly. Whenever she caught his gaze, he looked away, as though worried she might read something in his eyes, a flicker of the past, a moment's guilt. She tried to read his silence psychologically, but gave up.

There was something different about him, she noticed. He had tidied his hair slightly, trimmed his beard.

'The new look suits you,' she said.

He seemed even more at a loss for something to say. 'Have you found him yet?' he asked eventually.

'Found who?'

His eyes grew impatient. 'Your Inspector Monteath.'

'No. Not yet.'

The tension between them did not dissolve. He stared at her again. With a completely expressionless face, he asked, 'Want some coffee?'

'That would be great.'

He moved to the coffee machine. She watched him push in the pods. He avoided her gaze, fiddling with the buttons of the machine. Why fool herself any longer that they were a functioning team, she thought, and that his frequent moodiness served any purpose at all?

'If we're stuck we should ask Bates for help,' she suggested. 'Perhaps get some more detectives on the case.'

'Over my dead body,' he grunted, and handed her a coffee.

He coughed but to her ears it sounded like a feint to keep from having to speak any more. He sat back down at his desk, read what he had written, crumpled it up and then started on a fresh sheet.

Maybe it was time to let another team take over the case completely, she thought.

'By the way,' said Morton, 'I found out from Barker that Llewyn has a holiday home near Loch Lomond. Some sort of log cabin.'

Herron stared at him in surprise. 'But that sounds like the cabin in the photographs. And Loch Lomond is where Reichmann is having his walking holiday. They must be together up there. It can't be a coincidence.' A note of irritation had crept into her voice. 'Why didn't you tell me straight away? I've been in this room for at least an hour. I kept trying to get a discussion on the case going. Maybe you think I'm not important enough to be told of any new clues?'

'No, not at all. You've got the wrong end of the stick.'

He was quiet again, and Herron waited for a further explanation.

'Don't you ever get tired of saying nothing?' she asked.

He looked at her thoughtfully, leaving her question dangling. 'I was never much of a speaker,' he said eventually. There was a measure of pain in his voice.

'But these silences are more exhausting than any amount of speaking.'

He made a noise deep in his throat that might have been an expression of agreement.

Chief Inspector Bates entered the room. He told them that he wanted to run through a few things before he could draw a line under the day. He leaned back in one of the seats, and surveyed Morton closely.

'No sign of Llewyn, I take it?' said Bates.

'Correct.'

'And none of Chisholm or Dunnock?'

'The same.'

Herron tried to swallow her exasperation at Morton's reticence. She threw a look at Bates, but he seemed unconcerned.

'No fresh leads?'

'Nope.' Morton's lack of subtlety should have offended the DCI, but Bates seemed to be enjoying it, as though it were all part of a secret game.

'What do you intend to do next?'

Morton shrugged and said nothing, playing his usual trick of avoiding discussion, of slipping past any questions thrown at him.

'We've a special request to ask, sir,' she said. 'We can't leave the investigation hanging another night without following an important new lead about Dr Llewyn's whereabouts.'

'You're preparing me for bad news, Herron,' replied the DCI, leaning further back in his seat. 'I hope you're not going to expose an almighty scandal at Deepwell or destroy the reputations of the fine people who work there.'

'We need to take Reichmann and Llewyn in for questioning as soon as possible.'

'On what grounds?'

'Conspiracy to obstruct the police, for a start. Also aiding and abetting a murderer.'

'What forensics do you have linking these men to any crime?'

'None, at the moment. But Reichmann has detected the whiff of something rotten at Deepwell, and he's circling the murder investigation. He wants to maintain the influence and reputation of the foundation at all costs. I suspect he's been in contact with Llewyn and has been obstructing the investigation from the very start.'

Bates pulled a disbelieving face.

'Reichmann doesn't deny that there was something amiss on Ward G,' said Herron. 'However, I think he's trying to contain it in order to protect the reputation of the foundation.'

'This is a murder investigation, and your prime suspect has been Chisholm from the very start. Yet you seem more interested in taking down the reputation of these psychotherapists. Llewyn's legal team will accuse you of maliciously pursuing him and ignoring the danger posed by Chisholm.'

'But Llewyn is the link between Chisholm and Pochard. If we track him down I'm convinced we'll find Chisholm and hopefully Laura Dunnock.'

'What exactly have you got on Llewyn?'

'I'm almost sure he was the last visitor to Pochard's house on the day she was killed. He was her supervisor, not her patient. Hence the "S" that marked his appointment time, and the absence of any notes by Pochard. It also explains why her broken nail was in the patient's seat. We can get DNA tests that might prove he was there.'

'Be warned, if you tarnish the reputation of highly respected individuals you can expect a very in-depth examination of you and your colleague's work and personal motivations.' Bates looked her up and down as he was speaking. 'In other words, if you expose their failures, they will do their level best to expose yours.' However, he sighed and conceded that perhaps there was a case for interviewing Llewyn and his Swiss friend since the investigation seemed to have stalled. He gave them permission to take the men in for questioning, but warned them, 'Remember to clear up your own mess if this proves to be another red herring.'

They left the station and Herron saw Morton check the inside of his jacket, as though he had forgotten something. The gleam of a knife was revealed in his hand, and the worried look passed from his face.

His grim expression reminded her of the seriousness of their journey. She should warn David she would not be home that night until much later. She did not want him ringing her mobile, or nagging her the next day, complaining that she had flown out of the house without a word of explanation. She rang home, knowing the call would be too brief, and only add to the mood of secrecy and uncertainty associated with her work, but she had no choice in the matter. She waited on the line, but no one answered. She tried ringing several times, and still no one picked up. She was transfixed by the sight of her home number shining on her phone. How odd, she thought. Surely, David, or her mother-in-law, would have heard and answered it by now. She tried David's mobile, but it went straight to voicemail.

She climbed into the passenger seat of Morton's car and told him they would have to call at her home. She would only be a second, she promised, and, anyway, it was on their way out of Peebles. Morton drove, obedient as a chauffeur, his mouth shut tight, still reluctant to be drawn into conversation. Unable to think of anything further to say, she concentrated on the darkness of the road, and the task ahead.

To her alarm, there was no sign of David at home, but Mrs Herron was busy in the kitchen.

'What's going on, Bernadette?' she asked. 'I rang and rang and no one answered.'

'The phone didn't ring here,' said Mrs Herron as she tidied away the dishes, not looking directly at Carla.

'I definitely rang this number. I don't understand how you didn't hear it.'

'Like I said, the phone didn't ring.'

Carla went into the hall and checked the phone. It appeared to be working. She knew that her mother-in-law was lying, and had probably seen her number flash up on the screen and decided to ignore it. She walked back into the kitchen, her anger rising.

'Where's David?'

'He went to the pub for a pint. He said he'd be back at ten.'

It was ten thirty now but Carla let it pass. 'I just wanted to speak to him and the children, that's all. I have to go away until the early hours.'

However, Mrs Herron did not appear to be listening. 'It never rang,' she repeated. Her small frame seemed stockier, to have grown in size, swollen by some hostile emotion towards Carla. Was it indignation at the life her daughter-in-law was leading, her freedom to come and go as she pleased, in spite of the children? Carla did not want to think of the negative judgements that had been made about her and brooded upon in her own home.

To Carla's dismay, Alice stepped down the stairs, looking sleepy and upset. 'I want a hug, Mummy,' she said.

Carla rushed to embrace her, feeling her plans dangerously slip off track.

'Did you have a good day at work, Mummy?'

'Yes, I did.' Carla gave her another hug and took her into the kitchen. 'Granny's here to look after you now. We have her run off her feet.' She looked up at Mrs Herron. 'Will you tell David I'll be home later, and that we're close to solving the case?'

'I'm not your secretary, hen,' said Mrs Herron. 'I don't mind looking after the house and the children, but I draw the line at answering your calls and passing on your messages.'

Carla realised that her mother-in-law had stopped calling her by her name, and had taken to regarding her with an insolent look. This evening, the phone had rung and Mrs Herron had blithely ignored it. Carla could tolerate bad manners but she could not bear anyone lying to her, especially in her own home. However, she and David needed Mrs Herron's help, at least for as long as the investigation lasted. She fervently hoped that the case would end soon. She had paid too high a price for David to feel happy and content at home.

The front door opened and David appeared in the hallway. He looked surprised to see Carla and his mother standing in the kitchen, confronting each other wordlessly, with Alice standing in between them.

'What's up?' he asked.

'There's been a breakthrough in the investigation,' said Carla. She thought of asking him why he hadn't answered his phone, but she was running out of time. 'I have to leave now.' She saw herself in a glass panel. A woman with flushed cheeks and a guilty look in her eyes.

'Can't it wait until the morning?'

'No, we need to check it out right now.'

'At least you're not going on your own,' he said, glancing out through the front door at Morton's car, its engine still running.

Was it a note of reassurance or a veiled accusation she heard in his voice? Alice kept distracting her, pulling at the hem of her coat, demanding her attention.

'You'd better get going then,' said David. 'You and your friend haven't got all night. But then maybe you do.'

She was aware of her mother-in-law watching her with close attention. She was searching for something in Carla's face, some signal or clue. She realised that Mrs Herron had taken complete possession of the household, of David and the children, and the only territory beyond her control was Carla herself. She gave Mrs Herron a curt nod, and hugged Alice goodbye. She was careful to do and say the right thing. She mouthed some tender words into David's ear. She grew self-conscious under the scrutiny of her mother-in-law. It was a relief when she finally slipped out through the door and ran to the car and Morton.

As he drove off, Carla looked back and saw her mother-in-law standing beside David, calm, and protective, firmly installed in Carla's sanctuary. Mrs Herron was a family person, rooted in domesticity, but did that make her a more complete or better human being? Carla wanted to be a complete person, a good person, even in one sphere of her life.

Morton sped off, a mute statue at the driving wheel, and for the first time she relaxed in his silence, the sheltering bulk of it, glad of the chance to focus her mind and do her job properly. He guided the two of them into the night, away from the glare of towns and cities, towards the distant lapping of water, and the shadow of a murderer moving within the shadows of a forest.

The rain pelted down on the journey north to Loch Lomond. All Carla could see through the windscreen were the blazing lights of cars and the wipers swinging back and forth.

Morton was the first to speak. 'Relax. Don't even think about making the breakthrough tonight.'

However, she had not been thinking about the case at all. Far from it, she had been thinking of the humdrum world of children and interfering mothers-in-law.

'You've got to stop thinking too much,' said Morton. 'Just let your thoughts float free.'

If only he knew of the deep annoyance gnawing at her, she thought.

Shortly after one a.m., they reached Loch Lomond and the forest where Llewyn's log cabin was situated. Morton braked sharply and swung the car onto a gravel track. The car rolled and bounced over the uneven surface. The lights of the shaking dashboard shone on Morton's face, but all Herron could see were his straggly hair and beard, and a pair of hooded eyes. Morton leaned closer to the windscreen, cradling the steering wheel in his hands as he concentrated on the dim track through the trees. 'We'll soon be there,' he said.

From the depths of the forest, a light blinked and then dis-appeared. Morton braked and the car jolted to a halt. He rolled down the windscreen and they listened to the rain and the wind stirring the branches. Morton took the initiative, pushed the door open and ran to the back of the car with surprising nimbleness for a middle-aged man who usually shuffled into the office. He pulled on his waterproof gear and threw her a spare raincoat.

As they hurried towards the source of the light, her thoughts really did seem to grow lighter, almost buoyant. She felt detached from her home life and stopped listening to the nagging voices in her ear. She could hear the countless drips of water percolating through the leaves, and Morton up ahead, encouraging her to keep following him, talking away in a consoling tone. Or was he speaking to someone else? Another person up ahead, a shadow, a presence, odd sighing sounds, a ghostly victim or the murderer himself?

Her phone rang suddenly, and her hand trembled as she held it to her ear.

'Shaw here,' said the voice. 'Where are you?'

'Near Loch Lomond.' She was slightly out of breath. 'Close to finding Llewyn's log cabin.'

'Is Morton with you?'

'He's ahead of me.'

'You might want to hold back.' She heard the worry in his voice and froze. 'I interviewed the staff at Deepwell about Monteath, like you said, and I found out...' His voice grew faint, broke up and then steadied again. '... Pochard's secretary went trawling through her work diaries. She was searching for an imaginary detective but she found a real one. A voluntary patient at Deepwell nine years ago.'

'Who?'

'Harry Morton. Apparently his treatment at Deepwell ended in 2009. Several weeks before the first mention of Inspector Monteath in any of the patient notes.'

When she digested the revelation, it somehow made sense. 'Everything must be interlinked,' she said in the calmest voice she could muster. 'Morton, Monteath, the confessions of the patients and Pochard's murder.'

'Either he's the missing thread, or it's just a coincidence,' said Shaw.

'Do you think he knows more than he's letting on?' asked Herron, hunching over the phone as if it might be broadcasting Morton's secret to the entire forest.

'I've no idea.'

'Nor have I,' said Herron, 'but I'm on his heels.'

'What should I do now?' asked Shaw.

'Your sense of timing is impeccable. I want you to get help and come here as soon as possible.' Her voice was firm and clear. 'We're at the south side of the loch.' She gave him the directions and told him to hurry.

'Perhaps you should find somewhere safe and wait until we get there.'

'No, I'm too close to the truth.'

She switched off the phone. Strange, she thought, how everything was falling into place just when she was at her most vulnerable. As if someone were skilfully pulling the strings in the darkness.

# CHAPTER THIRTY-THREE

She put away her phone and listened hard but there was nothing to be heard above the distant lapping of the loch. The rain stopped. She stared at the black opening in the trees through which Morton had disappeared. The feathery pine branches that had engulfed him stirred in the breeze but were completely noiseless, their darkness tumbling towards her.

She stepped cautiously along the track, the trees walling her in, until she came to a small clearing and could make out the outline of the log cabin. It looked exactly like the one in the photographs. She positioned herself behind a pine tree and watched the cabin for several minutes. Then she drew closer. There was enough light from the moon and stars to guide her towards her destination. She walked as quietly as she could, wondering where the hell Morton was. The blinds were tightly drawn on the windows but there appeared to be no light emanating from within. The night gave nothing away. It was as if the cabin was hibernating and had somehow enfolded Morton in its darkness.

Even the surrounding trees appeared to be in a deep, motion-less sleep. She found a little storehouse next to the cabin, freshly painted and locked. She reached out to touch one of the cabin's windows and felt a slight warmth. Somebody had been heating the place. She pressed her ear against the glass and listened, but heard nothing. She withdrew into the shadows again, and wondered what she should do next. Shout for Morton or start banging on the cabin door? She had not planned to lose her colleague so abruptly. The safest thing would be to go back to the car and wait for reinforcements, but she hesitated. She was annoyed at her indecision. Perhaps Morton was standing somewhere amid the trees, deep in thought. She whispered his name, her voice sounding timid.

She tried to tune in to the landscape as though it were a crime scene. She spotted a collection of stones shaped like a cairn at the far edge of the clearing. She drew closer. One of the rocks had a greyer pallor than the others. A rock with mangled hair and roots of blood spreading over the other stones. She gasped, feeling sweat burst onto her forehead, her eyes sliding over the sickening sight. A disembodied head lay nestled on the pile of stones, its eyes closed, its face frowning, as though it were listening to something deep within the stones. But the head was far beyond listening, far beyond the reach of words. In the nearby bracken, she found the rest of the body, slumped in defeat, as though it had dragged itself through the undergrowth in order to keep up with the head but failed.

Sinister and deranged, she thought. Again, she felt that the location and the way the body had been left were part of the killer's motive. An outburst of madness that was somehow part of a meticulous plan. She saw a framework in operation. The lines of trees, the glinting body of water, the head and body abandoned at a loose cairn, a tableau of murder, and paths everywhere, wriggling through the undergrowth. A stage based on the pseudo-confessions of the patients from Ward G, the same stage that had been photographed numerous times by the psychotherapists at Deepwell. This wasn't a murder conducted on the spur of the moment, she thought, as she retreated slowly from the clearing, making sure that as little as possible was disturbed for the forensics.

She heard a twig snap behind her and gave a start. She turned round and saw a figure standing at the fringe of trees with his back to her. She recognised Morton's long raincoat, but for some reason he was ignoring her, his hands plunged in his pockets as though he did not give a damn for her or the investigation. She switched on her flashlight and shone it upon him, but he hunched down his head.

'It's me,' shouted Herron. Why won't he speak? Why was he being so secretive? She started talking to him hesitantly, approaching him with caution, imagining that he had turned into Inspector Monteath. His silence was as unflinching as ever. She felt her anxiety return. Something told her that the moment of greatest danger was approaching. What else could Morton's silence mean? Was it a warning signal against some unseen danger?

The figure coughed deeply, painfully. However, it was not Morton's cough, it was an old man's racking wheeze. Nor was the face that turned towards her Morton's. It was the face of a man she had seen only in photographs, gaping back at her, unmoved by her presence and the probing light of the torch. Finally, she had tracked down Dr Llewyn, but what was he doing wearing Morton's raincoat?

'Who are you?' said Llewyn. 'What do you want?'

She introduced herself and asked him what he was doing.

'I came here because Chisholm called me,' said Llewyn. 'He wanted to admit to what happened to these poor women.'

'Why did he do it?' she asked. 'What could justify killing them? What really happened on Ward G?' The questions appeared to confuse the psychotherapist. 'Did you make Chisholm follow your wishes?' she asked.

'Sometimes during therapy, I would direct him in subtle little ways. But only ever in the interests of the therapeutic process.'

'And to kill these women?'

'Billy always liked to impress. He was prone to satisfying other people's wishes to gain their approval. He could make himself believe that he had been involved in events that he had dreamed up.'

'Such as Pochard's murder?'

Llewyn sighed. 'She was dragging my life's work into the gutter,' he said, his face sagging with contempt.

'And you wanted to protect your reputation?'

He frowned. He had not liked that question. 'All this is like a bad dream, but somehow not as clear as a dream. Everything made sense in Chisholm's fantasy forest.' A look of sadness passed over his face. 'I have to go now,' he said.

She heard the wind rush through the trees behind her, a sense of the air quickening, and the needles of the pine trees bristling. Llewyn's gaze was fixed on a point behind her, and she wondered what he was staring at.

'You have to stay here,' she warned him.

Llewyn stiffened and crouched in the darkness, and then a sudden blow to the back of her head made her stumble to the ground, her vision blurred. A part of her tried to save herself, searching for defences, wielding her torch, but her arms and legs had other notions. She could hear a man's heavy breathing upon her. The next blow left her sprawled upon the ground.

Before she slipped into unconsciousness, an image came to her.
She saw the great dark dome of the forest settling over her, the
tall trees poised upright and their prickling shadows invading
her body, while far above in the night, a violent storm raged.

# CHAPTER THIRTY-FOUR

Carla awoke, sightless and powerless, plunged in darkness in a space which she sensed was small and enclosed, not knowing for sure, in spite of the heavy rustling movements beside her, whether she was alone or not. She could tell that she was lying on her side with her hands and feet tied, and that a gag had been placed across her mouth. Was her blindness due to the blow to her head? She was aware of a trickle of blood from her scalp, and a dull pain in her neck, but she was unable to take an inventory of her injuries. One part of her body felt much colder than the other, a coldness that was like sinking slowly into mud.

She heard a gasp beside her, and the sound of a body struggling against ropes. She had a companion, close enough to hear the person's laboured breathing, and a smell of deodorant mixed with smoker's breath that she recognised as Morton's. The discovery did not reassure her. It made her feel more like a doomed captive. During the entire investigation she had carried on blindly, struggling against hidden forces.

Everything she and Morton had done to date felt like a rehearsal for this final struggle in the dark.

She tried to communicate through the gag, but all that came out was a series of muffled grunts. By accident, she kicked Morton's leg. She sensed his body grow quiet and alert. He grunted back at her. It sounded reassuring. For several moments, she listened to the measure of his breathing, the little rasps and sighs, the stale air their lungs exchanged, as though they were finally having a conversation, really talking together at last. However, she was glad that neither of them could express themselves in words because that would have betrayed the true extent of their fear. Before, she had always been anxious to understand what was on his mind, frustrated by his moroseness, his ability to turn away and sweep out of the room without saying a single thing, and now that he was just this heavy lurking presence in the darkness, so close she could smell his breath, the sense of his inner life was overwhelming.

He grunted again, but this time she heard the fear in his throat. Something, she did not know what, had made him afraid. Then she sensed it, too. The coldness in her body was beginning to rise. From the far end of the chamber came the trickling sound of water flowing. In a flash, she realised the diabolical fate that awaited her and Morton. She twisted her legs, squirmed her waist, smacked her head off a wall, rapped her shins against Morton's body, and clawed with her bound hands at the sides of the cavity. Morton's body thrashed against hers, too, neither of them willing to occupy this watery grave. The investigation had turned into this final struggle of their bodies for air, the story of two detectives outwitted by a murderer, but unwilling to yield to death. The sound of the water rose, echoing cavernously, rushing and splashing against their twisting bodies.

Amid the frenzy, the rough coughing of their breaths, something passed between them. She heard a deep sigh from Morton, a final anguish, and then a slackening as his body relaxed and grew limp. She sensed his efforts change direction, his body pushing itself under, diving towards oblivion. She gasped for air. If he succumbed first, would that somehow give her leverage, enough to push herself out of the grave?

She could not let go. She had two children and needed to live. She was part of something bigger than just herself, a family, that might be part of something even bigger, a grand plan in life that was difficult to discern at the best of times, but she knew her role in it, and that was to care for the ones smaller and more vulnerable than herself. She wanted to hold out for as long as she could. She focused all her thoughts on lifting her head out of the water, feeling Morton's body hunch up below her, pushing her upwards. His body felt rock solid, and its intention was clear. Words were unnecessary. He had understood the grand plan and knew that she was meant to live. She thought she was witnessing his final breaths, that he was going to die beside her in the darkness.

The water rose around her mouth and nose, and she struggled more wildly, choking and spluttering as she tried to lift her head higher. She swallowed more water and hacked as her throat and nostrils stung. Almost her entire body was submerged now. She could feel the water streaming up to her eyes. She was frantic for air. She gulped and retched but was unable to fill her lungs any longer.

# CHAPTER THIRTY-FIVE

From somewhere beyond, Carla heard the click and creak of a door opening, and the pad of hurried footsteps. She shouted through the gag and choking water, but her efforts drew no response. There was a rush of air above her, the sense of the confinement lifting, and then a weightlessness overcame her. Suddenly she was breathing again, her mouth and nostrils spluttering water.

A voice spoke with the calm authority of the emergency services, giving orders, which were obeyed by a set of invisible hands that pulled her out of the water. Shadowy figures helped her to her feet and up a narrow set of stone steps. She could not control her shivering, and the exhaustion left her bowed over, as though she had just completed a long painful journey to arrive at this spot. She mumbled her grateful thanks and urged them to help Morton, as they untied the ropes and removed the blindfold and gag.

'Here, Carla, take this.'

She inclined her head, hearing a familiar female voice. Some-one wrapped a coat around her shoulders. Her vision had not fully returned. She felt detached and disorientated. Water gleamed everywhere as she blinked at the churning vision of her rescue party. A small thickset woman floated into view, as light as a bubble against the darkness of the forest. That voice and that domineering shape with its low centre of gravity. It could not be. Somehow, it must be an illusion, she told herself. She pulled the coat around her shoulders. It was identical to one she had seen before, in her own home. She peered into the murk again.

The coldness of the water and her near drowning had jarred her body, and her mind was numb. She hunkered down, pulling the coat more tightly around her, willing her thoughts to settle, content to let the emergency services do their job and look after her and Morton. But the sight of the familiar collar of the coat brought her out of her trance again.

'Lucky you found us,' she said to the ambulance crew. 'Did Constable Shaw raise the alarm?'

The men and women kept moving, helping Morton onto a stretcher, the detective moving slowly, all his vigour drained. She wanted an answer but none was forthcoming. Someone offered her a cup of tea from a flask, steam swirling in her face. Morton stirred and moaned on the stretcher.

'How did you know to come here?' she asked again. 'Did Shaw send you?'

The shapes busied themselves, urgent but indifferent to her enquiry.

However, her question was important, and the scene did not make complete sense to her. The thickset woman appeared again. She was not part of the rescue team. She was just watch-ing. Carla stared back at her. The woman drew closer, brushed

Carla's face with her hand, helped fix the coat around her shoulders. Carla resisted like a child.

'Say something,' she demanded.

'It's only me, hen,' said the woman.

'Only you?'

It was her mother-in-law's voice that spoke back to her, talking hesitantly, with maximum caution. 'Poor Carla. I followed you in the car after you said goodbye to David. I came here and tried to find you in the darkness. When I heard you scream I knew something bad had happened. When Constable Shaw turned up I was able to show him to the cellar door.'

Carla stared at her, startled that of all the people she knew, her mother-in-law was the one who had helped save her and Morton's lives.

'But why?'

'I wanted to know what you were up to. You looked so distracted and flushed. I thought you were having an affair. I could see that you were obsessed by some secret, and I thought what else could it be but a man.'

Carla gave an incredulous laugh that was more of a gasp. She never thought her mother-in-law could be so suspicious and calculating. Critical, perhaps, of her dedication to her work, but not so suspicious that she was prepared to follow her for several hours through the night. A mother-in-law's distrust, that was the reason she was still alive and not a floating corpse in that godforsaken cellar. However, in the circumstances, it was difficult not to feel overwhelmed by gratitude to the woman.

Carla tensed as Mrs Herron made to rub her shoulders. 'I'm fine, Bernadette. I can take care of myself. You should go home now.'

'If it's OK, I'd rather stay.'

'No, this is a crime scene. If you like, one of the police officers will travel home with you.'

'OK,' replied Mrs Herron and turned to leave.

'Just a second.'

Her mother-in-law stopped.

'What exactly did you see in the forest?'

Mrs Herron furrowed her brow. 'I saw a man pulling you
and your colleague along the ground. He was dressed in black
with a hood. I think I saw another figure. Someone stepping
out of sight, and hurrying down to the loch shore.'

The running figure had to be Llewyn, thought Carla. And
the man who had hit her and pulled her body into the cellar?
It must have been Chisholm.

'I was wrong, Carla,' said Mrs Herron. 'I didn't realise this
was what you were doing. I couldn't get a picture in my head
of you as a committed detective. But I have now.'

Carla met her gaze. She tried to smile but it felt uncomfortable. She was aware of a flow of sympathy from her mother-
in-law, and found it difficult to cope with. All she wanted to
do was close the investigation, not wallow in sentimentality.

She remained at the scene for several hours until the police
and the forensic team arrived. She was sitting in Morton's car
with a blanket around her shoulders, when someone brought
her a fresh cup of tea. It was Bates.

'We have a lot of questions we need to ask you,' he said.
'But we understand you may not be able to answer all of them.
Morton is recovering in hospital. I've spoken to him, but he is
unable or unwilling to say anything.'

She nodded, and said she would try her best.

'First and foremost, was it just you and Morton who came
here?'

'Yes.'

'No one else knew where you were going?'

'No one.'

He gave her a look that suggested he was not sure if he could believe her.

'No one,' she repeated. 'When we got permission from you, we left immediately. Not even you knew where we were headed. No one else was involved. Shaw rang when Morton disappeared, and I told him to get help.'

'What about your mother-in-law? How did she get here?'

'On the way, we stopped at my house. My mother-in-law decided to follow us for reasons only she can explain.'

'Did you speak to her or your husband about what you were doing?'

'No.'

'Llewyn's suitcase and clothes are in the log cabin, but he's disappeared again. Looks like he decided to do a runner rather than face the music.'

'And what about Reichmann?'

'No sign of him, either.' Bates grimaced and looked over at the cabin. 'What the hell was Llewyn doing here? Is he behind what's lying up at that cairn of stones? We haven't identified the victim yet, but it appears to be Laura Dunnock.'

'Before I was knocked out, Llewyn said he was able to direct Chisholm and make him believe that he had acted out his fantasies. I was about to arrest him.'

'What drove him to do such a thing?'

'He was afraid of his reputation, his life work, being ruined.'

Bates grew silent, while the network of suspicions reformed in his head.

'Maybe you were right all along,' he said, staring at her attentively. 'I thought we were after a madman, not the psychotherapist meant to be looking after him.'

Bates's manner suggested he was keen to close the case. He searched Carla's face as though urging her to provide the conclusive clues that would solve the murders but none were forthcoming. All Carla could think of were the figures of Chisholm and Llewyn, a psychotherapist and his patient running through the forest.

Shaw appeared. 'Morton is feeling much better,' he said. 'He's fully conscious right now, but the doctors need to keep him under observation. They say he has a severe concussion.'

Carla felt a wave of relief and thanked Shaw for helping to rescue them.

'He asked to speak to you, Carla. He wants to know if you picked up his knife.'

'His knife?' asked Bates. 'What the hell was he doing with a knife?'

'He said it was missing. He thinks he lost it after he was knocked out.'

'I haven't seen it anywhere,' said Carla.

Bates checked with the other officers at the scene, and confirmed there were no reports of a weapon being found. 'Chisholm or Llewyn must have taken it with them,' he said. He put out a call, warning that the two fugitives were probably armed with a knife.

They stared at each other, looking uneasy. The wind picked up, enlivening the branches of the trees, their darkness pierced by the swinging flashlights of the search party. Carla felt the coldness of the flooded cellar creep over her again. She watched the lights flickering in the murk, hoping that they would penetrate a passage through the darkness.

'Can you remember anything about the person who struck you?' Bates asked Carla.

'I sensed the presence of someone.'

'Can you explain that?'

'I felt it before at Deepwell on Ward G, and at Pochard's house. Something in the pine trees.'

Bates watched her, saying nothing. She thought she wasn't making sense but the DCI appeared to consider her words carefully, as if she were on the brink of something crucial.

'Tell me, Carla, why do you think Llewyn or Chisholm didn't just lift Morton's knife and kill the both of you?'

She could not answer that. She had not had time to work out the killer's motives. But it struck her that stabbing them did not belong to their attacker's landscape of events, the sequence of grisly images that lay scattered throughout the confessions from Ward G.

Bates asked her to give it some thought. She remembered an image from McCrea's confession, a description of a dark pit with the bodies of two detectives thrashing like snakes knotted together. It might almost have described the macabre death the attacker had in mind for them. Had his tormented mind fallen back on a familiar image?

'I've called in help from the local police force,' said Bates. 'Roadblocks have been set up around the south side of the loch. Officers have also taken up positions at all the entry points to the forest, and are approaching from the east and west following the lie of the land. Chisholm and his psychotherapist will be hunted down. We'll find them soon, mark my words. You've no reason to worry about your safety any more.'

He and Shaw stood against the backdrop of the forest, the sky above them full of pricking stars. The trees waved in the wind, their branches clustering together and whispering, not words but murmuring sounds that Carla understood as a form of primitive warning. There was something shrewd about the shadows, beckoning her to listen more carefully. Was it the effect of her head injury or the near drowning? The wind abated and then picked up again. But the sound of the trees was insistent, urging caution in a language she understood deep inside. She had the strong impression that there was something out of kilter with the way the night's events had unfolded. What else might Llewyn have said if she had not been knocked out? What were they up to with Morton's knife, and why hadn't they used it on them?

'I doubt that we'll find Chisholm alive,' said Bates.

'Why?'

'Do you think Llewyn would have helped him commit these murders, and then allowed him to carry on with the rest of his life? No, this fantasy in the forest needs an ending. Llewyn would have made sure of that. Once he knew you and Morton were on his trail that was the end of him.'

Bates made Carla travel with him to the hospital. He did not want her driving alone, even though she insisted she was fine. The DCI was preoccupied. His urgent driving revealed his anxious state of mind.

'You should have called in reinforcements as soon as you lost sight of Morton,' he chided her. His concern sounded more than professional, the note of tension in his voice signalling the grave danger she had risked.

A nurse had just finished checking Morton's blood pressure when they found his bed on the ward. He looked as though he had no idea where he was.

Bates stared at him with a hard grimace. 'Feeling any better?' he asked.

Morton tried to sit up in bed, but the effort seemed to nauseate him and he sank back onto his pillow. He stared around him as though he were on a strange island, washed ashore by a huge wave. No one spoke and the quiet between the three of them grew tense, or at least it felt so to Herron, like some kind of endurance test, with Bates and Morton waiting, hoping for her to break first. Yet another silence in which they were in charge. Morton shut his eyes. He needed more than silence. He needed sleep.

'The staff here will take care of you both,' said Bates eventually. 'I'm heading back to the forest. If you need me or remember anything else call me.'

When Bates had left, Morton opened his eyes, leaned over and grabbed Carla's arm. 'Get me out of here,' he croaked. In spite of the strain, his voice was insistent. 'I need to be sure the search is handled properly.'

'I can't. The staff have you under medical supervision. You're not fit to go anywhere.'

He slumped back. 'Who were the other people in the forest?' he asked.

'I was talking to Llewyn when someone knocked me out,' she said. 'It must have been Chisholm.'

'Who were the others?'

'My mother-in-law followed us there. She helped raise the alarm. She was joined by the emergency services.'

'Who else?'

'Shaw was there. He rang me while we were in the forest. He found out that there was more substance to Monteath than anyone thought.'

A stillness came over Morton. 'Clever Shaw. What did he find out?'

'The patients started reporting sightings of Monteath about nine years ago. Something happened at that time. Something that triggered their delusions.'

Morton pushed himself up in bed slightly. The blanket

slipped from his shoulders, revealing a bare chest marked by deep red bruises. 'What was it?'

'They met someone on the wards. A real detective.'

'Did Shaw find out the real detective's name?'

'Yes. He was a voluntary patient there for about six weeks. Dr Llewyn was in charge of his care.'

'The timing could be a coincidence.'

'I don't think so.'

She stood over him. She could see in his eyes, even drugged with exhaustion, the realisation that soon he must tell her his story, not as a confession like those told by the patients on Ward G, but in a form of words that would reveal the truth.

'I have a right to keep that time of my life private,' he said.

'Of course, but I still want to know what happened to you in Deepwell. What you saw and heard. It might have a bearing on the case.'

He swivelled his eyes round the blank walls of the room, and then he looked at her. He was unable to hide it any longer. She could see it in his expression. His face was marked, ridged with heavy lines of emotion. For a moment, she wondered if he would be able to survive revealing himself through this look of desolation, if she would survive it herself. He held on for several moments, but the lines on his face only deepened.

'Nine years ago, I was in a bad way,' he said. 'I'd been fighting it for months. The terrible feelings and thoughts that were building up inside me and would not let go. Hoping they would pass. But things grew unbearable. I was divorced, drinking too much, bad with my nerves. A real pitiful state. Bates made me go see the police psychologist. As it happened, she was being supervised by Dr Llewyn, and she recommended that I meet him.' He looked up at Herron and met her gaze. The tightness in his face had slackened its grip. 'I told him so much about myself, all the intimate details, until there was nothing left of me. The next thing I knew he had persuaded me that a voluntary stay at Deepwell would be in my best interests.'

She could see how Llewyn at the height of his career had cast a long shadow over the careers of many professionals and their patients, influencing their decisions and controlling their lives from the home territory of his therapy room.

'I have a question for you,' she said. 'You don't have to answer it right now.'

'I understand what you're saying.'

'What happened while you were in there?'

'I remember very little, and that's the truth. I was on strong medication to wean me off alcohol.'

'Were you ever a patient of Dr Pochard's?'

'No.' He lay slightly slumped in his bed. She sensed that he would not be able to take any more questions about Deepwell.

'That's enough for now,' he said.

He looked relieved when she nodded and said nothing. He shut his eyes in exhaustion, and shifted in the bed. She reached over and gently drew up the blanket to cover his chest, almost touching his bruised skin.

He opened his eyes suddenly. 'Tell me, who else was in the forest?'

She had seen no one else, she explained.

He grew agitated. 'Someone took my knife. I need to get back to the forest.' There was desperation in his voice, but his eyes glinted with determination. Here he was, recovering from a near drowning, reduced to a weakened state in a hospital bed, still trying to be a detective, following some impulsive hunch.

'A search party are combing the forest right now,' she said, trying to reassure him.

'Where's Bates?'

'He had to hurry back to the scene. Did you see who attacked you?'

'No.' He groaned as if in pain. 'I'm OK,' he said, but his breath had weakened. 'The thing is, there were others in the forest.'

'Who? Reichmann or Barker?'

A frozen look came over his face. 'I don't know,' he mumbled. 'I saw others watching.' He scanned the ward. 'Just point me to the bloody exit, Carla.'

'What's up? Why are you so anxious to leave?'

He turned away from her. He was damming up again. However, beyond his usual reticence, one thing was abundantly clear. Morton was scared. He kept looking at the gap between the curtains as if expecting Chisholm to pounce at any moment. He glanced at her with a dark look in his eyes, and for a moment she thought his silence was going to swoop down and seize her like an ice-cold bird of prey. The only sound between them was the air conditioning and the hum of the monitors. His eyes roamed around the cubicle and then fixed upon the wall.

She needed to think more clearly, troubled by the feeling she had glimpsed certain clues but had not fully understood them. The scene at the log cabin with Llewyn wearing Morton's coat had felt so well planned that it suggested a sequel, an invitation to go deeper into the forest. The monotonous tones of the air conditioning began to soothe her tired mind. Slowly, the forest disappeared from her thoughts, like something that no longer concerned her. Then, someone put a hand on her shoulder. She had fallen asleep. She looked up and saw that it was Bates.

'Where's Morton?' he asked with more than a trace of anxiety in his voice.

The detective had disappeared from his bed. They checked the toilets and the waiting room, but there was no sign of him. None of the harried-looking nurses had seen him leave. Somehow, he had slipped away. Bates told her not to worry, that Morton could look after himself.

'I came to tell you that we found Chisholm,' he said. 'We followed his tracks to the loch edge and found his body covered in blood with Morton's knife in his hand. He'd used it to slit his throat and had already bled out.'

But Chisholm's death had never been part of his fantasy or hinted at in any of the confessions. Was it because the murderer had no longer been in control? Then she remembered Bates's comment about Chisholm having to die. Could Llewyn have made Chisholm take Morton's knife knowing that he would use it on himself? With a twinge of fear, she thought about Reichmann again. She rang his mobile number once more, and this time when he did not pick up, she left a message for him. Her clear instruction was that he should present himself at Peebles police station for questioning in the morning, or else a warrant for his arrest would be issued.

# CHAPTER THIRTY-SIX

News reporters and cameras blocked off the open area in front of Peebles police station, but there was no sign of Reichmann the following morning. A temporary barricade had been set up with security guards in force, and Herron had to show her ID to get through. It struck her that the station itself seemed under threat, like Deepwell Hospital. She had already grabbed some newspapers and once safely inside she perused the front pages, which were filled with news of the dramatic events in the forest overlooking Loch Lomond. One photographer had managed to get to the loch shore not long after Chisholm was found, capturing the moment when a detective with long hair and a thick beard had crouched over the former patient's body as if searching for something. Although the detective's face was hidden, Herron could tell it was Morton. He must have left his hospital bed and gone straight back to the forest. What had he been looking for? Perhaps he had bent down to listen to the dead man's mouth, hoping for a final confession from his departing spirit. Herron would have liked to have heard what Chisholm might say from beyond the grave.

Herron slipped out to the back car park and rang Morton's number. To her relief, he answered almost immediately.

'Where are you?' she asked. 'Are you all right?'

'Better than I was, but not yet fit to listen to Bates shouting orders.'

Were you ever? thought Herron. 'The boss has been trying to reach you.'

'Yes. I've seen his messages.'

'Where did you go to last night?'

'Back to the forest,' he said, but would not explain any further.

'Am I right in thinking you're following an important lead?'

'Everything is still unclear, but right now the last place I want to be is in a hospital bed. I've waited years for a big case like this, and I don't want anyone at the station thinking I'm injured, or unable to see the investigation through. Tell the rest of the team that I'm busy tracking down the other members of Llewyn's holistic society.'

He might be unwell, but he was the same old Morton. Secretive and contrary.

'Any sign of Reichmann or Llewyn?' he asked.

'None. Bates has agreed to issue a warrant for their arrests. Right now he has the entire police team searching for them.'

Morton was silent.

She updated him on what the forensics had found in the forest and in Llewyn's log cabin. Most significant was a diary they found inside a field guide to Scottish birds. It expressed the hope that future generations of psychotherapists would base their work on what Llewyn had learned on Ward G. Chisholm and McCrea were just two of the countless patients he had dosed with high levels of benzodiazepines and subjected to extensive therapy, convinced they were suppressing memories of abuse and horrible crimes. However, they were his star patients, fed increasing amounts of tranquillisers. 'Bates says that the contents of the diary explain why Llewyn organised the murders,' she told him. 'Not everything that has happened at Deepwell, but enough for a court of law to comprehend.'

'What about Barker and the other staff at Deepwell?'

'They're distancing themselves from Llewyn and Sinden's research. All of the therapeutic programmes have been wound down. They're erecting a concrete wall between themselves and Llewyn's doomed reputation.'

No response from Morton.

'Are you sure you're all right?' she asked. 'The doctors said they wanted to keep you under observation. You suffered a severe concussion.'

'I'm all right.' However, she could hear the strain in his voice.

She wondered what exactly he had seen in the forest, his claim there were other people there. It reminded her of another detail from McCrea's pseudo confession. His claim that there were more figures spying on him, checking under the stones in the cairn.

'Perhaps you should really be in hospital,' she said. 'It would be the safest place.'

'No. I've something important to do. By the way, say thank you to your mother-in-law for saving my life.'

'She followed us because she thought we were slipping off to have an affair.'

Morton grunted. 'She must fancy herself as a private investigator.' He paused. 'I want you to take the rest of the day off, Carla.'

'What?'

'That's an order.'

'But the investigation is nearly over.'

'I just want you to lie low. And make sure I can reach you on this phone.'

'But you're the one who should be lying low, not me. You're the one who needs help.'

'This is important, Carla. You have to listen to me.'

'I don't understand. What are you not telling me?'

'I can't say anything more at the moment.' He spoke in a low voice as if concealing the conversation from listening ears. 'I might be completely wrong in what I saw last night but I have to check it out. God knows, the whole thing might have been an apparition. If that's the case, it's better no one else knows about it, not even you.'

'Surely I can be of some help? There must be something I can do.'

'I don't think so. Just make sure I can reach you later.'

This wasn't right. What if Morton was imagining things, what if his behaviour was caused by concussion and he was inventing his own suspects and plots? She must stop him. Even his voice sounded strained and odd. Then she heard some sounds in the background with Morton, a hoarse voice asking him for something.

'Wait. Who's that with you?'

The hoarse voice spoke again. It sounded vaguely familiar. Was it Dr Llewyn?

'Sorry, Carla, I have to go.' Morton sounded tense.

'Don't hang up,' she said sharply. 'You have to tell me what's going on.'

'I've already told you.'

'But if you know the whereabouts of Reichmann or Llewyn you have to tell me.'

'I just asked you had there been any sign of them.'

'You're not telling me the truth.'

'You don't understand what is going on, Carla. The grave danger that you're in. I want you to drop the investigation and go home right now.'

She had never heard him give an order in that manner. Usually, he made them as suggestions, helpful ways to guide her along the right path.

'If you think I'm in danger you have to tell me what has alarmed you.'

'Go home, now, Carla.'

'I see. So that's the way it is. I have to do what you want, and you ignore everyone else.' She wondered who it was he was trying to save her from. Perhaps he might need her help later on as part of his plan.

'I don't want you to do anything. That's my point. I'll call you when things are clearer.'

The line went dead. Carla stared at her phone. What the hell was going on with him? Didn't he feel, as she did, that they were a team, bonded together by their near-death experience, vindicated by their suspicions about the staff at Deepwell when others doubted and criticised them? What was he up to, fleeing the hospital and staying away from everyone? And the person with the hoarse voice, could it really be Dr Llewyn? She deserved to be told what exactly he was doing, to be informed of his plans, not ordered to take the day off. She dialled Morton's number, but the line went to voicemail.

She clenched her jaw and returned to the incident room. Morton was clearly demented. Why should she obey his orders and put up with his stubborn moods any longer? There was no way she was going home, not now, with Bates trying to take over the investigation, running around and giving orders to everyone with a triumphant smile on his face. The DCI was the worst type of boss possible, eager to pinpoint and blame subordinates when investigations stalled, and quick to steal the praise when things went well. Once this case was over, she would put in for a transfer, she thought. Anything to get away from these dysfunctional male detectives.

She was about to ring Morton's number again and leave an angry message when Shaw approached her.

'Are you OK?' he asked, sensing her tension. He glanced at her mobile phone but Morton's name and number had disappeared from the screen. 'A call came through for you early this morning. Derek Cavanagh wants to speak to you urgently. He said something about remembering one of the members of the holistic foundation.'

Herron called Cavanagh's number, but there was no response so she drove as quickly as she could to his house. She was standing at his porch, trying to place another call to Morton, when Cavanagh's wife answered the door, her face lacking its usual composure. 'I need to speak to Derek,' said Herron. 'He rang the station early this morning.'

'He left an hour ago. To meet a friend.' Her voice was tense and low. There was a breathless quality to it Herron had not heard before.

'Did he say where he was going?'

'He mentioned the park.' Deborah Cavanagh heaved a deep sigh. 'He was very agitated when he left. I haven't seen him behave like that for years. He wouldn't say who he was meeting.'

The park lay half a mile away. She drove, keeping an eye out for the psychotherapist in case he was walking back home.

The place seemed deserted but there were several cars parked at the entrance. She got out and ran along a gravel track and into the trees. She followed a path that sloped gently towards a small man-made lake, letting her instincts guide her. She had come here a lot when Alice was younger, spending hours feeding breadcrumbs to the ducks and throwing stones, watching them sink slowly to the bottom. She thought of ringing Morton again but decided against it. She stopped and listened, hoping to hear the sound of Cavanagh's booming voice, but all she could hear was the wind. Here she was again, peering through trees, prying in the shadows. She set off down a path that ran like a slender thread along the edge of the lake. She stood and stared at the water, and then at the trees behind her, thinking of all the recesses in the park where Cavanagh may have met his friend. She heard a car door slam shut from the park entrance, and then the acceleration of someone leaving in a hurry. She hurried back through the forest and came to a small clearing.

The sun came out, casting long shadows, and then she saw Cavanagh standing with his back to her. She called out his name, but he did not answer. There was a creaking noise from the branches above, and his body turned slowly. She moved towards him and then halted. His stiff posture seemed to suggest he was keeping a firm grip on himself, but that at any moment he might fall over like a dummy. She waited for him to say something, watching his body turn fully towards her, and then she felt faint, seeing his head drooping awkwardly, his eyes cast down, a rope coiled around his neck and tied to a branch overhead.

For a moment, she hesitated, wanting to call Morton or run away, but then her training kicked in. She checked the body for vital signs. There were none, and then she phoned the emergency services. She kept guard at the scene until the ambulance arrived. When the paramedics took his body down, she saw his wedding finger glinting in the sunlight. She noticed that he was wearing it on his left hand, rather than on the right, as he had done at their first meeting at the birthday party. She checked the fingers of his other hand and saw the band of exposed skin where the ring usually sat. She stared at the dishevelled state of Cavanagh's clothing, the scuffed earth around the bottom of the tree. Had there been a struggle before he died, some sort of final tussle in which the ring had slipped from his finger, and then been replaced, incorrectly, by the murderer? She warned the paramedics that the patch of ground around the tree was now a crime scene.

Morton was correct, she realised. She was in grave danger.

# CHAPTER THIRTY-SEVEN

At the police station, Herron brooded upon Cavanagh's death. Who was the member of the foundation that he had wanted to speak to her about? She checked with Shaw to see if he could remember anything else about Cavanagh's message, but he had not taken the call. It had been relayed to him by one of the receptionists.

She spotted Bates in the corridor. The chief inspector was in buoyant form, marching towards her without slowing down, as if she was invisible to him. At the last moment, he stopped and smiled. He told her he was convinced that the solution of the case was easily within reach, and that Llewyn would be soon caught.

'What we need to do now is clear the mud that Llewyn has thrown our way,' he said. He had organised a case meeting to take place later that day, so that they could prepare answers for a press conference scheduled for first thing in the morning. He had kept the reporters at bay long enough, and now was the time to enlist the public's help in tracking down Llewyn, and anyone who might be assisting him, such as Reichmann.

Herron said she was going back to the first murder scene by the waterfall.

'Why?' said Bates, frowning slightly.

'I don't know,' she replied. 'I don't think there's anything else I can do in the meantime.'

'What do you mean?'

She shrugged. 'I just need time to think.'

Bates's phone rang and he broke off the conversation.


The odd gust of wind, the dreary flap of branches, and the shedding of dead needles were the only sounds in the forest. Creeping along the track to the clearing, Herron felt a sensation of secrecy and narrowness, her body and mind closing up. In the distance, she could hear the torrent of the waterfall as it charged down the hillside. It started to rain heavily. The trees turned to silhouettes and then vanished in the downpour. The thunder of the waterfall grew louder. It seemed to plummet through the forest, spreading towards her like a surging tide. She felt as small as a lost child, and thought of running back to her car for shelter.

This is loneliness that I am feeling, she thought. She told herself she had a family and a good job, and that these were bulwarks against solitude, but why did she feel so isolated at home, and so lost in her role as a police detective? The mysterious depth of her feeling gave her a sense of determination to explore it further, and she pushed on.

The wind picked up and the entire forest seemed to tip in one direction, leaning towards her like a slow-moving giant, all those thousands of branches and millions of pine needles turning in obedience to the invisible force of moving air, pausing now, seething together, waiting for the command. She stood very still, in a posture of intense concentration. *I'm at my best when the forest turns its silence towards me.* Pochard's words ran through her mind and suddenly made sense. Everything became fathomable and still. The rain stopped, and the path opened into the clearing. The cairn of stones and the writhing tree roots looked sharp and clear in the aftermath of the downpour. She could see the waterfall spilling down the hillside. Again, that sense that McCrea and Chisholm were not murderers, but witnesses, forced to endure a long and terrible look at their darkest fantasies.

Her colleagues were searching for the wrong man in Llewyn, she was certain of that. But who had murdered Pochard and Dunnock, and possibly Cavanagh? Who could be capable of such brutality and cleverness? What was the combination of memories and words that were welling up inside her, and who were they pointing towards?

If only she could spell out her thoughts to Morton right now when they were fresh in her mind. She needed his shrewdness. No one in her working life as a police officer had been kinder to her, she realised, than this middle-aged detective who never smiled in her company, but whose presence was like a guiding hand, a churlish big brother, a defender who seemed to understand the professional pressures she laboured under as an inexperienced female detective. She knew that if she relayed her ideas to him they would become clear-cut and comprehensible.

She took out her phone and rang his number, but he did not answer. She tried again. The rain picked up, and standing there, listening to the waterfall, she thought of the disturbed fantasies of the patients on Ward G and the professional dreams of therapists like Sinden and Llewyn inextricably entwined and writhing together like the gnarled tree roots at the foot of the waterfall. She closed her eyes and allowed all her doubts to flow away from her, willing the crime scene to open up, if only for a moment or two.

Slowly, it dawned upon her. It did not feel like an overwhelming moment of clarity. More a train of thought hinting at a deeper insight. Something Sinden had said about his reputation at Deepwell, the way he had looked past her, as though he were complaining to an invisible audience, and the fact that Pochard never saw patients after six p.m. She had imagined that the moment of breakthrough would be a climactic moment, a dam bursting, but it was not like that at all. It was smaller and shallower. It reminded her of when her waters broke before the birth of Alice, when there was so little water she was not entirely sure the important moment had arrived. However, when they had stopped, she knew something crucial had changed, and that deep within her body, her sweet baby was beginning to pulsate with a new force.

All she had to do was make a few checks and find some firm footholds for her suspicions. She rang Dr Barker and asked him two questions. The first was about the plastic trays Reichmann had mentioned in his letter to Dr Pochard. The second was about the members of the holistic foundation. Barker's tone on the phone was acid-like. He protested and seemed on the verge of swearing, but then his voice grew aggrieved and defensive. After she had secured the information she was looking for, she thanked him and he replied she was welcome. This time he did swear.

She made her way back down the track. The trees had returned to stillness, hushed against the sky, but an undercurrent of shadows flowed along the path. She hurried to her car, feeling the darkness travelling alongside. She had to bide her time, she told herself. She tried to control the flush of excitement and wondered if she would be able to sit through the investigation meeting that Bates had urgently called. She was about to climb into her car when her phone rang. It was Morton, and his voice sounded agitated. She told him about Derek Cavanagh's death and what she had found out from Barker, and then Morton reiterated his warning that she was in great danger. He spoke at length. She asked a few brief questions when he had finished. He gave her the location of where he was hiding and warned her not to ring him or try to make contact in any way until the appointed time. He seemed to be under considerable pressure and she wondered if he was in danger of having a breakdown.

# CHAPTER THIRTY-EIGHT

The case meeting had already started when Herron slipped in at the back. Next to a projector screen showing photographs of Llewyn and Reichmann sat the chief inspector, looking sharp and alert, and extremely sure of himself. He kept glancing around the room to make sure he had everyone's attention. Herron felt a wave of irritation at the way he had taken over an investigation that he had interfered with and almost derailed. Bates was a great improviser, and with Morton gone, he had no one to challenge his place on stage.

'There are still several question marks hanging over the case and I have a press conference first thing in the morning,' he said. 'The reporters will be baying for answers, so I'd like to serve up the solution on a plate, with Llewyn caught and in custody. Case done and dusted. I've issued warrants for Llewyn and Reichmann's arrests and given their details to the press. Every police officer in the Borders is on the alert, and we have several squads following up every lead.'

Herron reported that neither Morton nor she could recall

anything about the person who had knocked them out. She mentioned her suspicions about the death of Derek Cavanagh, her fear that he had been murdered to prevent him from revealing the identity of the murderer or an associate.

'Everything points to the fact that Llewyn must have had assistance from someone else associated with the foundation,' she said, 'and the most likely suspect at this stage of the investigation is Professor Reichmann.'

She had worked out one piece of the puzzle though. The mysterious trays that Reichmann had asked Pochard to keep secret were related to the way in which medication had been dispensed on Ward G. She had confirmed with Dr Barker that the trays contained blister packs of daily doses, which would clearly reveal the unsafe levels of tranquillisers and antipsychotics dispensed to the patients in conjunction with Llewyn and Sinden's memory therapies. However, they had been removed from the ward along with the written medication records while Barker was on leave and Llewyn was covering for him, and could not be located. Barker had described the levels of medication as mind-bending, and said they would have induced severe hallucinations in the patients.

Bates rose to his feet, and congratulated Herron on her detective work. 'Llewyn and Reichmann will be tricky to capture,' he warned. 'They aren't mentally damaged like Chisholm, though clearly it would be difficult for a rational person to understand the murderous lengths they have taken to save their reputations. Their self-images are of intellectually gifted men forging new understandings of the criminal mind. They aren't mad. They are simply arrogant fanatics prepared to experiment on vulnerable men and lock them away from the world because of confused memories that probably never occurred.' He propped his hands on the table and leaned forward, staring at each of the officers in the room. 'They have been ready to sacrifice the freedom of their patients to prove their theories. They have sought justification for their behaviour from a small, cult-like group of psychoanalysts. They have been prepared to bully and harm the career of anyone who disagreed with them. When pushed into a corner, they have become desperate. Faced with the ruin of their reputations, they have hatched a clever plan to use Chisholm as a cover to get rid of their enemies.'

There was nothing more to say at this point, said Bates. Police with the help of the media would be scouring the Borders for Llewyn and Reichmann, who could no longer rely on the support of their fellow therapists and the corridors of Deepwell as a safe refuge from judgement.

Before the meeting closed, Bates asked if anyone had heard from Morton.

'Not a thing,' said Shaw. 'He didn't look great when I saw him last in the hospital.'

'What the hell is he up to?' said Bates. 'It's not like him to do a runner at a crucial stage in the investigation.'

Herron pondered for a moment, and then made up her mind to speak. 'He rang me earlier this morning,' she said. 'He sounded confused and paranoid.' It was the unvarnished truth, nothing more. She wanted to show her discretion and professional approach. It was her duty in the circumstances. With as little fuss as possible, she relayed her suspicions that Morton might be with Llewyn, and may even have helped him evade arrest.

'Good God,' said Bates. 'I knew he was a contrary bastard but this is a step too far.'

'What should we do now?' asked Rodgers. 'Issue a wanted notice for Morton as well?'

Bates shook his head. 'Morton is a seasoned detective. We

can't risk ruining his reputation and that of the police force by letting the media get wind of this. Besides, if he sees his wanted picture online he's likely to become completely unhinged.' He turned to Herron. 'Have you been in touch with him since?'

She explained that she had kept trying to ring him all afternoon. He had eventually replied with a brief call in which he had revealed the location where he was hiding. However, he had asked her not to reveal it to anyone.

'If you don't have anything more sensible to do,' said Bates. 'I suggest you bring us there right now.'

'It might be best if I approach him alone,' she said. 'If he's confused, the sight of a squad of officers might unsettle him further. What do you think?'

'Let's do that, then. I'll send Rodgers and Shaw as backup. They'll keep a safe distance behind you, but close enough to help you in an emergency.' A worried look fell across Bates's face. 'If he does have Llewyn, you have to convince him to give the doctor up.' He shook his head. 'I've never known Morton to behave like this before. Never ever. He mustn't be in his right mind at all.'

# CHAPTER THIRTY-NINE

The darkness of the valley threatened to swallow up the road. Herron drove cautiously, leaning over the steering wheel, checking her mobile phone to ensure she still had a signal and could be contacted if anything were to go disastrously wrong.

After several miles, she turned off the road and onto a lane. She slowed down until she saw that Rodgers and Shaw had followed her, and then she drove on. The branches of the fir trees leaned out of the night, sweeping over the track, raining down pine needles onto the bonnet of the car, as it rocked over potholes.

The shell of an abandoned-looking cottage swung out of the shadows. Her headlights flashed across the building and then she brought the car to a halt. She killed her lights and waited a while. The cottage seemed sunken in silence, and there was no sign of her backup.

She hoped she had understood Morton's intentions and projected them correctly onto what she knew of the murder plot. Their foe was extremely ruthless and powerful, and he could easily vanish into the protective shadows of his profession, no matter how strong her suspicions were of his guilt.

She slipped out of the car and peered through the cottage windows, but they were sheets of blackness. It was a well-chosen hideaway. A fugitive could have stayed hidden here for months.

She pushed the front door and it gave way. She eased herself inside, half expecting a rough hand to grab her from the darkness. She stopped in the cramped hallway, trying to discern what might be human amid the moaning sounds of the wind and the creaking of the house. She fervently hoped there were no fatal loose ends she had overlooked. Then she heard the sound of a foot slowly pressing onto a creaking floorboard. A light blazed on, revealing dank walls and a flurry of shadows, and a German-accented voice floated through the cottage interior. 'Watch your step, Sergeant Herron. This place is a mess.'

Reichmann appeared with a gun in his hand and directed her into one of the back rooms, where she found Morton sitting hunched over a seat, his arms tied behind his back, his mouth gagged. He lifted his gaze to her and she noticed that his eyes were red-rimmed from exhaustion, but his look was as piercing and direct as ever. In the opposite corner sat Llewyn. He was staring at his feet and seemed reluctant to meet anyone's gaze, a lonely old man who had believed in an unreliable psychological theory and created an unreal world around it.

Oddly, Reichmann showed no signs of being perturbed by her arrival. There was almost a trace of sympathy on his lined face as he pointed the gun at her and directed her to an empty seat. 'Welcome to my little therapy session,' he said. 'I believe we have some more guests still to arrive.'

Beneath the professor's calm smile, she could see the tension that pulled at his facial muscles, the practised gaze of his eyes and the intensification of his pupils, which suggested he was using every ounce of his professional charm and skill to pit against the darkness of the task ahead.

She followed the direction of his gun and sat down on the seat. Reichmann looked at his watch, and kept his gun trained on Herron.

'Did anyone follow you?' he asked.

'Two officers are in a backup car further down the lane.'

'Normally we psychoanalysts don't like to accept late arrivals, but in this case we'll have to make an exception.'

Herron's phone began to ring, but Reichmann warned her not to answer it. It rang a second time, and then it went quiet.

Reichmann stood in the middle of the room and began speaking as if reciting a rehearsed speech. 'Unfortunately, Sergeant Herron, you've followed the examples of Jane Pochard and Laura Dunnock in signing your own death warrant. You and Morton know things you should not.' He paused and his voice rose with a note of hysteria. 'We are living in a time of great change to the world of psychiatry. When the values of psychoanalysis are being undermined by new approaches. To the great detriment of humanity, I must say.' He looked at Herron intently. 'Do you understand the predicament that I am in?'

She was unsure what she was meant to say or do at this point. She glanced at Morton. Something about his gaze told her that she was understood and valued, and was here to play an indispensable role in the final unravelling of the mystery. She had to hold on to the belief that she had done the right thing in coming here, but where were Shaw and Rodgers, and why hadn't they radioed in reinforcements?

Reichmann sighed. 'Sadly, all this is due to my failure to keep an eye on what has been going on for years at Deepwell. The patients who were doped with medication to levels beyond intoxication and encouraged to confess to crimes they most likely never committed, and then were kept locked away on Ward G. Exploited because their worst fear was they would be taken off their tablets and dumped back on the streets.' Reichmann raised his gun and pointed it at Herron. 'Unfortunately, sacrifices have had to be made to preserve the good reputation of the hospital and the foundation. I regret I will have to add to those sacrifices, tonight.'

There was an unreal quality to Reichmann's voice and the concentration of his gaze. Herron closed her eyes and waited for him to fire the weapon, but nothing happened. Instead, the tread of a footstep in the hallway interrupted Reichmann. A figure stepped carefully into the room.

'Detective Chief Inspector Bates,' said Reichmann, lowering his gun. 'Where have you come from? Sergeant Herron said that two officers followed her here.'

'I decided to tail her instead,' said Bates, scanning the room, taking in the figures seated against the wall. He appeared slow to respond to the fact he was facing a gunman and three hostages. 'I've been listening in to your little session, Eric. Don't worry, I haven't called in the reinforcements.'

Reichmann looked surprised at the DCI's appearance, but the two men clearly knew each other and had some sort of understanding.

'I hope it's not a bad time to visit?' said Bates with a smile.

'Not at all, Simon,' said Reichmann. 'It's always good to receive another trusted member of the holistic foundation. Even if the circumstances are a little unusual.'

The DCI's first name, thought Herron. The puzzle of the letter 'S' in Pochard's appointment diary had been solved. Bates had been a member of the foundation all along, and known to Pochard, as well as Reichmann.

'Until this moment, professor,' said Bates, 'I had no idea of the extraordinary lengths you would take to protect the reputation of the society. I have to commend you for your loyalty and thoroughness.'

Reichmann nodded. 'I've decided to put an end to the scandal threatening our society. Once and for all.' He raised the gun towards Herron and paused. The silence in the room grew so dense that Herron's ears began to ring. She hunkered in her seat. The professor turned and smiled at Bates. 'I hope you don't mind me finishing off your handiwork, Simon.'

'Be my guest, and if my own efforts have inadvertently inconvenienced you, then I apologise.'

'What do you mean, your own efforts?' asked Reichmann.

'It's a pity I didn't think to include you from the start, Eric. I would have preferred to have you with your ruthless streak as an accomplice, rather than pathetic old Llewyn and that poor bastard, Chisholm, but then you were in Switzerland, and I had to act quickly.'

Reichmann appeared to be buying himself and his hostages more time. He lowered his gun a little. 'You've kept your role in this cover-up a secret, and I commend you on that. You have gone above and beyond your duty to the foundation in trying to erase all traces of the scandal on Ward G. But why did you risk everything? After all, it wasn't your career or reputation that was on the line.'

'That's not exactly true. You see, Dr Llewyn and I have been working together secretly for years. In an unofficial capacity, of course.'

'What do you mean?'

'He was a trusted supplier of suspects. I had lots of unsolved crimes on my books. Thefts by housebreaking, assaults, sexual offences, and even the odd murder. You could say we helped each other out in our careers. I presented the details of the crimes to Llewyn and he used them in his memory recovery sessions with the patients at Deepwell. By and large, they confessed to the crimes and my success rate soared. Everyone was happy with the outcome. The patients stayed at Deepwell under Llewyn's care where they could enjoy whatever medications they were addicted to, free of the fear they would be dumped back onto the streets. Llewyn, the old fool, thought they were all guilty. He knew we were operating along blurred boundaries but he believed that the end justified the means, and all the time he was enhancing his own reputation in the world of psychiatry.'

A smile played on Reichmann's lips. 'So you had to make a judgement as to what was in the ultimate interest of two institutions: Deepwell Hospital and the police force?'

'Correct,' said Bates. 'I tried to persuade Pochard and Dunnock to drop their campaign against Deepwell but they could not be trusted. So I had to kill them.' He glanced at Herron and Morton and seemed to grow impatient. 'Now, if there is any way I can assist you in your plans to dispose of these failed detectives I am more than willing to do so.'

'What plans?'

'I mean the steps you have taken to deal with—'

Reichmann snorted. 'Let me assure you, I have taken no steps at all.'

The puzzled look on the DCI's face gave way to a cold blank expression. In the meantime, Morton had slipped his hands free and removed the gag from his mouth. He rose from his seat and fixed his gun on Bates. 'It's not your show any more, boss,' he said. 'I'm arresting you for the murders of Jane Pochard and Laura Dunnock.'

'Don't worry, Chief Inspector,' said Reichmann. 'You're in

fine company. The best minds on your force also suspected I was capable of killing to protect the reputation of the foundation. No doubt the press and the public would have fallen for it, too. Fortunately, Morton persuaded me to set up this little ruse to extract a confession from you. Think of it as a novel form of therapy.'

Bates stared at Reichmann, slack-jawed. He whose career had thrived on securing confessions had just been duped into giving up his secrets. 'You mean…'

'I mean, this was all a trap. Inspector Morton kindly agreed to arrange listening equipment to record every spoken word and transmit it to officers from neighbouring police forces who right now are making their way here from their nearby vantage point.'

A look of fear spread across Bates's features, eating into his customary swagger like acid. With a considerable physical effort, he pulled himself together, steadying himself against the wall as though trying to adjust to the changed weight of forces within the room.

Reichmann resumed speaking. 'Dr Llewyn is a failed psychotherapist but not a murderer; I knew that from the start. I played along with the idea that he posed a significant threat. However, in reality, Llewyn was like a blind old spider trapped at the heart of a web he had created but had lost control over, one that was being secretly manipulated by the murderer. I was reluctant to launch an official investigation into the foundation because I did not want to tear down the web. Otherwise, the murderer would have gone scuttling into the darkness for ever. I made my own enquiries and worked away quietly in the background. Every time I touched the web, the murderer did not reveal himself. I realised his sensitivity was far greater than my own, but that he was hiding somewhere close by.'

He turned to Bates with his gun. 'So I had to trap some prey in order to trick you into revealing yourself.'

Herron tensed and waited, holding her breath. Reichmann had planned his trap with great precision, pulling Bates into his own web, and now it would drag him down in its fall. With two guns pointing at him, Bates had only one escape route, and that was out the door and into the forest, where police officers were waiting to arrest him.

'The only failed detective in this room is you,' said Morton, as he placed a set of handcuffs on Bates. 'The root or source of madness is not always where you expect to find it. Billy Chisholm was a totally blameless and vulnerable individual who you cast as a scapegoat to preserve your reputation at all costs. You must have enjoyed the twisted logic of it all. A murderer eager to confess but completely innocent of the whole gruesome business and ignorant of the true motive for the murders.'

Bates said nothing. Perhaps it was because he had said too much already. His lips were grey and he stared at Morton with bulging eyes.

'Until a few weeks ago, you were a fully signed up member of the holistic foundation,' said Morton. 'You had a perfectly good working relationship with the psychotherapists at Deepwell, until Dr Pochard decided to lift the lid on what was really going on. The threat to your reputation, the undoing of all those investigations you had taken the credit for, was more than you could cope with. None of the cases would have held up in court if brought in for a retrial. Pochard was your therapist and confidante. She saw you out of normal hours and kept no notes of your sessions because of your high rank in the police force. You tried to persuade her against bringing her complaints. You thought she would bow to your demands, but she refused and so you turned violent. That is most likely how it happened. Afterwards, you saw the opportunity to frame Chisholm and thus you began to re-enact the details of his confessions.'

Searchlights lit up the room and silhouettes floated across the walls. A police officer appeared, shining his torch in Bates's face, and still he said nothing.

'Alistair McCrea's confession was unexpected. It threatened to derail your plans,' continued Morton. 'Perhaps this was when you decided you would have to incriminate Llewyn as well, and make it look as though Pochard's supervisor was the killer. Then when Carla reported her suspicions about Derek Cavanagh's suicide, I knew we had to act fast. Cavanagh must have remembered that you were a member of the foundation and believed it would have a bearing on your investigation. You found out that he had contacted the police station this morning, and made sure he wouldn't reveal your secret.'

Every individual has a particular look of surprise when the moment of final defeat arrives, and Bates's was something special, like that of a showman whose enormous circus tent was falling around him, his eyes white and jerking at every shadow in the room as Morton kept talking, so close he was almost whispering in his ear.

'Last night, I happened to remember something that took place years ago when I was a voluntary patient at Deepwell. I was deep in therapy and heavily dosed with medication. You came swaggering towards me as if you owned the place. When I stepped aside, I gave you a nod of recognition and called you "sir", but you barely glanced at me. You looked irritated and threw your shoulders forward, and kept marching down the corridor. Later, when I asked what you had been doing on the ward, one of the nurses smirked and said you were pulling off another conviction. She'd hinted that you'd cracked loads of cases on Ward G without a single shred of evidence. I'd completely forgotten the conversation until last night in the hospital, seeing you on the ward, staring right through me with those eyes that never smiled, the way you threw your weight around as if you would destroy anyone who stood in your path.'

More light filled the window, and the buzz of police radios intensified. A heavy calm descended as officers crowded into the room and led Bates away, his back upright, his neck stiff, bundling him out through the front door and into the fathomless silence of the forest.

Morton turned to Herron, his face suddenly grey and haggard, as if all the strength had drained from his body. 'I'm sorry to have put you through that,' he said, 'but I had to hear the truth from Bates's own lips.'

'You could have told me your suspicions earlier. Back in the hospital. I thought we were a team, but you kept almost everything to yourself.'

Morton shook his head. 'If I had told you the truth, Bates would have sensed something was up. He would have launched open warfare on us, and covered up his tracks completely.'

Herron recalled her first visit to Deepwell and its hushed corridors. It seemed like a dream or a distant memory merging with a dream. McCrea's confession had seemed so mysterious and deranged, yet she had been drawn in completely. She had even believed in the existence of Inspector Monteath, not realising he had been another delusion manipulated by Bates to control the patients on Ward G, and also herself, urging her to find the body of Dunnock and the false clues he had planted at Llewyn's log cabin. She was just like Sinden and Llewyn, only more lost. Would anyone, police detective or psychiatrist, be able to understand everything that had happened on Ward G?

'I've missed important leads,' she said. 'Even when they were staring me in the face. I made mistakes.'

'No, quite the opposite,' said Morton. 'You penetrated all the layers, the delusions, the lies, the enormous wall of resistance at Deepwell, straight through to the reality hiding beneath. Right from the start, you knew the murderer existed, and you hunted him as though your life depended on it.'

He looked her straight in the eye, and she returned his gaze. For the first time, she felt as though they were communicating on the same level. Then he turned away, signalling that was the end of their conversation, and there was nothing more to say.

# CHAPTER FORTY

The room was plunged in darkness and those gathered inside listened with hushed breath to the sounds of two people plotting on the other side of the door. There was no longer a need for silence, and a murmur went through the huddled figures. Someone gave the command. It was time to close the circle around the child now, the figures drawing together tightly. The door flew open, and a little girl squealed with excitement as the shape of a candle-lit birthday cake swung into view and everyone began singing 'Happy Birthday'.

Bearing no hint of the stresses and strains she had been through, Carla laid the cake on the table and beckoned her daughter to blow out the candles. The other parents and children cheered, and David took some photographs. Alice laughed aloud, and said it was the best party and the best cake ever. Everyone watched her with a smile. Even David looked at ease, and seemed genuinely interested in chatting to the other parents.

For the first time in a week, Carla was able to tune in to what was going on at home. The preparations for the party were hassle-free – gone were the silent reproaches and simmering anger between her and David. They had bought decorations and devised party games, including a treasure hunt around the house, light-hearted and excited like children. Her mind was no longer distracted by work. It seemed that the world of pine forests had given her back her old life without her having lost or sacrificed anything.

She ran to and from the kitchen, seeing to the guests, serving drinks, preparing food and interacting with Ben as he sat at the table in a baby-chair, gurgling and banging a spoon. Everything around her was connected to her life as a mother and wife, nothing else. Perhaps limits were inevitable, she thought, part of life, just as there were freedoms to be found in even the most tightly confined roles. Contentment wasn't characterised by pursuing one thing; it was shaped out of giving and taking, and allowing other people the space to be themselves. She was fortunate she had found the room to be herself and push herself forward in life.

David came into the kitchen and watched her closely, meditatively. He drew near and leaned towards her. 'Is this the life you've been dreaming of?' he asked. 'A successful investigation under your belt, promotion beckoning...' There was a new tone to his voice, a hint of admiration she had never detected before.

Finding it difficult to hold back a smile, she hid it by bending over Ben. The truth was the investigation had left her feeling vindicated, exalted even, but also exhausted. 'Perhaps I've had too much of what I've been dreaming about,' she murmured.

David began sliding slices of half-eaten birthday cake into the bin, and then he placed the rinsed plates in the dishwasher.

'I'm going to book us a holiday,' she said. 'What about two weeks in Andalusia? We'll hire a farmhouse in the mountains and do lots of hiking and swimming.'

'Sounds good to me.' He had finished loading the dishwasher and now he was placing the tab in its compartment. 'You know something; you still haven't told me why having children made you want to be a police officer.'

Why had it? Because having children had taught her to be braver and more truthful with herself, had made her stop making excuses to cover for her weaknesses, and prove she could do better with her talents. She was about to tell him this, but something about the stiffness in his facial expression made her stop. She felt a draught of cold air and caught the whiff of a smoker's breath. She glanced at who he was staring at and saw Morton standing in the hallway. The detective did not take off his coat. He just stood there, hanging back from the door like one of those childhood friends you're not supposed to play with.

'I tried ringing but no one answered,' said Morton.

'What is it?' she asked, feeling a familiar excitement take hold as she read in his eyes the dark details of a crime scene.

Morton beckoned her to follow him. David looked at her sideways, and said nothing as she stepped into the hallway. She took a quick glance into the sitting room where the birthday party was still in full swing. She hesitated, trying to establish whether anything had changed from the last party she and Alice had attended, but clearly nothing had. All the pieces had been put back together, the overexcited children, the harried parents chatting about schools and their work–life balances amid the waves of laughter and screams. Alice was even wearing her red princess shoes again. She wanted to bask in the merriment a moment longer, but she was the one who had changed.

'What's wrong?' she asked Morton. 'I thought we'd closed the investigation.'

'Yes, we have,' he replied. 'But this is a new murder case. The forensic team is there already, waiting for us.'

She put on her coat and told David she would be back, but not when. She felt a secret confidence well within her. A true detective was one who could close her eyes, and throw herself into a new investigation without once glancing back, letting things take her where they will.

Her last thought as she ran to the waiting car was to wonder what she would dream about later that night when she slipped into bed, her mind tired but racing with visions.